THE SULPHUR SPRINGS CURE

THE SULPHUR SPRINGS CURE

JEFFREY ROUND

Cormorant Books

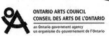 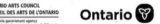

We acknowledge financial support for our publishing activities: the Government
of Canada, through the Canada Book Fund and The Canada Council for the
Arts; the Government of Ontario, through the Ontario Arts Council, Ontario
Creates, and the Ontario Book Publishing Tax Credit.

LIBRARY AND ARCHIVES CANADA CATALOGUING IN PUBLICATION

Title: The Sulphur Springs cure / Jeffrey Round.
Names: Round, Jeffrey, author.
Identifiers: Canadiana (print) 20230562817 | Canadiana (ebook) 20230562825 |
ISBN 9781770867284 (softcover) | ISBN 9781770867291 (EPUB)
Subjects: LCGFT: Novels.
Classification: LCC PS8585.O84929 S85 2024 | DDC C813/.54—dc23

United States Library of Congress Control Number: 2023949973

Cover and interior text design: Marijke Friesen
Manufactured by Friesens in Altona, Manitoba in January, 2024.

Printed using paper from a responsible and sustainable resource,
including a mix of virgin fibres and recycled materials.

Printed and bound in Canada.

CORMORANT BOOKS INC.
260 ISHPADINAA (SPADINA) AVENUE, SUITE 502,
TKARONTO (TORONTO), ON M5T 2E4

SUITE 110, 7068 PORTAL WAY, FERNDALE, WA 98248, USA

www.cormorantbooks.com

For my mother, Loretta Marion Round
And her parents, Abbie and Henry White

If you ever get cripple,
let me tell you what to do.
Lord, if you ever get cripple,
let me tell you what to do.
Take a trip to Hot Springs
and let 'em wait on you.

"Hot Springs Blues" by Bessie Smith

-1-

SUCH STUFF AS
DREAMS ARE MADE ON

THE OLD WOMAN lifts her head from the pillow, feeling confusion
and a muddle. A luminous dial on the bedside table reads 12:43
a.m. The edges of a dream that seemed at once both dangerous and
inviting are only now beginning to recede. She flicks on the lamp
and gazes around. Things take a moment to register. The year is
2009 and her name is Violet McAdams. She is in the bedroom of
her home on the outskirts of Victoria, British Columbia. Of course
I am, she thinks. Where else would I be? *Who* else would I be? She
feels both relief and a huge disappointment on registering this.

Outside, the sky is restless. A branch taps furtively at the
window. It reminds her of the dream. Only a few minutes earlier,
she'd been back on the grounds of the Sulphur Springs Hotel in
the summer of 1939. It's the third night this week. Each time,
she dreamed of lifting the stone that covered a crevice in the wall
bordering the hotel grounds like some inquisitive teenager bent on
discovering a secret. In fact, she *had* been a teenager at the time.
Only her name was Violet McPherson then. And she certainly had
discovered a secret. But all that was a very long time ago.

For a moment, she glimpses her former life from a distance.
She sees that plucky fourteen-year-old running across footbridges,
ducking under hedges, and darting through woods.

And lifting stones.

The past is always with her these days. Maybe it's because of the impending move. After more than forty years, her house is to be sold along with most of its contents. There will be little left but memories once she disposes of the property and relocates to the McPickell Residence for Seniors. Just thinking of the name rankles her. She might as well be pickled once she moves there.

But, yes, it would explain why her memories have started to unravel. The dreams have been very insistent of late. Vivid, almost angry at times. All those shadowy faces and figures from the past clamouring to get at her. Why now, when she's about to leave it all behind? Seventy years have passed since that dreadful day when her childhood ended, leaving Violet stranded on the shoals between youthful innocence and the knowledge that follows in the wake of experience. And soon her little life is about to be rounded with a much bigger sleep than any she has ever known. On days like this, she doesn't feel ready for it.

She struggles to sit up. Her rheumatism has been getting worse of late, making her hands and feet a battleground most days.

There is a tentative knock at the door.

"Come in, Claire."

Her niece peeks in, sees her propped against the pillows, and smiles sheepishly. "I'm sorry, Aunt Vi. I thought I heard you cry out."

Violet tries to recall. Had she cried out? Her head is still a bit fuzzy. The answer doesn't come.

"I might have," she admits.

"Is everything all right?"

The memory of the stone intrudes with excruciating clarity. Violet looks around her as though the reason for it might be writ, large or small, on the walls of her bedroom. Slowly, she shakes her head.

"No. I think I can say with some certainty that everything is not all right." She tries but fails to keep the crankiness out of her voice. "I wish it were."

She can still hear the voices. She wants desperately to shake them off and drive them away, but these days the dead aren't so easily appeased. Not that they ever were.

Claire sits on the edge of the bed, matronly concern written across her forehead. She'll get wrinkles that way, Violet thinks. Her mother — Violet's younger sister, Elizabeth — was just the same. And so was our mother, Maggie, though for some reason I was born with tougher skin than the two of them. Well, the devil looks after his own.

"Is there anything I can do?" Claire asks.

"Such as?" Violet's voice is querulous.

What she wants to ask is, Can you fend off these ghosts and make them leave me in peace? Can you tell them to drop dead — again? She reminds herself that Claire is here to help with the move. It won't do to snap at her for no good reason. In fact, Claire, the youngest of her five nieces and nephews, is the only one who offered up her time when Violet announced her decision. *It will keep my mind off the divorce*, she'd said. Violet had protested briefly, though she knows Claire would never have made the offer if she hadn't meant it.

"Don't worry about me, dear," Violet says. "I suppose I'm fine."

Suppose? Which is it then — am I fine or not? Just seconds ago, she'd declared she wasn't fine at all. It won't do to be wishy-washy. Claire will think she's getting fuzzy headed. She might even tear up. That would be far more aggravating than the matronly concern she's trying at this moment to express.

Claire reaches over and gently rubs the skin on the back of her aunt's hand. Violet looks down at the wrinkles and liver spots — old age in all its glory. She withdraws the hand. She hates being treated like a fading flower. Sympathy's wasted on me, she thinks. I'm old, not delicate. Besides, "old" isn't something you can help being, otherwise I'd never have got old. I'm still a tough nut underneath it all. Just try cracking me.

"Shall I make us some nice chamomile tea?"

Claire asks this in a way that Violet would find patronizing in others. For some reason, her niece can get away with it.

Despite the girl's meekness, Violet trusts her intentions. She can't be doing this to get a larger share of the estate — there won't be that much to leave. Besides, she has made it clear that everything will be divided equally among all her nieces and nephews. When the time comes, of course. She hasn't heard the wingèd chariots yet. In any case, why not? She loves them all equally, not a bad apple in the bunch, though she's always felt a stronger connection with Claire. If what the Buddhists claim is true, then Claire must have been someone Violet was fond of in another life. And who can say they're wrong? It makes sense, in a way. She far prefers life's profit-and-loss ledgers to add up properly. Give a little, get a little. It should all be made clear when we arrive in the world: Take what you like, but don't forget you have to pay for it when you leave.

"Tea, Aunt Vi?"

Violet looks up.

"Chamomile? To help you sleep?"

Before she can answer, the tapping resumes at the window. Violet turns to look. They're here — all the long-lost dead. She can't see them, but she can feel them. Still, she's not afraid. She pats Claire's hand.

"Why not? Would you mind?"

Claire smiles, glad to be of use. "I'll be right back."

When her niece is gone, Violet looks around the room. Shadows cover the walls. She knows they're waiting for her. Lately there seems to be nothing but ghosts to keep her company.

"Come on then," she challenges. "Don't hang back in the shadows. Show yourselves."

The room remains hushed and unchanged. She hears Claire moving about downstairs in the kitchen, opening cupboards and clanking the kettle against the sink. Violet's eyes roam the walls, pausing over a sepia photograph of her mother from the 1930s. Maggie is wearing a long-sleeved dress with a lace collar. Her expression is inscrutable, just as she often was in life. She has a book resting on her lap: *A Noble Lord* by Mrs. Emma D.E.N. Southworth. Violet read it once several years ago, surprised to have unearthed a copy in a second-hand bookshop. A soppy romance. Well, that's what they wanted back then before they had television to pollute their minds.

The branch taps at the window again. *Ah, there you are!* it seems to say, as her mother might once have said on discovering Violet hiding beneath a hedge. *You can't catch me*, Violet would have replied. *Wrong*, her mother would say, grabbing and tickling her till she screamed with delight. But it's not delight she feels now.

Outside, the wind tosses the leaves about, the world unfurling in the soft contours of night. Changing, always changing. There's a pulse that runs through everything, in darkness and light, in winter and summer. You can feel it, Violet thinks. Birds migrate, plants grow, tides ebb and flow. Change unceasing. You can't hold it back. It's the natural order. But what of the unnatural order? What of an early death? What of a death by design? These things aren't part of any order she understands.

She turns from the window and tries not to think of the stone. It's like *not* thinking of a white bear. She'd heard it was an exercise the great acting coach Stanislavski asked his pupils to attempt during their classes with him, to show how pitifully weak the mind really was. They all failed. So, too, the stone has a great hold on her dreams lately. She'll be damned if she lets it disturb her waking life too.

Keep calm, she thinks. Claire will be back with the tea soon and the conversation will resume with talk of everyday things. They can talk about what needs to be done to ready the house for the sale: cleaning and packing, repairing the fence and trimming the garden. In fact, a good deal more than just memories has accumulated in forty years. Sometimes the reminder of the past is a pleasant relief; at other times it's a torment. One has to choose one's memories as much as the right moment to let them in. Otherwise, they bring misery.

She looks over the photographs again, scrutinizing the faces of her ancestors, some of whom she barely remembers and others not at all. There is a portrait of her grandfather, frowning sternly down at her. He's seated at a desk and dressed in a suit and bowtie, an accounts ledger in one hand, as though prepared to meet the Day of Judgment in good order if not good cheer. Next to him is a replica of the McPherson family coat of arms and, underneath, its motto: *In patience lies wisdom.* Just words, she thinks. Like most children of her day, Violet was raised on these so-called truisms: Cleanliness is next to godliness. Patience is a virtue. And so on. Even then, she suspected that certain kinds of moral uprightness had little to do with godliness and virtue, and far more to do with hard-won strength and overall endurance. Like a stone — a hardness that was in itself considered a virtue. Can't make a stone cry. Can't wring tears from a stone. What was so good about being a bloody stone then?

Don't think about the stone.

Some of the portraits are more than a century old. That's older than I'll ever be, she thinks. And thank goodness for that. There's no great art to living long — the art is in living well. Not that she's lived any better than most — if she had, there might have been more to life, both for her and Edgar. Children, trips abroad, and all the things that other people had seemingly effortlessly. But never mind all that. It's too late to complain. And to what purpose? *If your problem has a solution, then why complain?* her father used to say. *And if your problem has no solution, then why complain?* He smiles down at her from the wall, as if he still lives on in some other place just out of reach.

Those beautiful, hand-carved frames were passed down to her from her parents. Had the carvers known their work would outlast the hands that made them? Had they understood how the frames took on lives of their own as they passed from carver to merchant, from seller to buyer? From one set of hands to the next? Probably not. Back then, people were too caught up in their day-to-day lives to notice the extraordinary around them. They were oblivious to how a face in a photograph could come alive again if looked at in the right light or how the youthful features of a woman who had withered and died long ago still seemed to glow with life in that brief moment when she sat in a hotel that has long since burned to the ground.

In the photograph, Maggie looks as young and vital now as she looked then. Violet wonders if she'd been wrong to hang that particular picture again after all the years it sat unseen, tucked away in a closet. When she'd retrieved it, it had seemed just another portrait in a frame — a moment in time that could never return. Not so now. It seems to be speaking to her. How long would the memories continue to haunt her? It has already been the better part of a lifetime.

She tries to recall what prompted her to place the photograph over her bed. Some sentimental urge, perhaps, though Violet considers sentiment suspect at best and treacherous at worst. Thinking about it now, she realizes that's when the dreams started. Why hasn't she connected the two?

The dead are gathering. They left her alone for years, but now they've come back to claim her. She senses them hovering in the shadows. Shape-shifters. Here come Ned and Julia, followed by Violet's mother and father. Don't they know they're ruining her peace of mind, giving her restless nights? Like photographs, memories are funny the way they bring back the dead and make them seem alive again. In a way, of course, it's because they are still alive whenever Violet chooses to recall them.

Nonsense. There's no "choosing" in the matter. Memories intrude whenever they damn well please. It's as if they have a will of their own. She can't help remembering the past any more than she can stop herself from dreaming about it. If she closes her eyes, she can still see the flat, grey stone that covered the cavity in the wall, can still see her hands eagerly pushing it aside and reaching down to the fateful slip of paper nestled on the bottom.

Why?

Why had she done it? What had driven her to meddle in other people's affairs? If she'd had a daughter like that, she would have throttled the nosy wretch.

The tapping starts again, more urgently now, sounding almost desperate against the glass. Never any peace! Is it prompting her to speak up or warning her to stay quiet? Does it want her to confess her awful part in the past or forever shut it out and let it die with her? It's been seventy years, after all. Seventy years that she has kept it all to herself. What difference could a few more years, or even months, make?

Blood will out.

Claire's footsteps return. The door flies open.

"Here we go!" Claire exclaims, a trifle loudly, as though to cover someone's social blunder.

Violet scrutinizes her niece's face. Has she been talking out loud, mumbling up here in her room all by herself while Claire made tea? When the ghosts gather, she sometimes does.

Claire sets the tray on the dresser, lifts the teapot, and pours. She extends a cup, smiling like a benevolent Angel of Mercy. Violet doesn't mind her gentleness too much. At least Claire is real flesh-and-blood company. She's grateful for that.

She sips her tea, then sets the cup on the side table.

"Feeling better?" Claire asks hopefully.

The question unsettles Violet.

"No, I'm not," she snaps, surprised by her crotchetiness.

A worried look steals into Claire's face. How did I age into this person? Violet wonders. How did I become this old crab! She recalls a handful of neighbourhood women, already ancient when she was young. She remembers watching them with scorn. Why would anyone let themselves grow into *that*? The faces lined with anxiety and frustration, the eyes clouded with suspicion and regret. Never a smile or a pleasant word. How could they let themselves get that way? As if willpower had anything to do with it. Though perhaps willpower has more to do with it than we realize, she tells herself. There aren't many eighty-four-year-olds living alone, still driving cars and doing their own shopping without help from others. At least, that had been the case until her fall the previous month.

It was inevitable. She'd always been careful, but the statistics finally caught up with her and down she went, like so many others her age. All the sensible shoes in the world couldn't have prevented it. She was lucky she hadn't broken anything. A slight sprain had been the worst of it, and that was mostly healed now.

"Probably the gin and tonics," she told her doctor, amused by his disapproving look. "Not the fall," she added, though she was tempted to let him go on thinking whatever he liked, the silly old bugger. "I wasn't drinking when I fell. I meant that was why I didn't break anything." She's convinced that a drink every now and then keeps her limber. And probably sane, too, if she thinks about it. But now they're all terrified the silly old bat is going to do herself in.

She smiles at the thought, then catches Claire watching her. What must this sensible young woman think of her old aunt? One moment she's crabbing about how terrible she feels, the next she's smiling to herself and staring off into the distance.

"Are you thinking what a doddering old woman I am?" she asks, catching the guilty look on Claire's face. "You are, aren't you?"

Claire quickly shakes her head. "No, I'm not thinking that, Aunt Vi. I'm worried about you. You seem distracted. Is something bothering you tonight?"

The question catches her short. What to tell this girl who is far wiser than most of the silly young things her age? Should she tell her the dead are haunting her? Should she say they crowd her dreams and won't let her rest in peace? Claire would think she was out of her mind for sure. That was bad enough, but if she claimed they talked to her, then she would seem positively barmy. Though in any case, it would help if they spoke plain English rather than all this tap-tapping against windows and blowing out of candles in the night. If only they would just come out and say what they wanted to say. But no, it's always the same meaningless signs and incomprehensible symbols.

Outside, the wind is almost a howl. There's a storm coming. A flash of lightning shifts the patterns on the wall, followed quickly by a second burst. For the briefest of moments, she sees Ned's face in the frame where her father's ought to be. In that fleeting instant she is actually frightened. Perhaps it's not so meaningless and incomprehensible after all. The flare dies and the picture returns to normal.

Claire's voice intrudes on her thoughts. "I know what it was like at Sulphur Springs," she says.

Violet is startled almost out of her wits. How on God's green earth could Claire have known about Sulphur Springs?

She turns to her niece. "What did you just say?"

Now it's Claire's turn to be startled, this time by her aunt's vehemence. She watches with evident concern. "I said, 'I know what it's like when you start thinking things.'"

Is it true? Had Claire really said that and not the other about Sulphur Springs? For one paranoid instant, Violet's mind seizes on some film she'd seen where an old woman's relatives try to drive her crazy by saying and doing things and then denying them. Was it Bette Davis? Elizabeth Taylor? One of those screen legends who also had turned into an old bat like her.

Claire nods. "It's as though our thoughts get out of control and we can't help remembering. I've had many sleepless nights since the divorce ..."

Violet feels a twinge of guilt. She's been so wrapped up in her own concerns she has barely given Claire's troubles a moment of reflection. That's really all ghosts are, she thinks — stray thoughts, memories unleashed in idle moments.

She nods and takes a sip of tea.

"Sometimes our thoughts get the better of us. They're like unwanted guests at a party. Once you let them in, they don't leave until they're ready. Do you think of him often?"

"All the time," Claire says softly.

Violet has heard only the bare bones of the story. It sounded to her like a simple tale of mismatched passions. The sooner you find out the better, of course. She'd like to know more, but out of compassion rather than curiosity. It would help her to understand what her niece went through. So far, Claire has kept it largely to herself.

"From the little you've told me, you're better off without him."

"You're right, of course. More tea?" Claire asks, changing the subject.

Violet holds out her cup. "Please."

Claire refills the cup and passes it thoughtfully back into her aunt's hands. "But what about you? Are you worried about having to sell the house? Is that what's been on your mind the last few days? Change can be a frightening thing —"

"I'm not afraid of change," Violet declares.

The worried expression returns to Claire's face. "You don't have to sell, Aunt Vi. Nobody wants you to give up your place here, but we have been concerned." She smiles guiltily. "Actually, the others asked me to report on you while I'm here."

Violet gives her a stern look.

"I'm not spying," Claire says defensively. "Any decision you make is up to you. If we need to, we've agreed to hire a nurse to come in and look after you on a part-time basis. We just want to be sure you're all right and know you're happy with your choice."

Violet nods. "So you *do* think I'm a doddering old woman."

"No, Aunt Vi, please don't say that."

She looks chastened. Violet felt the same having to tell her own mother she would need to be taken care of by somebody else, and at a far younger age. Maggie had become too much to handle alone. Violet had learned to stagger duties, looking after her mother along with her teaching schedule, but by the end there always had to be someone on hand, and so it was eventually recommended that a care home be sought. Violet had been desperate to move on and start her own life. Edgar had proposed to her by then. He'd agreed to wait for as long as it took. Kind, patient Edgar. And they *had* waited till it was inevitable before suggesting it. But it was still no easier for all that.

Poor Maggie. Violet had looked after her through nearly twenty years of illness, the last few on her own after her father died. Elizabeth had gone off to school by then, but she'd at least had Edgar. It had been far more difficult than anyone could have imagined. For her mother to lose her motor skills was as great a tragedy as having that brilliant mind imprisoned in a withered body. Both had dwindled slowly, neither kindly. But Maggie had clung on, the muscles turning to mush and trapping her mind like a bird in a cage, flitting dimly back and forth till she finally died.

Tap-tap!

The branches again. Would they never give her any peace? Was she doomed to end her days plagued by things she would rather forget? *O Guilt, thou'rt a pitiless master!* The past was like a shadow that took a step with your every step and breathed with your every breath, reminding you of all you could never be free from.

But why *should* I be free? Violet wonders. Why should any of us be expiated for the sins of our youth? Nevertheless, the sentence has been mine and I have borne it all my days. And now those days are dwindling, their numbers running out like sand in an hourglass.

Still, they haunt her, all those things that never will be.

"That's Grandmother McPherson, isn't it?" Claire asks, looking up at the portrait of Violet's mother. "I don't recall seeing it before. Where was it taken?"

For a moment Violet doesn't reply. It's a simple question and there is only one answer, but it takes her a while to find the strength to speak the words.

"It was at a spa just before the war, right before she was diagnosed. We had gone there seeking treatment — a sulphur cure — before we knew what she had. It was called the Sulphur Springs Hotel. It had beautiful gardens."

"The Sulphur Springs Hotel." Claire quietly repeats the words as though trying to place them in her memory. "Where is that?"

"It was in Dundas, Ontario. It doesn't exist now."

Claire nods, as though to say she understands all that it says about time and decay. "It looks like a lovely place," she enthuses.

"It is — or rather it *was* — a very lovely place." Violet's hands are shaking. She moves to pass her cup to Claire. "I think ..."

Claire takes it from her, watching with concern. "What is it, Aunt Vi?"

Tears spring to her eyes. Imagine! After all these years, she's finally crying over it. She reaches for Claire's hand and squeezes hard, as though she must never let go or she'll be lost forever.

"I think I killed someone there."

The teacup falls to the floor.

2

FAMOUS LAST WORDS

VIOLET WATCHES CLAIRE'S face for a reaction. When it comes, she has to fight an urge to laugh aloud. The girl's expression is that lugubrious. What must this prim young woman think of a disgruntled old rebel like Violet, especially now that she's just confessed to murder?

She glances at the dresser mirror. Floating over the gold-trimmed hairbrush and manicure set, gifts from her long-dead mother, Violet sees her fourteen-year-old self silvered over in the glass. The girl watches back with a curious, unblinking scrutiny. Does that youngster feel any compassion for her aged self? Does she even recognize the bloated caricature she's become? What should she say to that teenager staring back at her with such defiance? She wants to warn her not to meddle in other people's affairs, to tell her she can't know the terrible things life holds in store for her if she does. After all these years, she still doesn't know how to reach the child she once was. The youthful image fades and Violet finds herself facing her own white-haired reflection.

Suddenly, it's all too much for her. Memories she hasn't dwelled on in decades come tumbling out. Claire sits, unmoving, as Violet begins with an account of her stay at the Sulphur Springs Hotel, prompted by her mother's misdiagnosis of a sprained ankle. It spills over into her unexpected friendship with the worldly Julia

Browne and her dislike of Julia's harshly featured mother, Enid. It doesn't stop there, however. She keeps talking, recalling all the sad, desperate people at the hotel hoping for some relief for their troubles.

It's all a great jumble, even to Violet's ears. Of course, it would be after being held back for so long. She pauses when she comes to the young man, Ned. She hasn't spoken his name aloud for years. Saying it brings him vividly before her again, almost as if he had just walked into the room and smiled at her in that cocky way of his. So handsome, yet so terribly devious. Finally, she gets around to mentioning the stone that covered the crevice in the wall — she can't hold back that little detail. It all comes back to her now. To all appearances, it was just a simple rock wall that wound around the property. Only it wasn't so simple. In fact, that wall was the reason for Violet's involvement. That was Ned's fault too, though she can't really blame him for it now any more than she would have done then.

Finally, she ends with an account of the night of the tragedy and her years of self-reproach. If only she'd never looked into that hole, if only she had never hatched the terrible plot that led her to meddle in the lives and affairs of others. If only, if only, if only. How nice it would be to live in the magic land of If Only.

The cup lies on the floor between them. Tea soaks the carpet. Surprisingly, Claire has resisted the urge to clean it up. Violet's recounting has held her attention far more than any worries she might have about the spill. She sits there with a pensive look on her face.

"Do you believe me?" Violet asks.

Claire's eyes dart away. "I ..."

"It's all right. You can tell me I'm a delusional old woman. Some days I think I am too."

The admission makes them both laugh and the mood lightens a little. It may be the first real laugh they've shared since Claire's arrival.

"And you said no one was ever convicted of the murder?"

Violet shakes her head. "As I've said, there were several suspects, but no one went to jail for it."

Claire thinks about this for a while. "Don't take this the wrong way," she says at last, "but are any of them even still alive?"

Violet gives her a sharp look. "Besides me, you mean?"

"Yes, of course, Aunt Vi. Besides you."

"I don't think so. I was the youngest one at the hotel. The only person I kept in touch with in all that time was Julia and, as I've already said, she died last year."

Claire nods. "If there's no one else to remember, then it shouldn't really be a problem, should it?"

Violet raises her hand and smacks the bed. "But it *is* a problem — a problem for me!"

"Yes, I see," Claire says meekly.

Violet sighs. She disdains timidity and meekness. If the meek ever inherited the earth, they wouldn't have a clue what to do with it. But it's clear to her that Claire doesn't really see. How could she? She wasn't there. She can't know what it's like to have lived with this terrible secret for seventy years, to go to sleep with it lying beside you on the pillow and have it taking up space in your dreams each night. No, Claire does not see.

"I'm not sure you do," Violet says, trying to sound civil. "This has been on my conscience all these years. I don't want to die without having settled it."

"But even if you did, how can you tell anyone if they're all gone?"

While this might otherwise be a valid and very sensible point, Claire's phrasing pricks her.

"They're not 'gone,'" Violet says. "They're dead. Need I point out the difference? Guests from a party are gone once the clock strikes midnight. These people are dead."

"Yes, I see," Claire says, again with infinite patience. "But what I'm asking is, how can it make a difference to anyone now? How would it change things?"

She's right — it can't change anything. It's seventy years too late to change anything. But it might allow Violet to die in peace knowing she's done something about it after all this time. Not that speaking about it is doing anything, really. If you've got something to say, better to come out with it than let it rot away inside you. That's what her father would say. If only Violet *had* said what she knew back then. But no — that wasn't right. She had tried to tell them. Both her parents and the police. If only she'd been *believed* back then, there might not have been all that subsequent bother afterwards. But what had she really seen? That's the question. It's why the memories persist in haunting her, even today.

Still, as Claire has pointed out, it's all water under the bridge. With no one but Violet to recall the events of that day what was the point in bringing it all up again? It's nearly two o'clock by the time Claire bids her goodnight. Violet listens to her niece's footsteps recede and her bedroom door close.

It's no surprise when she doesn't sleep. She tosses on her bed like a ship on a turbulent sea. The wind moves restlessly outside the window. Before long, the branch starts up again. It seems to be tapping something in Morse code — not that she could decipher it.

The ghosts parade by in the shadows, all those long-dead faces, looking even now as though they're alive still. There's Ned, so striking in his soldier's uniform, which she had seen him wear only once. Now here come Violet's mother and father. Her father is already worrying about her mother's health, though Violet hadn't seen it at the time. Maggie laughs off his concern, as she always did. It wouldn't be for another year that the terrible wasting disease made itself known implacably, ending Maggie's career as a tennis player along with so many other things.

Now here's pretty Julia Browne, who befriended Violet and shared her concerns over all that happened in that momentous time at Sulphur Springs. Violet once envied her, but life hadn't gone so well for Julia. She'd never really known her father and her mother had been difficult and cold. Later, she'd made first one bad marriage and then another. For some reason, rotten luck had plagued her, even though she'd been born to relative prestige and social grace, if not outright wealth. If anyone ought to have had it good, it was Julia. How ironic that life should be so unkind to the ones who seemed to have the most to enjoy.

Violet, on the other hand, has had a long and mostly uncomplicated life, apart from her mother's illness. Her biggest regret was that it had seldom been exciting, except during that brief time at the Sulphur Springs Hotel. All because her mother had turned her ankle playing tennis. Moments after winning a strenuous game, Maggie collapsed in front of the entire field. Violet's father had rushed onto the court to help. Afterwards, the doctor said she'd sprained her ankle. A hasty and inaccurate diagnosis, as it turned out. With a tournament coming up in the fall, they had done everything they could to get her back on her feet, but progress was painfully slow. Eventually, someone told them about Sulphur Springs and its miracle cures. The McPhersons were on board a train in a week, steaming across the province to a place Violet had never heard of before, hoping to get her mother's ankle back in shape.

Violet's father stayed with them the first week, but he returned home before the tragedy. A pity, really, because he'd had such acute powers of observation. He saw something odd about Ned from the start. But he left, and Violet and her mother had stayed on without him. That was when Violet got mixed up in it all, dragging others down after her.

Poor Julia — had she ever forgiven her? Of course, she must have done. Otherwise, she would never have asked Violet to be a bridesmaid at her wedding to that lout whose name she never could remember. Harry ... Larry ...? No, it was Perry. It had been a dreadful mistake, Julia wrote later. Especially when Perry returned home from the war and found himself a father. He'd been unprepared to settle down after all he'd been through. The divorce hadn't really come as a surprise to anyone. It was followed not long after by Julia's second marriage to an older man who would now probably be classified as a latent homosexual. From the beginning, he'd shown Julia almost no affection, but, for better or worse, she stuck with him till he died nearly thirty years later. Violet suspected it had only been for her daughter Brenda's sake. To her credit, though, Julia never complained. Perhaps in a way she hadn't been so unhappy after all. It was hard to know for sure when news was largely confined to the occasional telephone call and letters sent back and forth across the country.

There had been a few visits after the war, then that was it. Eventually, Violet had moved far from her friend's orbit, all the way from Fort William to Vancouver Island. Yet somehow the letters continued, spanning the years and keeping the memories alive, growing less frequent only in the last decade, when they turned up mainly at Christmas and for the occasional birthday celebration. Imagine — a friendship lasting nearly seventy years. That was far longer than most marriages.

She occasionally wondered if it was just the tragedy that had kept them linked out of a shared sense of guilt. Julia was the only one who understood the full extent of Violet's involvement in the affair. Otherwise, why would two women who knew each other for such a brief time have kept in touch for so long afterwards, with only a handful of visits in all those years? It was funny how those old bonds had endured, right up until Violet received the letter saying Julia had died. On reading it, Violet felt relief as much as sadness knowing the troubled path her friend's life had taken. She'd always wondered if the events of that fateful summer had contributed to Julia's unfortunate choices later in life. No doubt a psychiatrist would have a great deal to say about it.

She feels anger rippling beneath the surface, thinking how she'd caused far more trouble than she cares to recall. No, sleep won't come now. After a moment, she pushes the blankets aside and goes to her closet, peering into its shadowy recesses. This is where she keeps the things that hold a special meaning for her. Most are things that could not possibly mean anything to anyone else. How odd to think that she has packed eighty-four years of a life into a space measuring two metres by three. On the other hand, Violet notes, she's been remarkably tidy about it all.

The top shelf holds her collection of hats. She brings down the red one with a partridge feather tucked into the band. It was Edgar's last gift to her. He always loved to see her dressed up. In fact, if she counted, she would probably discover that he bought her more hats than she bought herself.

On a lower shelf are shoeboxes containing letters and photographs — a lifetime of memories tied up in string. Without her glasses, she can just make out the name JULIA in felt-tipped marker on one of them. Her fingers ache as she pulls it out and carries it over to the bed. The correspondence spills onto the sheets, envelope after envelope, going back nearly seventy years. It will all end up in the dumpster soon. How can her life have dwindled to this? With Julia dead and Violet soon to follow, no one will ever know what these handwritten notes once signified. Nor will they care. And why should they? People have their own lives to live without worrying about the mistakes someone else once made.

She retrieves her glasses and the world swims into view. She tugs Julia's last letter from the envelope — it seems to resist — then flattens it on her lap, taking care not to tear the thin blue tissue she always wrote on:

Dec. Whatever

Dear Violet,

Forgive my missing your birthday this year. Time has taken such a funny circuitous route around us, but here I am writing to you again. Where has it all gone? Damned if I know!

I'm suffering from the usual aches and complaints we oldies get — diabetes, a bum ticker, and all the rest. I'll spare you the litany — I'm sure you have problems of your own. We could probably both do with a Sulphur Springs cure. Ha-ha.

I am still on Bridlewood in Dundas with my daughter Brenda and my grandson Bryson, who is the light of my old age. He's a detective in the police force. He moved back to help us out. We're lucky he can tolerate this tribe of matriarchs.

As you noted, we have all kept the family name. Brownes we are and always will be. It's quite the circus here some days when we're all together. You once said life had been dull for you. It's ironic, but you may never know how much I envied your so-called dullness.

Anyway, cheer up! You know what they say: We'll all be dead soon. When my time comes, I'll be ready, though it would be wonderful to see you one last time. I keep imagining you showing up at my door unannounced. And how welcome you'd be! Do you think it could happen?

With Fondest Regards and Best Wishes for Christmas,
Julia

P.S. Did you ever figure out who killed you-know-who? If anyone could, it would be you. I've always said that Violet McPherson got to the bottom of things!

It had been their last correspondence. Before Violet got around to replying, Julia had the heart attack that took her off almost immediately. A blessing, no doubt, as it was probably how Julia would have hoped to go. Fast and sure, not to burden anyone. Without looking, she knows the next envelope contains the letter from Brenda saying her mother had died.

As she refolds the letter, it slips from her grasp and flutters to the floor. With her achy joints, it takes her a moment to bend down and pick it up. She finally gets it in hand and finds herself re-reading the postscript: *P.S. Did you ever figure out who killed you-know-who?*

At the same moment, the branch taps its mournful message again. Violet looks up. The moon is emerging from behind clouds, big and round and low on the horizon, just as it had that terrible night. Afterwards, it had seemed an omen. You'd think that after all these years she'd forget a detail like that. But no — that night has etched itself onto her memory forever.

Tap-tap!

There it is again. The dead are calling her.

She refolds the letter and slips it neatly inside the envelope, placing it on top of the shoebox of correspondence. There's an unsettled feeling in her gut, like heartburn or a belch slowly making its way up and out. For a moment, Violet feels she might be sick. Something to do with the chamomile tea, maybe. She's always hated it. Why she let Claire make it for her she doesn't know. Her hand covers her mouth to make sure nothing escapes.

Surprisingly, what comes out is not a belch, but a cry. At first, it's a dull croak, but then she finds her voice — or it finds her — and she calls out as loudly as she can muster.

Within seconds she hears the creak of the floorboards. It's as if Claire has been expecting her call. Without waiting for her niece's timid knock, Violet calls out. "Come in here, Claire. I need you."

The door opens. Claire enters, eyes wide, a tangle of hair around her pale moon-face. She looks like a silent film star. Constance Talmadge or Lillian Gish — all vulnerability and startled innocence.

"Does your computer work at night?" she demands.

Claire blinks quizzically. "My laptop?"

"Yes. Does it work at night? I mean, can it connect with that Internet thing? Or do they shut it down?"

"No, it's always on."

"And is it true you can purchase things on it?"

"Yes, nearly everything."

"Airplane tickets?"

"Definitely."

"Good. I need you to book me a ticket." Violet's mind is doing double time now that her plan is in motion.

"A ticket, Aunt Vi? Are you going somewhere?"

"I'm putting off the estate sale and going to Sulphur Springs." Violet eyes her niece for signs of insurrection. She detects nothing but genuine curiosity. "I will probably have to fly into the airport at Hamilton. You'll need to check to see if that's still the closest one."

"All right."

Violet waits a beat.

"I don't mind going alone, but I would prefer it if you came with me. That way, you can be sure I won't fall." She gives Claire a sidelong glance. "And you can report on me to your brothers and sisters from there, if you like. If you have nothing better to do, that is."

After a moment, Claire smiles.

3

WHAT A DIFFERENCE A DAY MAKES

VIOLET RISES EARLY and makes a grand spread — eggs, peameal bacon, and pancakes with loads of butter and syrup. Not to mention plenty of coffee. The kind with caffeine. It's a hearty Canadian breakfast. Her appetite, so feeble of late, has returned with a vengeance. This is food she would normally avoid, but after last night's confession — not to mention all the undernourished-looking spirits parading before her eyes between midnight and dawn — a hearty morning meal is more than appropriate. Seventy years she'd been waiting to tell someone! That alone deserves a feast.

She watches her niece come down the stairs and take a seat at the table. Poor Claire looks as though she is paying for her lack of sleep. Not surprising, what with Violet carrying on about ghosts and murder and airplane tickets till the early hours. If her niece thinks she's totally lost it, she won't be surprised.

"I left a message for the solicitor," she says.

Claire looks at her with glassy eyes.

"To tell him to put off the sale. I figure it can wait a week or two."

"Yes, of course." Claire nods.

Violet reaches over to pour a cup of coffee and gently pushes it across the table. Claire stares at it as though she has never seen coffee before. After a moment, she silently dumps three teaspoons of sugar into the cup and stirs.

"Is everything still fine from last night?" Violet asks.

"Yes. I got the ticket confirmation," Claire replies. "It came through after you went to bed." She hesitates. "Are you sure you want to go through with this, Aunt Vi?"

"You mean in the cold, clear light of day you're hoping that maybe a little sanity has set in and made me change my mind?"

Claire smiles woodenly. Has this girl never been teased before? Perhaps the divorce has stolen all her joie de vivre.

"I wouldn't say that," Claire replies. "In fact, I was rather hoping you hadn't."

Violet reaches out and squeezes her hand. "Good. Because we're going." She nods at the food on the table. "You'd better eat. This won't keep till we get back. I've ordered a taxi to take us to the airport. It will be here in an hour. I'm already packed."

After a brief sleep, she'd woken with renewed excitement. Picking out some of her favourite outfits — clothes she hadn't worn in years — she was delighted to discover they still fit. For all she knows, they might even be back in fashion. There is a burgundy dinner jacket she's always loved, along with the lapel pin Edgar had given her on their forty-ninth anniversary. Sadly, he hadn't made it to the fiftieth. She wonders why it's taken so long to find a reason to wear it again. Strange, she thinks, how you just pack up your life in boxes and closets and wait for things that might never happen.

Claire gives her a funny look. "The others ... my brothers and sisters ..."

"Yes?"

"They told me things would be pretty dull out here." She smiles mischievously. "I guess they weren't counting on a murder investigation to shake things up."

Violet detects a spark in the girl.

"You ain't seen nothing yet!" she says with a wink.

After breakfast, while Claire is upstairs packing, Violet washes the dishes and puts them away. No dishwasher for her — she still does some things the old-fashioned way. The house will be fine to sit empty while she's gone. She's thankful she has spared herself that one old-lady affectation: a houseful of mewling cats to find shelter for whenever she leaves home, which admittedly hasn't been often since Edgar's death.

She looks over at their wedding photograph on the sideboard. The years stretch behind her like a canvas, spotted here and there with scenes and people she has encountered along the way. The one thing that always stands out is her time at Sulphur Springs. She wonders what Edgar would have thought if she'd spilled her terrible secret to him all those years ago. Would he have been shocked? Probably. Despite his sense of humour and his quiet sensuality, he had been quite prim in his way. If anything, he'd conspired to maintain their life together to be as uneventful as possible, circumscribing it with order and propriety, giving the neighbours nothing to gossip about. The most memorable event in their married life had been the move from Nanaimo to Victoria once Maggie had gone into a home. The rest had been quietly contained in living out their days one at a time.

That hadn't been so difficult. In keeping with her Scottish heritage, Violet has always kept her business to herself, including any mention of her involvement in a scandal-ridden affair that occurred so many decades ago. It wasn't cowardice that prevented her from speaking about it all this time; she might easily have done so without repercussion. That she'd ever been involved in such an event was shocking enough, but was it not somehow even more shocking that she'd kept it from her own husband all those years? In so many ways, she and Edgar had been completely honest and open, not sparing each other life's uncomfortable and, at times, difficult details. But this? Violet shakes her head. Trite phrases like "It just never seemed the right time to talk about it" do not really cover the truth of it. The simple fact is it hadn't been anybody else's business. Despite his admonition to speak up at the time, even her father had advised her to keep silent about it afterwards. And that was precisely what Violet had done. Till now.

Shocking as the murder had been, it hadn't affected her personally. Or had it? How many years has she fought to keep it buried inside her? How long has she hidden the truth at the back of her mind waiting for ... what? For someone to come forward and say, "Do tell us, Mrs. McAdams, what really happened on that long ago evening at the Sulphur Springs Hotel, an evening that ended with one person murdered in cold blood and another the prime suspect?"

What could she have told them? No more than she'd told the Dundas police at the time, which is that she had seen the pair together after one of them claimed to have left town. But what had she actually seen? A silhouette, a profile in the dark as they grappled together in the sulphur springs. But that was all she'd seen before turning tail and running like a scared rabbit, hoping they hadn't seen *her*.

Violet certainly hadn't felt inclined to stick around once she realized what they were up to that night. What might have happened if she'd stayed? Could she have prevented a death? Not likely. In fact, if anything, it might have been she, Violet, who had ended up murdered. Odd, but she's never seriously considered that until now. In any case, it's far too late to ever know for sure. If going back there can do anything, it might help atone for her silence all these years. It might possibly make up for not having made the effort to see Julia one last time, for not visiting that friend of her youth and talking over those days once again. Yes, it might do that. Time will tell.

She shakes her head. This is just fantasizing out of some misplaced sense of guilt. Even if she had gone back to visit, what would she and Julia have had to say to one another? In truth, they'd been thrown together by chance that summer at the spa in the days leading up to the war. It was only the memory of what happened in that brief time — that and a modicum of fondness for one another — that had kept them in touch all those years until Julia's death.

A toot of the horn announces the cab's arrival. Violet halts in her reveries and looks up to see Claire standing at the foot of the stairs. Her niece has undergone a transformation. Her hair is done and her face is alight with excitement. Maybe the subject of murder is a turn-on for her. Though that might be putting it a bit too vulgarly, Violet chides herself. It may just be the prospect of travel.

"I'm ready, Aunt Vi," Claire declares. She clutches her suitcase with a vigour Violet hasn't seen in her till now.

"You are indeed," she says. "And good for you."

Standing before the hall mirror, Violet dons the red hat — the one Edgar gave her — and matching calfskin gloves. Claire watches with something like admiration. Violet catches the girl's eye.

"I may be old, but that's no excuse for not having a sense of style."

Claire's eyebrows shoot up. She positively beams.

"You look very stylish, Aunt Vi," she says.

Yes, Violet thinks, her niece has definitely caught a sense of adventure.

BY THE TIME the taxi drops them at the airport, Violet, too, is tingling with excitement. She hasn't felt like this in years. Inside, the terminal is the usual drab affair of lineups and people clutching suitcases so desperately you'd think they'd packed their entire lives into them. And maybe they have, she thinks. We're all escaping from something.

Claire bypasses the long lines and takes them to an electronic check-in kiosk. She inserts a piece of paper into the machine and something beeps. Amazingly, in less than a minute they're checked in. Violet realizes how out of touch she's been — who knows what sort of transient mindset people have got themselves into nowadays. They probably went off on world adventures at the drop of a hat.

There's a moment of consternation when Violet sets off an alarm at the security port. She sees the curious faces of the security guards watching her. Are they looking at her as a possible terrorist? She'd be the perfect foil for it, disguised as a harmless little old lady.

For a moment, they all stand there looking on in surprise until a young woman with an oversized wand comes up and traces her outline to see what mysterious item she has failed to remove or possibly hidden on her person. It can't be jewellery, Violet thinks. She'd taken it all off and set it in those plastic bins rolling down the line to the X-ray machine.

Then it occurs to her.

"It's my hip," she says.

The wand zips down to her left side. Sure enough, it sets off a loud beeping. There is a collective sigh of relief. They all share a laugh as they agree the culprit is the pin from her hip replacement. She and Claire collect their belongings and soldier on. There are no further barriers on this side of the lineup. What there is, however, is store after store and restaurant after restaurant. It's like a mini shopping mall of boutiques and cafés.

Travel is certainly looking a lot more convenient than when she was a girl. You can even get a good gin and tonic at a bar before your flight, she notes. And she does just that. After a brief stop in Charlie's Jazz Spot, they proceed to the boarding gate. If their plane leaves on time, they'll be in Hamilton by early afternoon. They can check into their lodgings in Dundas in time for a late lunch. And that, she realizes, is definitely something to look forward to.

Thinking of it now, she imagines a resort not so very different from the Sulphur Springs Hotel — an elegant, genteel establishment, the sort of place where retired ladies and gentlemen might spend their leisure hours reading or discussing business and politics. She envisions a well-stocked library with a grand piano and a real wood-burning fireplace, not one of these tinselly affairs with flashing lights and plastic logs that fools no one. And, while she's at it, she wants the piano to have actual keys that make real sounds when depressed, not some lumbering elephant carcass missing all of its insides.

She is feeling nicely relaxed as they board. She and Claire have plenty of time to get comfortable. Together, they watch the flight attendants demonstrate the proper method of buckling seatbelts and donning oxygen masks, though she suspects they'll need more than oxygen in the event of an emergency. Maybe another gin and tonic. Looking around, Violet realizes that she and Claire are the only ones taking this in. Perhaps the others are so well versed in travel procedures they know the instructions by heart.

When it comes time to turn on the entertainment screen and don her earphones, she's positively amazed by what is available. She quickly dismisses the selection of action movies and romantic comedies and turns instead to the radio. The sounds of Celine Dion on channel 8 fade into a Healey Willan canticle, a girlhood favourite, on channel 9.

Even more surprising, the flight leaves on time — none of this dawdling about on the runway for hours that you hear about on the radio all the time. She's flooded with relief as the plane surges forward and the earth drops away beneath them. For a moment, everybody falls silent as the upward thrust catches them in its grip.

With a tinge of remorse, Violet thinks how easy it would have been to get on a plane and visit Julia at any point in the last decade, despite Edgar's warnings about the perils of travelling. He would have been worried about bomb threats and hijackings, gently admonishing her for wanting to go all that way for a visit when they could just as easily talk on the telephone. And far more safely, in his eyes. Men! Instead, she'd waited till her friend was dead before making the return journey.

In less than a minute, they're surrounded by clouds. Then, just as suddenly, they break through into the bright blue space above. Conversation resumes all around them. How glorious! she thinks. I should have done this years ago.

4

THROUGH VERDUROUS GLOOMS AND WINDING MOSSY WAYS

DUNDAS VALLEY WAS a marvel to behold. Lush greenery caught the eye and refused to let go. According to geological surveys made the previous century, the valley was formed by the gentle scouring of pre-glacial rivers. Then came the not so gentle ice, carving out the U-shaped basin even more thoroughly until it lay a full hundred metres below nearby Lake Ontario.

According to local lore, the original Scottish pioneers settled in the valley because its rolling hills and rushing streams reminded them of home. It was here the first McIntosh apples were farmed and also here that the famed sulphur springs were discovered and hailed for their miraculous curative powers. More than a century later, the community still resembled the original settlement built by those hardy Scotsmen.

Fourteen-year-old Violet McPherson reached a gloved hand toward her father and stepped from the train. Her eyes looked crystalline, especially when she was excited. It was a sign of intelligence, her father said. Once she had alighted on the platform, she turned to watch him assist her mother, noting the care he took to avoid any strain on her ankle.

If his wife would have allowed it, Clive McPherson would have carried her bodily from the train, but Maggie McPherson was too independent for such gestures. When she stood securely on the platform, he released her with a smile. Violet saw the earnestness in his gaze. Clive McPherson was a big man. Many found him intimidating, but his gentleness could be heard in his voice and discerned in his level-headed approach to life. People said he resembled the English poet Siegfried Sassoon, a war hero, while Violet's mother looked like the American film star Carol Lombard. Violet had overheard a neighbour saying so just the other day. Around the neighbourhood, Maggie and Clive were said to be a "handsome couple." Violet knew who Carole Lombard was — she'd seen her movies at the cinema — but she'd never seen a picture of Sassoon. She imagined that Sassoon and Lombard would make such a glamorous match that they would fall immediately and madly in love, were they ever to meet.

In reality, the McPhersons were a hard-working couple. They weren't overly well off, but they had not had it as bad as others during the long dark days of the Great Depression, only now ending. Clive had secured a job as a high school biology teacher, while Maggie maintained a steady tour of the women's tennis circuit. Occasionally there were winnings, but the take was never large. The past year had been her best, but she was now in her thirties. It wouldn't last. Somehow, they managed with whatever life offered. In truth, they considered themselves blessed. Perhaps, if they'd known what lay just ahead, they might not have believed themselves so lucky. In the years to come, Violet thought it fortunate that fate conferred on hard-working and idle humans alike the gift of being blind to the future, allowing no hint of coming joys or incipient tragedies, so as not to spoil tomorrow's pleasures or darken today with a dread of what lay ahead. To Violet, who had so far been sheltered from its hardest blows, life might otherwise have seemed far crueller and the present more poignant than it did at that moment, caught up as she was in the mad rush of adventure carrying her to a place she had never before seen.

On leaving the station, her father hailed a cab and gave the driver the address for the Sulphur Springs Hotel.

"Very good, sir. You'll enjoy it, I'm sure," the man said, swinging their bags into the trunk of his car. Then he noticed Violet's mother's limp. "Has the lady hurt herself?"

Maggie McPherson turned a glamorous smile on him. "It's nothing," she said, allowing only that she'd been experiencing some trouble with her ankle since playing a game of tennis.

"In fact, my wife is going to the spa for treatment," Clive McPherson answered. "She's a tennis champion."

The driver gave her a serious look. "Is that a fact, now? Well, whatever ails you, madam, I'm sure you'll come away cured," he said with cheerful optimism, and nosed the car onto the road. "Those waters are good for almost anything that ails a body. My mother-in-law spent time there a few years back for her rheumatism and she was practically cured in a fortnight."

"Is that right?" Clive asked.

"Yes, sir. They're a miracle, those waters. Just you wait and see. That's why me and Ellie — the wife — moved here, to be close to the springs. She's had the occasional twinge of arthritis herself. Whenever it flares up, she just goes for a dip in the waters."

The cab edged down a hill and sped along beneath a canopy of trees. For a moment, the sky disappeared from view as if a veil had suddenly been drawn across the sun, turning the landscape into a vista of oncoming twilight. Had Keats's celebrated nightingale made it to North America, it might have felt right at home here. Then the cab headed up again and the world winked back into sight.

The trip was a mere ten minutes from the station to the hotel along the dusty back roads of Dundas Valley. Violet was used to the stark landscape around Fort William, where towering Jack pines thrust scraggly arms skyward in the rocky, barren landscape. Now, as the cab whisked them onward, the valley unfolded in a forest of winnowed boughs and meadows gleaming like an emerald sea.

They passed through a gate in a low rock wall and pulled up before an arresting limestone façade. Violet found herself slightly awestruck. The hotel's windows faced in all directions to catch the full effects of the sun. From the brochure, she already knew that Judge Emond Browne had built the place as a family dwelling in the late-1800s. The Browne family had lived here ever since, eventually converting their home into a hotel and managing the springs publicly after the judge's death. Despite its bright exterior, there was a gloominess about it, as if it doubted its right to exist in this fairy-tale valley next to a legendary spring whose miraculous waters were becoming known far and wide.

The cabbie sprang to open their door. Maggie stepped out first, followed by Violet. The branches of bur oak and poplar swayed overhead as if in welcome. A waterfall spilled into a pool filled with water lilies. At its centre a herring dipped its beak below the surface, speared a fish, then spread its wings and soared upward.

Maggie looked around and nodded approvingly. "It's every bit as lovely as the photographs."

Violet sniffed the air. There was a faint odour, as of something burning far off.

"What's that smell?"

"That's the sulphur water that will cure your mother," her father replied. "You'll get used to it."

The front door opened. A tall, bespectacled man in a vest and pinstriped suit emerged and introduced himself as Mr. Willoughby, the hotel's director. With his wire-rimmed glasses and greying hair, he looked more like a bank manager. The sort that would turn you down for a loan as quick as give one, Violet thought. He directed the cabbie to bring the McPhersons' bags into the lobby as he accompanied the new arrivals to the front desk. A woman with thin, unsmiling features glanced up at them.

"May I introduce Mrs. Enid Browne, the spa's owner?" said Willoughby. "Mr. and Mrs. McPherson from Fort William."

"You've come a long way." She stood and shook Maggie's hand, then Clive's. "Welcome to the Sulphur Springs Hotel.

"Thank you," Maggie said.

"We're delighted to be here, Mrs. Browne," said Clive. "We've heard wonderful things about your spa's curative powers. My wife has an important tournament coming up in a month and we want her to be as fit as a fiddle."

"Rest assured, Mr. McPherson, we will do all we can for your wife."

"And this is Violet," Willoughby continued, turning to the girl who had pressed herself against the wall until she was almost hidden from Enid Browne's gaze. "She looks as though she would make a suitable companion for Julia."

This was the first Violet had heard about a companion of any sort. She was disinclined to accept Willoughby's statement. How did he know what sort of playmates she liked?

"She's a lovely child," Mrs. Browne said, though her smile did nothing to convey warmth.

Violet knew the things that hid behind a smile. She knew with unerring certainty, for instance, that she would not have wanted this woman for a teacher. She'd be the sort to rap your knuckles if you whispered to a classmate during lessons. She recalled how Miss Budge, a grade six teacher, had spanked Teddy Wilson for talking out of turn. She'd called him to the front of the class and made him bend over, striking him three times with her yardstick. At first, Teddy had shown no reaction. Then suddenly, he burst into tears. They were all too shocked to say a word. Violet had thought it cruel of Miss Budge to spank Teddy in front of the class, but she thought it even crueller when the others taunted him about it till Miss Budge threatened to strap the very next person who said a word. They'd all kept mum after that. Enid Browne seemed almost certainly of that type.

Willoughby excused himself and stepped out of the lobby, only to return a moment later pushing a wheelchair.

Maggie looked at it and laughed. "Is that for me?"

"Yes, Mrs. McPherson. For your convenience only."

Violet thought her mother would refuse, but she acquiesced and sat in the awkward-looking contraption as Willoughby accompanied them down the hall. At the far end, he stopped to unlock a heavy wooden door. They entered a large suite with a king-size bed and a bay window. Afternoon sunlight nestled in the corners. Violet looked around for a second bed, but found none.

"Where will I sleep?" she asked.

"Right next door, darling," her mother said with a smile. "You get your very own room."

This was a surprise. Violet realized it must have entailed considerable expense on her parents' part, something she'd deduced from the murmured discussions they had when paying bills: what to pay off right away and what could be put off till the following month. Her father took her hand as they exited and followed Willoughby back along the hallway to an adjacent door.

The room was outfitted with an armoire and a four-poster bed beneath a green canopy. On the walls, frilly ferns had been stencilled around a gleaming pond watched over by a poky-looking beaver and a family of deer, including a fawn with exaggeratedly large eyes. A fountain sparkled in the background. These, she decided, must be the mystical sulphur springs. It seemed a magical rendering of a secret world.

Willoughby set her suitcase by the bed.

"It's wonderful!" Violet exclaimed, hugging her father.

It was hers for the week ahead, he told her. Once he returned home to prepare for the school year, Violet and her mother would share the larger suite. For now, she was on her own. She secretly hoped that if she waited till the right moment to ask, her mother might let her keep this room for the duration of the stay. It hadn't yet occurred to her that her mother might need her help when her father left.

Since her collapse on the court, Maggie McPherson had come to depend on others far more than was usual for her. She had taken to asking Violet for help when she found it difficult to reach something on a shelf or, once, when a shoe had become too tight for her to remove. Violet thought it a surprising show of dependence for someone as plucky and determined as her mother.

Once they were settled, the McPhersons returned to the lobby where Willoughby waited to take them on a tour of the hotel grounds. Twittering noises filled the air. Just past the reception desk, Violet saw a towering gilt cage housing several canaries.

"Do they actually sing?" she asked, pressing her face close to the bars while the startled birds flitted from perch to perch.

"Only in the morning, miss," Willoughby replied.

"And probably only when curious young ladies keep their distance," her father added.

"Shall we start the tour?" Willoughby asked.

Violet walked alongside her mother as the wheelchair crunched down the gravel drive. A loving hand had shaped the gardens. There was heather and hydrangea and hanging, grape-like wisteria clusters. Beneath a far window, a swath of pink spikes caught Violet's eye.

"Look, Daddy! *Digitalis*," she cried.

Her father turned to where she pointed. "Yes," he said. "You're right."

"Good heavens! Is that some sort of bug?" said Maggie McPherson.

"No, it's your daughter's fancy way of saying 'foxglove,'" replied Clive.

"And over there is monkshood," Violet said in a hushed voice.

Nearly hidden behind a row of thorny roses could be seen a tall, malevolent-looking plant with dark, hooded flowers.

"Yes," her father said. "And as you know, monkshood can be highly dangerous even to touch."

Willoughby examined the flower with a look of alarm. "Goodness. I hadn't noticed it before. The young lady will have to be careful prowling about the gardens."

Clive McPherson gave a little laugh. "No need to worry about Violet," he said. "I'm a botanist by training and Violet has been coached thoroughly as to which plants must be avoided. She can tell poison ivy from poison oak, and even has a fair knowledge of which mushrooms are edible and which are not, though she will never" — here he shot a meaningful look at his daughter — "attempt any culinary adventures without me on hand to verify her choices."

"A botanist, sir? Then you will no doubt appreciate our gardens. We have a wide assortment of plants acquired from around the world."

"Indeed, I have been noticing, Mr. Willoughby."

As they walked, Violet spied a young man in overalls and a checked shirt leaning on a shovel. The taut features of his tanned face were nearly hidden beneath the brim of a grey felt cap. He seemed to be watching them with barely concealed amusement.

"Afternoon, Mr. Willoughby, sir," said the young man.

He had a slight accent. Not as though he were foreign, Violet thought, but as if he came from a different part of the country. His vowels sounded knotty.

"Good afternoon, Ned," Willoughby replied. He turned to the McPhersons. "Ned is our resident gardener," he said, with a coolness that suggested he wasn't impressed with the young man.

"And occasional bathhouse attendant, as required." Ned doffed his cap in a comical manner. Curly brown hair spilled out from underneath it as he stood there openly regarding them.

"This way, please. We're nearly at the end," Willoughby said.

They left Ned standing there with his shovel and his open stare. When Violet turned to look back, he winked.

They continued on to a small fountain with a bathing nymph at its centre. Violet was beginning to wonder who was responsible for the grounds. Surely it couldn't be the dour Mrs. Browne, whose appearance and demeanour did little to suggest an interest in beautiful things. On the other hand, Ned the gardener looked too young to have created such opulence. Perhaps it was a tradition carried on from a time when the judge lived there.

Willoughby came to a halt. The sulphur springs were still a bit of a walk from the hotel grounds, he informed them, and therefore best left till the following day, but the paths around the hotel made for an impressive walk at any time of day or night.

"Are they safe?" Clive asked. "Violet is a bit of a wanderer."

"Oh, yes. Have no fear," Willoughby replied. He turned to Violet. "Not a *shrinking* violet then, I gather?"

"No, I'm not," Violet said coldly, having heard the comment far too often to find it amusing.

Willoughby turned to her parents and clasped his hands. "Well then. This is the extent of our tour today. But feel free to roam at your leisure."

Maggie took hold of her husband's arm. "Looks like we'll have plenty to see and do while we're here, won't we Clive? You and Violet can explore the gardens while I do my exercises and consult the doctors about my ankle."

"And while you are taking the waters, Mrs. McPherson," said the hotel's director, "I suspect little Violet will have a very nice time getting acquainted with Mrs. Browne's daughter, Julia."

Violet disliked being called "little" but did not say so.

"Does she like dolls?" she asked.

"I suspect Miss Julia is a bit beyond the doll stage, miss," Willoughby answered, "but she'll still make a fine playmate for you."

Violet felt her face heating up. It had never occurred to her that anyone might be "beyond the doll stage." If that were so, then why did her mother show such interest when she brought Baby Gabby and Baby Henrietta to the table for an imaginary tea party? She seemed to be as pleased as when she presented her report cards showing all her As and A+s.

Willoughby nodded to Maggie. "The girl, Julia, would make an excellent sitter, if ever you have need of one, Mrs. McPherson."

She smiled. "Thank you, Mr. Willoughby, but I doubt I'll have need of one. I won't be doing much wandering about on this ankle. My husband will be leaving once I'm settled, so it looks like I'll be doing a lot of sitting myself." She looked over at Violet. "And Violet is pretty mature for her age, you'll find. I seldom need to leave her with anyone."

"A big girl, are you, miss?" asked Willoughby.

"I'm almost fifteen," Violet told him, annoyed that he would have mistaken her for younger.

"Well, there you are then," he said with a laugh, and turned his gaze to the sun. "It's just going on two o'clock, I believe."

Clive McPherson checked his watch. "Indeed, it is."

Willoughby nodded. "I'm about to ask you to do something unusual, sir. Please don't be alarmed. At Sulphur Springs we like our guests to relax and forget all about outside concerns and anything beyond these grounds while they're here. We encourage you to leave the modern world behind and enter fully into our tranquil, healing environment."

"Goodness," Clive said, putting an arm around Violet's shoulder. "You're not going to ask us to give up our firstborn, are you?"

A bewildered look crossed the director's face. "Not at all, sir, but I am going to ask you to give up your watches — temporarily, of course. These devices can be disruptive to a curative state of mind."

Maggie McPherson looked surprised. "But how will we know what time it is, Mr. Willoughby?" she exclaimed. "How will I keep my therapy appointments? And — my goodness — however will we know when it's time for dinner?"

Here, Willoughby looked up at the sun again. "One develops a wonderfully accurate sense of time after being here only a short while. All appointments are finished at four o'clock, giving you plenty of time to retire and dress for dinner, which is served promptly at six p.m. each day, followed by an hour of music. A dinner bell is rung at precisely five forty-five, although guests are welcome to gather for pre-dinner cocktails in the dining room beginning at five thirty."

"How civilized it all sounds," Maggie McPherson joked.

Again, Willoughby did not catch the humour. "Yes, I suppose it does." He turned expectantly to Violet's father.

Clive McPherson handed over his watch on a chain. "I'm trusting you to look after this, Willoughby," he said. "It's a family heirloom."

His wife unfastened her wristwatch and held it up. Willoughby pocketed both of the timepieces.

"Have no fear. I have never lost a single timepiece in all my years at the spa."

They arrived back at the lobby, deserted now. To the right of the desk stood an imposing grandfather clock.

"That clock will always tell you the correct time," Willoughby said. "If you are ever in doubt, follow it and you will never go wrong."

Violet regarded the large brass numerals and long pendulums encased in a solid-looking wooden box with woodland scenes carved into it. She wondered if it, too, had belonged to Judge Browne.

"If all else fails," Willoughby continued, "there is a sundial in the garden — but of course that works only on sunny days."

He bowed and took his leave.

"Eccentric little fellow, isn't he?" Maggie said, watching him go. "And what a strange rule."

"But a good one!" Clive declared. "So long as we get our watches back, I won't have any problem adhering to it. I am liking this place more and more."

-5-

A SEA OF BRIGHT RED ROSES

THAT AFTERNOON, WHILE her parents attended a consultation with the spa physician, Violet decided to explore the hotel grounds. She put on a tartan skirt and blouse, exchanging her buckle shoes for sneakers, a far more practical getup. Apart from the miracle springs with their lure of mystery, she was curious to learn what else might await. There could be caves — she'd seen the ridges of hills in the distance during the cab ride in. There might even be horses, though she had so far seen nothing that looked like stables. The closest to that had turned out to be a gardening shed.

Daydreaming of adventure, she rounded a corner and nearly collided with a girl a few years older than herself. Her hair was straight and black, her face pale. She stood nearly a head taller than Violet. Casual slacks and a blouse emphasising her breasts gave her an adult look. Clearly, she was a young woman and not a girl. This, no doubt, was Julia Browne, the hotelkeeper's daughter. With crashing clarity, Violet understood what "beyond the doll stage" meant.

The young woman's face took on a look of practiced congeniality. Despite her pleasant expression, there was an air of sadness about her.

"Hello there. You must be Violet." She extended her hand. "I'm Julia."

They shook.

"Mr. Willoughby told me your family had arrived. Perhaps we could have a tea party with dolls later."

Violet flushed, glad she hadn't worn her Shirley Temple dress with its pink frills. If you could be beyond the doll stage, then there was probably such a thing as too cute. "Actually, I'm pretty much beyond the doll stage now."

"Oh — that's a relief." Julia flashed a smile. "I'm sick to death of dolls. For some reason, I get saddled with all the youngsters who show up here with their parents wanting to play childish games. I'm glad you won't be anything like that."

"Not at all."

"Good. Do you want to see the grounds? Our gardens are famous."

Violet was quietly astonished that someone her own age could claim to have famous gardens.

"I've already seen some of them. Why are they famous?"

"Many of the plants were imported from Europe and Asia. People come for miles around to see them. Sometimes plants disappear from the beds."

"Disappear how?"

Julia gave her a wry look. "With a shovel and a burlap sack, is my best guess."

"You mean people steal them?"

"Sometimes. Though why they can't just go out and buy their own is beyond me. Never mind that. Let's go."

Julia flipped her hair over her shoulders as she turned. Up ahead, she stopped abruptly to point out a patch of small purple flowers bordering the garden edge.

"There are lots of big flowers here, but I love those tiny ones. Aren't they pretty?"

"Yes, that's *vinca minor*. Its common name is periwinkle."

Julia gave Violet a sharp look then burst out laughing. "If you say so."

"I do say so. It produces reserpine, which is a medication used to treat high blood pressure. My father's a botanist. That's how I know these things."

"That's very interesting, but I'll tell *you* something. Periwinkle is called the Flower of Death. Do you know why?"

"No. Why?"

"Because its vines used to be woven into headbands for dead children when they were buried."

"That's —"

"Creepy?"

"No. It's clever!"

Both girls smiled at the same time. They walked on, with Julia pointing out her favourites and Violet giving the Latin names for the ones she knew. They came to a halt beside a gazebo. Violet looked around.

"Where are the others?" she asked.

"What others?"

"The other children. You said —"

"There are no others right now. Just us. But don't worry," said Julia. "We'll find things to amuse you. I'm sure that won't be difficult. I can tell you're clever."

They walked in silence till they arrived back at the front of the hotel.

"Why did you say I'm clever?"

"I know a smarty-pants when I see one."

"I'm not a —"

"Oh, yes you are." Julia smirked. "It's nearly tea time. Let's get ready."

She turned and headed inside. In the lobby, Julia pointed to the grandfather clock.

"I'm in charge of clocks. Every morning I set the time and wind it with this key." She pointed to a large brass key fitting. "For me, it really is a grandfather clock. Judge Browne was my grandfather, and this was his estate."

"I thought so when I saw it."

"You see? You *are* clever!"

"It's a beautiful clock," Violet said. "What was your grandfather like? Was he nice?"

"No! He was a nasty old bugger. He never had a kind word for anybody."

For the second time in fifteen minutes, Violet was shocked by Julia's admission. She'd heard boys at school use words like that, but none of the girls she knew talked that way.

"Old people can be very trying," Violet said, repeating something she'd once heard her mother say.

"Can they ever!" Julia exclaimed, turning and heading down a long hallway. "Come on! His portrait's in the library chapel. You can see for yourself."

The library lay in shadows. It was filled with walls of books and heavy, old-fashioned furniture — what her mother sniffingly referred to as "Victorian." To Violet's approval, it also contained a grand piano and a gaping fireplace nearly tall enough for her to stand upright in.

A door at the far end led to a small chapel with mud-brown walls and heavy velvet drapery. A sign overhead read The Hermitage. Inside were seats for a dozen people. The overall effect was oppressive and stale, as if the room had been closed up too long. Behind a dais hung an oil portrait of a man in judge's robes.

"This is my grandfather, Judge Emond Browne," Julia said with mock formality, as though introducing them.

The judge's expression was gloomy. It reminded Violet of the look on Enid Browne's face. The portrait gave the impression that the sitter wanted to appear menacing. He seemed part of that mysterious kingdom of virtue and righteousness adults often spoke of, particularly when pointing out the flaws of children. These were the ones who would inherit the earth, according to her Sunday school teacher, Mrs. Johnson. Violet had long since decided that if Heaven were filled with people like that, then she was in no hurry to get there. And what of the others? The ones who wouldn't spend their eternity alongside pious judges and prosperous businessmen? She imagined them as the sort of men who leaned against buildings, smoking cigarettes and shirking their responsibilities. Clearly, these were not the stances of the meek and mild. When she'd spent time with the Holy Book — which hadn't been often — it was the more vigorous and warlike Old Testament that she preferred. Less meekness and mildness and more of the high and mighty.

If truth were told, Violet felt more inclined to side with the heathens, the ones who defied the plagues of God and questioned His edicts about sacrificing this and not eating that. She would not be inclined to save anyone who sacrificed a living animal, for instance. Or worse, someone like Abraham, who would willingly kill his own son. As far as she was concerned, the Bible got most things backwards.

Violet's mother was surprisingly old-fashioned about such things, despite her modernity in other ways. She had balked when Violet asked to be excused from attending Sunday school, seeming to regard the church as an offshoot of social functions. In her estimation, attending church built character. "Violet already has plenty of character," her father said, making Violet feel he was rooting for her against the unwanted burden of church-going. But then, her mother laughed and she wasn't sure after all.

Both parents encouraged her in the basic values: honesty, compassion, and responsibility, but it was her mother who encouraged her nightly prayers, asking the Lord to take her soul if she should die in her sleep, an event Violet felt highly unlikely. As she saw it, there was God and then there was something called the "Godhead," a word she had heard the minister use once. She imagined the first as an impossibly old and cranky man at the farthest ends of the universe, someone who quietly amused himself by watching over the affairs of humans, while the second was untouched by those same humans, if aware of them at all. She preferred the latter, if she had to believe in something, but nature was her true religion. Birds and mammals and insects. She'd held a snake in science class once. Its yellow eyes gleamed as its tongue slithered in and out. Sarah Bradley had screamed, but Violet liked the feel as it wrapped itself around her wrist. She especially liked being praised afterwards by her teacher on how calm and brave she had been.

At ten, she'd declared herself an atheist. Her father, who shared her scientific bias, had been amused. Her mother was perturbed. She tried in vain to inspire religious feelings in her daughter, telling her of the supposed glories of Heaven. It had a sky that was bluer than blue, she said, and it was more beautiful than anywhere on earth. Was it more beautiful than the rugged shores of Lake Superior that seemed to spread forever northward? Violet asked. That and more, Maggie assured her. It was everything you ever wanted. It contained your favourite chair and food and all your best friends. Even your pets. Violet tried to imagine sitting in a rocker with Peaches, her cat, while holding onto a slice of blueberry pie. It sounded all right, but something was missing. She added an entire library, including a set of Nancy Drew mysteries with more titles than actually existed, since she'd read them all twice, but even that didn't feel right somehow. Eternity meant forever. How long before she got bored?

"She's only ten, Clive," her mother argued. "Don't you think that's a bit early to encourage her to make such a decision?"

"I don't think we have any choice," her father responded. "We can't make her believe in something she doesn't agree with. Besides, it shows her ability to reason through what she's been told. If nothing else, it will make a good scientist of her. Anyway, there's nothing to say she won't change her mind later on. If and when she does, I'm sure God will forgive her."

"Why does she always go too far?"

Her mother had sighed a great deal in the days following Violet's declaration, but left the subject alone after that. She knew her daughter's stubbornness too well. That wasn't the end of it, however. In fact, it was the beginning of Violet's drive for independence. It was her sarcasm that got her in trouble next. One day at dinner she'd made a comment to the effect that her teacher, Miss Budge, was so unattractive that no man would ever marry her.

Her mother's eyes narrowed. "Miss Budge might be a perfectly nice person inside. It's not her fault if she's plain. You mustn't be uncharitable to others."

"But it's true," Violet protested. "Aren't I always supposed to tell the truth? Isn't that what the Bible says?"

Maggie just shook her head and changed the subject. Her father looked amused, but said nothing. She preferred it when he took her side in things, but she knew better than to push him too far.

"Don't argue with your mother, please," was the harshest of his admonitions.

Argument or not, Violet believed strongly in virtuous mothers and barren spinsters. Her mother was kind and beautiful. Miss Budge strapped her pupils and wore gingham and blunt shoes, with stockings rolled halfway down around her ankles. In Violet's view, such a woman would never be chosen to bear children or be loved by a devoted husband. This appealed strongly to her sense of apocalyptic happenings and a stern biblical justice meted out to the wicked. She felt the sting of victory in taking one of her mother's own weapons and turning it around on her.

"There's honesty and then there's charity," Maggie said, shading Violet's black-and-white beliefs into tones of grey. "Knowing when to tell the truth is almost as important as how you tell it. You'll learn this in time. If you're simply saying things to be smart or mean, then there's no point in saying them."

"Martin Bowman said I was a show-off in class. That's mean, isn't it?"

Her mother looked coolly at her. "It may have been. I wasn't there. Were you showing off when you should have been doing something else? Like your schoolwork?"

"I can't help it if I'm the smartest person in the whole school."

"If you are the smartest," her mother said, "then you needn't show off to prove it. It will be apparent to everyone."

"That's what I said," Violet declared, and flounced off, feeling superior.

Standing there before the portrait of Julia's grandfather, Violet felt a tug at her sleeve.

"I'll bet you're a good sleuth," Julia whispered.

In fact, Violet thought herself an excellent sleuth. She once found a missing pencil case a classmate had dropped inside an apron pocket hanging on a peg. While everyone else had been looking on the floor, Violet had looked up instead.

"Yes, I am pretty good," she said. "Why?"

Julia's eyes flashed. "Because there's a mystery going on in this hotel right now."

"Really? What is it?"

"I'll show you. Come on!"

Violet found herself standing with Julia inside a high-ceilinged kitchen with large wooden counters and a long, black stove at the far end. Soot-darkened stovepipes ran up and out through a hole in the wall. Julia nudged Violet and pointed to an open doorway. Cupboards stretched from floor to ceiling, stacked with cans and bowls and an electric stand mixer.

"That's the pantry," Julia said.

"That's quite obvious," Violet said. If Julia thought her a smarty-pants, then why not prove it? "So, what's the mystery?"

"Go in and tell me what you see."

Violet stepped into the narrow space and glanced around at the shelves. She turned back to Julia. "A lot of tinned goods and rows and rows of jam in jars."

Julia crossed her arms. "What else?"

She looked at the counter. "There's also a pan of brownies."

"Right. And do you notice anything unusual about them?"

"Someone's been eating them before they've been taken out of the pan. They've been clawed apart with a fork instead of cut with a knife. Which probably means someone's helped themselves."

Julia gave her an admiring glance. "Very good. I always said girls make better sleuths than boys."

"Who ate them?" Violet asked.

Julia held her gaze. "That," she said, "is the mystery. Someone comes in and steals the brownies when no one is looking."

"They're being stolen?"

Julia nodded solemnly. "Someone comes in and helps themselves right from the pan. It's usually when Cook's taking her break. Then there's not enough for dessert later. It happens every other day. Mother is getting extremely annoyed with her for leaving them out, but Cook says she can't take them from the pan and put them away until they're cool."

Violet thought of the severe-looking Enid Browne. She felt far less inclined to solve a mystery if it meant helping the harsh, unsmiling woman. On the other hand, she very much wanted to impress Julia.

"Can't you just wait outside the door and see who comes in?"

"Tried that," said Julia. "Whoever it is doesn't come near the place when I'm parked outside it."

Violet nodded. "I think we should lay a trap and get to the bottom of this."

"I'm with you there. What do we do?"

"Leave it to me. I'll think of something."

"Okay, Miss Smarty-Pants, I'm counting on you." Julia grinned. "I have to go now. My mother will be looking for me to help get tea ready. I'll see you tonight at supper. Then later, if you like, we can feed the dogs."

"Dogs?" said Violet. She hadn't seen any dogs. "How many do you have? What sort?"

"Hounds. There are three of them. We keep them in a kennel in the woods behind the hotel. You'll hear them kicking up a great fuss precisely at eight o'clock. That's when I feed them. Dogs always know what time it is."

Violet headed down the hallway. She knocked on her parents' door; there was no answer. She went to her own room and lay on her bed to read. A clinking sound from outside caught her attention. Her window overlooked a rock garden. To the left stood a small forest of sunflowers. Tall and gaunt, they reminded her of hunchbacked old ladies, though that was probably just more of her uncharitable thinking, she knew. She couldn't help thinking such things, even if she knew not to say them in her mother's presence. To the right lay a wide swath of roses, fully fleshed with blooms.

Violet raised the window frame and stuck her head out. Beyond the rose beds, a carpet of lawn flowed on to the forest. Someone coughed. Turning, she saw the gardener, Ned. In one hand he held a hoe, in the other a cigarette. He spat on the ground. One of the unholy, she thought.

He put down the hoe and picked up a ball of baling twine, unravelling it and measuring it out in strands of equal length. Done, he took out a pocket knife and began to slice, then brought the lengths over to the roses and laid them out on the ground. He began to tie up the bushes.

She was just about to turn away when he glanced up at the window and startled her by waving. She shrank back inside the room, feeling her heart beat wildly. After a full minute, she looked again. He was gone, but she would always remember his forget-me-not blue eyes flashing at her over a sea of bright red roses.

THE SILVER SWANS

VIOLET HAD JUST turned eighty when she was approached to join the Silver Swans. Or, rather, when she was first approached by Sheila Dufresne, who claimed to represent the group and was considered its de facto spokesperson. The title was largely self-appointed, as Violet later learned. This was at the downtown YMCA, where she had begun to take regular exercise at the pool on the advice of her physician, on Wednesdays between three and five, the hours designated for seniors and members with special needs. The prospect had seemed unlikely at the time, as she was far past the age when she thought she'd ever join anything again, except for her ancestors.

On the afternoon in question, Sheila was coy in her approach. Violet had been at the shallow end of the pool, while Sheila was treading water at the deep end. When she spied Violet, she waved as though she had just recognized an old friend. She came swimming up to her, waving and bobbing while trying to keep herself afloat.

Violet looked around; there was no one else she seemed to be waving to.

"We've seen you here a lot over the past few months, I think?"

Sheila was particularly good at turning any statement into a question. It was as if she thought the person she was addressing needed to recognize the need for the asking more than Sheila required an answer. In fact, this was true. Sheila seldom asked a question for which she hadn't already formed an answer; whether it was correct or not hardly seemed to matter to her.

The veracity of her question-statements aside, Sheila seemed eager to appropriate anyone who ventured into the group's territorial waters, so to speak, like a one-woman conscription committee.

"You may have done, yes," Violet ventured, not wanting to commit herself to something she couldn't back out of politely, though good manners were not the extent of her resources for dealing with the socially inept. "I like Wednesdays for the quiet."

She was hoping the woman might take this as a hint that she preferred her own company, so she could get on with things and get back home to Edgar. She might also have added that the quiet she preferred seemed to end abruptly at four p.m. every Wednesday when the pool suddenly filled with a group of elderly women who talked non-stop till their time was up at five p.m. She could have, but she refrained from saying so.

"I thought so," said Sheila, extending a hand. "I'm Sheila."

"Violet."

They shook, water dripping from their arms, as Violet found herself wondering how long the intrusion would last.

"I can always recognize a fellow devotee!" Sheila declared, with an enthusiasm that transported her beyond the everyday world of hellos and goodbyes and nice-to-meet-yous. She seemed to want to include Violet in her elation.

We'll see about that, thought Violet, for she had suddenly recognized Sheila as one of the women who took regular exercise on Wednesdays — the blabbers, as she thought of them — with one woman in the centre who always wore a large sombrero. Waterproof, no doubt. But then, one never knew with eccentrics.

The group trooped in at four o'clock and engaged in an aquatic exercise program that involved the use of long, tubular flotation devices, which they manipulated as they moved about, some flu-idly, others awkwardly, in the pool.

"They're noodlers," Violet overheard one woman say to another in the change rooms.

The woman she was talking to gasped. "That terrible thing they do with catfish?"

The first woman laughed. "What? Oh, no. Not that, dear. The other kind of noodling."

Violet was totally confused. There were two types of noodling? She wasn't even sure what the first was, but she definitely had not heard of the second, the one with catfish.

She had gone home and looked it up on the Internet. There it was, in black and white, and some colour. Noodling was a form of fishing using one's fingers and sometimes, in the male popula-tion, one's genitals, as a way to attract catfish in order to catch them by hand. Violet had shuddered, not wanting to imagine the consequences if things went wrong. On the other hand, she thought, if it did, you might count the human race lucky to be rid of the potential for procreation by the sort of people who did such things. Darwinism, wasn't it called?

"You should join us," Sheila was saying now, as they faced each other in the pool. "We have loads of fun and afterwards we all go out for a tipple."

When Violet looked blank, Sheila said. "You know — gin."

"I definitely know what gin is," Violet assured her.

"It's aqua-fitness. Aerobics in the water. It's very good for you," Sheila assured her. "I'm sure you'd love it, don't you think?"

How would I know? Violet wondered. But in fact, she had been intrigued. Not so much at the prospect of joining a group of older women — assuming they wouldn't turn out to be the ghastly, silly type — but at the prospect of having a coordinated program of exercising that would help with her increasing mobility issues. For she had found her rheumatism to be gaining ground with each passing year.

"We're called the Silver Swans," Sheila informed her.

Violet recalled the Orlando Gibbons madrigal *The Silver Swan*, a favourite when she'd sung in a choir. The lyrics had been penned by that world-famous poet, Anonymous, referring to the belief that swans were silent for their entire lives, breaking into song only as they were dying, giving rise to the expression "swan song." Sheer nonsense, of course, like so much of what the human race believed.

The tune floated through her head now:

The silver Swan, who, living, had no Note
When Death approached, unlocked her silent throat.
Leaning her breast against the reedy shore,
thus sang her first and last, and sang no more:
"Farewell, all joys! O Death, come close mine eyes!
More Geese than Swans now live, more Fools than Wise."

Unlike Gibbons's single-note beauty, however, these birds never stopped their warbling. Perhaps they'd be better off calling themselves the Gabbling Geese, she thought, but held back from saying so. She knew to keep her sarcasm in check thanks to her mother's urging, having long since learned where it could lead.

"But don't confuse us with the other group of oldies that meets on Thursdays," Sheila added. "They're called the Spring Daffodils. They dress all in yellow." To Violet's recurring blank look, she added, "They do an amusing geriatric version of synchronized swimming. You wouldn't want to join them, now would you?"

No, Violet thought, she certainly wouldn't want to be a Spring Daffodil.

"Say you'll come," Sheila urged.

"What if I just came to swim with you, but not use the, um, flotation devices?"

"Then we would probably hiss at you," Sheila replied with a wicked grin.

"That's geese," Violet said, thinking she'd been right all along.

"That's what we are! Angry geese, if you want to know. Left alone, abandoned, forgotten. By husbands, children, work colleagues, friends. You name it, they've let us slip between their fingers. But we prefer to call ourselves the Silver Swans, having one last grand go of it."

Whether this group would turn out to be the Fools or the Wise of Gibbons's composition, Violet was inclined to reserve judgement. She agreed to join them for a try-out on the following Wednesday. To her delight, she found them rather enjoyable.

One thing led to another. Violet soon found herself looking forward to her Wednesday afternoons with this unconventional bunch. Edgar, noting her enthusiasm, asked her about it. When she told him where she was going, he wondered if he might join them one day.

"They sound like a lot of fun," he said.

"Oh, no," Violet hastened to say. "It's women only. That's half the fun of it. I'm sorry, but that's what it is."

"Isn't that a bit sexist?" he'd grumped.

Violet nodded. "Totally, darling. And unapologetically so. Now forgive me, but I mustn't be late."

And off she went to join her fellow Swans, who began each session by forming a circle around their leader, Kaye Harding, the woman with the sombrero. She wore it as though it somehow distinguished her from all the others. Don't be fooled, Sheila harrumphed when Violet asked about her. Kaye was only leader because they let her be.

"That and her stupid sombrero," she said. "She thinks it makes her look important because she wears it in the pool."

The hour passed quickly: Step right and turn, now lift, two-three-four. Step left and turn, now lift, two-three-four. All that tilting and twisting, making those squeaky sounds with the noodles. I'm not sure where this is getting us, Violet found herself thinking one day, but it's an awful lot of fun. Silly fun. The type of fun I should never have given up.

They followed Kaye in her sometimes gracious, sometimes furious motions, twirling the noodles overhead, then digging down as though they were stilts, jabbing the ends toward the pool bottom while kicking up with their heels.

Violet surprised herself by turning a full somersault in the water one day, coming up spluttering and laughing. Goodness knows I could never do this again on dry land, she thought. It reminded her of the ease of movement she'd felt in her youth. If Edgar only knew what he was missing, he'd be even more jealous then.

"ARE YOU ENJOYING yourself?" Sheila asked one afternoon over gin and tonics at the bar next door to the Y.

"I'm only sorry you didn't ask me sooner," Violet said.

"I knew you were one of us!" Sheila cried.

They laughed to recall how earlier that afternoon a woman named Meena Nanda had caused a ruckus at the pool when they all thought she was drowning.

"I was sure she was having a heart attack," Sheila laughed.

Meena had got the floating tube trapped between her legs and couldn't pull it out, resorting to flapping her water wings and flailing around till they rescued her.

"Most excitement I've had in years!" Meena shrieked later in the bar.

Violet had become comfortable enough by then to share a few things about herself with the others. This was usually late in the afternoon, when they were on their third gin and tonic. It was still sharing, Violet felt, even if they wouldn't remember much of what she'd said the following week.

"I've been thinking about murder," she said, apropos of nothing.

She'd been having more of her sleepless nights, the ghosts crowding in on her with their accusing spirit eyes. Conversation stopped at the table. All eyes were on her. Human eyes.

"Who are you thinking of murdering, dear?" asked a woman named Sydney White, who they were all slightly afraid of because of her fierce scowls. "Is it a daughter-in-law?"

"Oh, no. It's nothing like that," Violet hastened to reassure them. She scrambled to come up with a reason. "I was watching a documentary on serial killers. It was very illuminating."

This elicited several minutes of excited conversation about killers and their raisons d'être. Nellie Bergeron had a real-life story about a neighbour who murdered his wife, making it look as though she'd committed suicide by locking her in the garage with the car running and a hose syphoning carbon monoxide through the window.

"Only it turns out she'd had suspicions he might try something when she found emails to a lover he was planning to leave her for." The lover, apparently, had been pushing him for some time. "When poor Esther found the emails, she sent them immediately to her lawyer, telling him to petition for divorce. The papers arrived the same day he drugged Esther and put her in the garage with the car running. Well, he couldn't very well argue himself around that one, could he? Eventually he confessed to killing her so she wouldn't take all his money. All very diabolical. And so sadly unnecessary," she clucked. "She had told her friend Sally only the day before that she was prepared to leave him without asking for a thing, just to make it easier on both of them, knowing what a selfish bastard he was. She said she would be glad to be rid of him and start her life over again. And just look how it turned out."

This elicited several thought-filled moments of silence.

"I think that sort of thing is more common than we realize," Kaye said. "Most of the time, when men kill, it's out of possessiveness. It's because they fear losing something. Either they fear losing their wives or girlfriends or they fear losing their money in spousal support."

It made Violet think of Ned. He'd been a cock-of-the-walk type, always thinking he had the better of the women around him. At times he'd acted almost as though he owned them.

"I think you're right," she said. "Men kill to possess, but in killing they end up losing whatever they're trying to hang onto."

Heads nodded all around. Several of the divorcées heartily agreed.

"It's true," said a woman named Miranda, who had flaming red hair and claimed it was natural, though they all knew it was dyed. "When we're young and they don't want to lose us, they do whatever it takes to hold onto us. But later, when we're older, they can't drop us fast enough."

No one argued with that. Violet quietly reflected how lucky she was to have Edgar, who loved and cherished her above all else. Goodness, he still bought her hats as though he wanted to parade her around and show the world what a lucky man he was to have her for his wife.

Of course, it helped that their sex lives had extended along with the years, though not quite at the same decibel level as in their younger days. Violet thought she would one day tire of the bother and declare that the race had been won, now and for all time. I'm done with all that, she might have said, but to her surprise, she enjoyed the intimacy, the closeness that still brought them together. They had been warned that a lessening of libido was to be expected, if not on one side, then on the other. When that happened, there were bound to be resentments. It jived with what the divorcées complained of: being cast adrift when the excitement died and the men moved on to new territory, though Violet knew well enough that it happened on both sides, women leaving husbands for younger or better-looking men. Nowadays no one was satisfied with what they had, always on the lookout for more.

She was thirty-two when she met Edgar. That was long past the age when most women married in those days, if indeed they intended to marry. Many were forced to choose between the obligations imposed by marriage and family and those of a profession. Women teachers were routinely expected *not* to marry. It was felt that they could not properly divide their attention between a family at home and the brood of children they were raising and guiding and giving direction to at school. Violet shook her head at the thought. There were so many things women were not supposed to do back then. She was more than thankful her parents had given her free rein to imagine what she could be rather than let herself be limited by societal expectations. She was also more than thankful she had met Edgar, who wooed her so gently and subtly that she almost didn't know it was happening. He'd been one of the doctors looking after her mother. Violet thought, naturally, that his interest was largely in Maggie's well-being, but, as it turned out, it went well beyond Maggie's personal care. Though he never stopped caring for Maggie right up till her last breath, he had, surprisingly, turned out to be interested in her eldest daughter as well.

It had taken Violet a while to figure it out, but on his third house visit in less than two weeks, during which he arranged to spend significant time alone with her discussing Maggie's care and treatment — time that seemed to extend well beyond the expected, for no obvious reasons — she popped the question: "Are you interested only in my mother, Doctor McAdams, or do I detect a slight interest in me as well?"

He had blushed and stammered, but, true to his nature, he hadn't lied. Only the truth hadn't come out in words so much as in a hasty series of noddings and turnings away, not to show his embarrassment.

"Then ask me out properly," she prompted, when she understood she'd been correct in her assumptions. "And I'll let you know if I'm interested in return."

He smiled and asked her out to dinner the following evening. And, of course, she had accepted. By then, she had a career underway as a teacher, like her father, although her subjects had extended to poetry and literature as well. She liked to say that biology had been her first love and Shakespeare her second. Finding a way to include a husband in her life while maintaining her own interests, however, had not proved as difficult as might have been expected. There had been resentments from others, of course, especially from other women who seemed to feel she had been given a special privilege. You can choose both too, she wanted to tell them, though as often as not they turned deaf ears to her words. Petty jealousies had been inevitable. Violet did her best to befriend the ones who envied her rather than let them secretly resent her success. And over the years there had never been any question of either her or Edgar tiring and leaving the other for someone else. That, too, was a success.

She smiled and swirled the gin in her glass. Memories.

"If men kill to possess, why do women kill?" Sheila wondered aloud.

"We like to think we don't, of course," Violet said. "We prefer to think that women are above violence, but that's not true, is it?"

"Anybody here ever try to kill anybody?" Sydney's voice rang out.

There was laughter and startled expressions. Several of the women looked around as if seeking complicity in the question.

Perhaps others, too, had thought such things, even if they hadn't had the nerve to go through with it.

"I've thought of it," said a woman named Beatta. "I had a mother-in-law I couldn't stand. She was jealous from day one. She eventually broke up my marriage."

"Hell, I wanted to kill Harry after he left me," said a woman named Carmen. "He convinced me we both were unhappy together and said we deserved a new start in life. I still loved him, but I knew he'd been bored with me for years. I thought it was my fault, so I gave him an amicable divorce. Not a cent of alimony. Then I learned he married his secretary six months later. He's lucky he's still alive."

It was true, they agreed. Women could be as violent as men. It was just a matter of whether or not they could go through with it. Violet recalled her mother telling her about a group of suffragettes who bombed the Rosslyn Chapel in Scotland in 1914, during what became known as the suffragette bombing and arson campaign. An older cousin, a member of the Women's Social and Political Union, had been one of those involved in the bloody struggle for women's suffrage, which eventually took several lives, including that of a fellow suffragette who ended up in the wrong place at the right time. All this had taken place between 1912 and 1914, ending only with the Great War. Her mother had decried the actions, but young Violet had been sympathetic toward both the cause and the group, whose motto was, "Deeds not Words."

"How much would you kill for?" asked Sydney, holding up her glass to them.

"Depends who it is," said Kaye.

They all screamed with laughter.

"But *why* do women kill?" asked Sheila, all innocence and giggles under her curiosity about bloodlust.

"We kill when we're thwarted!'" Meena exclaimed.

Heads nodded around the table as woman looked to woman and saw things there they had till then only suspected might lie deep inside themselves. One by one, they murmured their agreement on the possibilities that lay within.

"And when we're jealous," added Sydney.

The table went silent again as all thoughts turned inward.

-7-

EVENING BREEZES

THE GRANDFATHER CLOCK chimed six times as Violet and her parents approached the dining hall. The sound was richly resonant, like a far-off church bell. There was something quietly reassuring in the way the tones hung in the air long after the last stroke had rung out that spoke of space and time and how things endured.

There was an atmosphere of expectancy as they entered the room. The floor to ceiling windows had been opened to facilitate a breeze. Tables were set with linen and silverware. All the niceties were observed. No one sat alone, solitary diners having been paired with others. A dress code was in effect. Violet's father wore a linen jacket and a tie. Her mother wore a dark-blue evening dress with a string of pearls. She was easily the most glamorous woman in the crowd and noticeably one of the youngest as they made their way to a table reserved for them in the middle of the floor.

The room was packed with older women. For these aging butterflies, diaphonous fabrics seemed the order of the day, as though someone had sent out a fashion edict: *All ladies over the age of fifty shall be required to wear crepe and chiffon.* Many had accessorized themselves with costume jewellery. One frail-looking thing had bedecked herself with a headpiece made of ostrich feathers, as though she were at a fashionable resort from a bygone era rather than a recuperative spa for invalids in the here and now.

The chief occupation of these ladies seemed to be to gripe about their surroundings. Complaints hung in the air like a distasteful odour. The room was too hot or too cool, the light too bright or too gloomy, the tea too weak or too strong. Violet thought of Goldilocks and her three bears. Looking around, however, she discovered that they had more than enough reason to complain. Many were crippled with arthritis or rheumatism, while others were simply aged and infirm. The room felt paralysed with mass inertia: Sunken faces, leaden pallors, and swollen limbs were the order of the day. Violet wondered how they'd let themselves get so far gone. Scenes of biblical retribution and apocalypse came to mind, but lacking all sense of proportion or place in the natural order. This was affliction, clear and simple. Violet couldn't help feeling sorry for most of her fellow diners.

Julia was seated with Mrs. Browne at the head of the room. She looked over and waved. Violet felt gladdened by her presence, as though together they represented everything that separated good health from infirmity.

"You've made a friend, I see," her mother remarked.

"That's Julia," Violet said. "She showed me the pantry this afternoon. I'm going to help her find out who steals the brownies. And she winds the grandfather clock in the lobby. She has to do it every day. She said she would let me do it one day."

The lie came out effortlessly, but Violet barely recognized it as such. There seemed little to prevent it from becoming truth.

"That's very nice of her."

The McPhersons were seated across from a woman whose hands trembled. She introduced herself as Sally McMaster. Rather than avoid mention of her affliction, she seemed inclined to talk about it. She'd been a psychiatrist's receptionist until the strange palsy had set into her limbs. Within a year she went from being a healthy, independent young woman to a helpless creature confined to a wheelchair. Not long after, her fiancé had abandoned her. She was just thirty. So far, none of the conventional doctors had been able to do anything for her. She had come to Sulphur Springs in a last, desperate hope of finding a cure. The intensity of her expression frightened Violet, who hated to think of people needing things beyond their reach.

On Violet's right sat Frank Larsen, an older man who spoke energetically to the others around him. Frank wore a pink riding jacket and a dress shirt with a cravat. He seemed wholly out of place among the crowd of misfits. In fact, he looked as though he belonged to a foxhunt rather than to this sad group. Violet wondered what had brought him to the spa. She soon learned, however. Whenever anyone addressed him, Frank swivelled his entire body to face the speaker.

He caught Violet's look of concern.

"My spine is fused," he told her.

"What does that mean?" she asked.

"It means I can't turn my head from side to side, like you."

"Does it hurt?"

"Not too much." He smiled reassuringly. "Not exactly a fun bunch, are we?"

Tongue-tied, Violet shook her head.

"You be a good girl and eat your vegetables, so you won't end up like this lot," he said with a laugh.

Violet turned to look at her parents. What were they doing here amid all these desperate cases? Was there something really wrong with her mother or was it just a sprained ankle, as everyone kept saying? She looked to Julia for reassurance, but Julia's attention was elsewhere.

A bell rang as a set of double doors opened to admit a gurney laden with large silver trays. The lids were raised to reveal a roast beef dinner with mashed potatoes, peas, carrots, and an expert-looking Yorkshire pudding. Steam wafted upward as the room filled with tantalizing odours. The server was a droopy-eyed young woman with rust-coloured hair. Violet recognized her as the maid going from room to room from earlier in the day — Julia had said her name was Celeste. Her outfit was tight, as though she had squeezed herself into it to emphasize her figure. She kept her eyes down as she went around the room rattling plates onto tables under Enid Browne's disapproving gaze.

They had just begun to eat when hurried footsteps approached. The door flew open to reveal a good-looking young man. At first Violet didn't recognize him; then she saw it was Ned, the gardener who had waved at her earlier in the day. He'd cleaned himself up and was wearing a jacket and tie. Heads turned at his entrance. He stopped to exhale a nimbus of smoke, then stubbed out his cigarette in an ashtray beside the door.

"My apologies," he said to the crowd, seating himself at a table alongside the director, Willoughby. "My sundial must have been off. I lost track of time."

A cloud darkened Willoughby's face as people laughed. The maid hurried over to put a plate in front of Ned. She smiled at him until she caught Enid Browne's stare and made a hasty retreat.

They had been eating for a few minutes when a tall, bearded man in a waistcoat and bowtie stood and cleared his throat.

"Ladies and gentlemen, please grant me a few minutes of your time to welcome you to the Sulphur Springs Spa and Hotel," he said. "I am Doctor Cheavers, the spa's head physician. I'm pleased to see some familiar faces tonight. You are a testimony to our work here. For the sake of the newcomers, kindly bear with me while I give a short talk on the curative properties of the sulphur springs."

All heads were turned to him.

"The waters on this property are rich in dissolved minerals, with some fifteen-point-seventy-seven cubic inches of sulphuretted hydrogen per gallon. That may not mean a lot to you, but what you should know is that among the important minerals the springs produce are chloride of sodium, sulphate of lime, and magnesium. All of these have proven healing and restorative powers. This is how Mother Nature provides it to us, as it comes served fresh from the earth."

Over in a far corner, a hand shot up.

"Yes, madam?"

"How much will we be required to consume each day to achieve the maximum results?" asked the woman, whose face betrayed her anxiety.

There were a few titters in the room. The woman looked around at the others with a perplexed expression.

"You see, it smells terribly and I'm afraid I shan't be able to keep it down."

"Then you are in luck, madam, as you won't be required to consume any." Doctor Cheavers smiled reassuringly. "In fact, if you drink our waters, you might get worse, not better. But you are going to spend a lot of time bathing in it."

"Ah! How clever," said the woman, clearly relieved.

"And I'll be there to help you out," came a voice from the back of the room. It was Ned's.

A few gasps were heard around the room, followed by laughter.

"Ladies and gentlemen, may I introduce our resident gardener and sometime personal attendant, Ned Barker," said Doctor Cheavers.

A few of the women fluttered their hands in applause.

Cheavers turned to Ned. "I'm sure your charm will go a long way toward entertaining the ladies while they are soaking up the cure."

"I like to see everyone get their money's worth," Ned said.

Violet saw Enid Browne's expression darken as she turned away.

"I gather that young gardener thinks himself quite dashing," Violet heard her father say.

Ned *was* dashing, Violet thought. It was written all over his face.

"He looks rather militaristic," said Maggie. "He'll probably be heading off to war soon."

"Perhaps you're right," Clive replied. "Just a lad kicking up his heels. I guess we'll have to put up with his hijinks, seeing how he's going to be a hero soon. There's no telling what young fellows like that have got into their heads these days."

Maggie smiled. "You weren't so very different in your day, dear. In fact, it was your wild-eyed charm that convinced me to marry you. Did I never tell you that?"

"It wasn't just my dashing good looks?"

"That too, of course."

Violet looked Ned over again. He did look ... What was her mother's word? Militaristic. She recalled rumours that another war was about to start somewhere in Europe, though some of her classmates claimed if it did it would be over by fall. It was practically all the other kids had talked about during the last few days of school. Violet had overheard snippets of conversation, especially from the boys, who were full of bravado despite being far too young to enlist.

"We gotta get the Gerries!" a boy named Michael Carmichael insisted in the playground during recess one day.

"Before they get us!" agreed another boy named Howard Everest. He mimed stabbing an imaginary enemy with a bayonet.

Violet wondered who the *Gerries* were.

"It stands for 'geriatrics,'" confided Lisabeth Scott, when Violet caught up with her before class. Lisabeth one day hoped to be a nurse. "That means 'old people.'"

That was even more confusing. Why would they have to get

the old people before they got us? Violet wondered. It wasn't long, however, before she learned that the actual term was *Jerries* with a J, not *Gerries* with a G, and that it referred to Germans. But by then, the war would be in full swing.

Still, Violet wondered, why did boys always want to fight? Wasn't it better just to disagree if you didn't like someone and get on with your life? Why did there always have to be fighting? All it seemed to do was get everyone fired up and then people got hurt. Usually the wrong people. Violet's Uncle Charlie — her mother's oldest brother — had died in the last war. He'd been just twenty and married less than a year. Violet tried to imagine what it must have been like to die at such a young age. She had seen other men, veterans of that war, sitting in wheelchairs selling pencils outside Woolworth's. Unlike her mother with her sprained ankle, they couldn't just get up and walk away when they pleased. Surely, *they* didn't think that war was a good thing. It all seemed stupid and pointless.

Doctor Cheavers's voice interrupted her thoughts as he reminded the guests about the importance of sticking to a regular schedule for bathing in the sulphuretted water. This, he maintained, was necessary to achieve the full benefits of its curative powers. He looked at Frank Larsen.

"Why, even you will be dancing before you leave, Frank," he said.

"If you can accomplish that, doctor," Frank replied. "I will put you in my will."

"Mark my words," said the doctor. "It will happen!"

There was gentle laughter. As Doctor Cheavers concluded his talk, a burst of applause went around the room. Relief had replaced the frowns and concerned looks on many of the faces. Even Violet's father seemed to place an inordinate faith in the waters and their so-called "miracle cure."

"But I don't see," Violet declared, "how just sticking your ankle in some smelly old water is going to do anything. I think it sounds dumb."

Her father smiled. "You'll see, Violet. It's not just sticking it into the water that is going to help your mother's ankle. Her skin is going to absorb the minerals and the heat from the springs will help work the minerals into her joints and tendons. All of that combined is going to help get her back on her feet."

"You mean it's like taking medicine, only Mom will absorb it through her skin rather than by swallowing it."

"Exactly, you clever girl."

Violet was proud to have grasped this fact, but the proof remained to be seen. The people around them seemed to have severe limitations in many ways. At the back of her mind lay a dread at seeing her mother end up like the others.

Dinner was over. Celeste returned and began to gather the dinnerware, stacking things haphazardly till they threatened to topple. She gave a cry as she nearly dropped a plate. Her efforts were being watched by several women at a nearby table. One of them, an older woman wearing an ermine collar — which to Violet's chagrin still had the ermine's face attached — and a feathered hat, had introduced herself as Mrs. Emily Hutchins.

She *tsk*ed. "Did you ever see anyone so clumsy in your whole life?"

"Never," replied her companion, a thin, demure woman named Miss Turner.

The maid seemed oblivious to their talk. Once the dishes were cleared, Ned helped Willoughby move the tables off to the side of the room, revealing a dance floor that had been hidden till then. The marble was overlaid with richly variegated tiles in a harlequin pattern as impressive as the floor in a cathedral. Mrs. Browne wheeled in a Victrola and set it up in a far corner. She wound the crank and lifted the needle, placing it with care on the edge of a record. The strains of a popular waltz filled the room.

Violet saw a sad, faraway look come into Enid Browne's eyes as a woman's voice began to sing:

Every evening you'll hear me call
That's when I miss you most of all
The breezes sigh and so do I ...

Maggie McPherson turned to her husband. He took her hand and returned her gaze. That's love, Violet thought. It wasn't yucky, as some of her classmates had said. It made her feel warm and fuzzy.

Down by the shade of the old oak tree
That's where you can always find me ...

The tune continued softly as some of the more able-bodied among the group got up to dance. Violet's father turned to her.

"Your mother will have to sit this one out, but I believe you are free for this dance, young lady."

He took Violet by the hand and led her to the centre of the room, where they eased into a waltz, gliding effortlessly around the floor. She felt glamorous to be dancing with her father as others looked on. He raised his arm over her head as she twirled. For a moment, she wondered if the other ladies were envious of her.

The song ended and another began. Violet and her father sat to soft applause. The maid brought out coffee. She wasn't pretty, but she had an exaggerated vitality. In fact, she seemed to have altogether too much energy for such a small frame. She reminded Violet of some of the girls in her class. She knew they were poor.

Some lived in tarpaper shacks on the outskirts of town. In school they were quiet, but outside they could be loud and aggressive. Their faces seemed permanently set in masks of defiance, as though they felt a need to prove something. It set them apart and made them seem wild or dangerous. Violet had never been able to make friends with such girls. She was afraid to approach them, knowing their roughness and loud laughter would be directed at anyone who got close. They seemed to be daring you to make contact with them so they could rebuff you.

The dancing had been going on for some time. Violet was beginning to be bored when a burst of laughter came from the back of the room. Ned had said something to Mrs. Hutchins, making her shriek. He smiled and put a hand on her arm.

"Can you guess what their little game is?" said a voice at Violet's shoulder.

She turned to see Julia looking down at her.

"Is it a game?"

"Oh, yes. It's very much a game." Julia's eyes flashed. She stared at the pair. "You'd think they could at least behave respectably in public, wouldn't you?"

Violet nodded, though she wasn't entirely sure what game Julia was referring to. It was as if she saw things that were invisible to her. Perhaps Julia, too, was wild and dangerous in her way.

"People should always behave respectably in public, even when they're playing games," Violet said. "It's rude not to."

Julia smiled and brushed Violet's hair from her forehead.

"You're young," she said. "But one day you'll understand. For now, go on enjoying being a child. It won't last forever."

"I'm not a child."

Julia paused. "Sorry, I didn't mean it like that."

Another burst of laughter came from the table at the back of the room.

"Come with me," Julia said. "It's time for you to meet the pack."

Violet looked over and saw that her parents were engaged in conversation with Frank Larsen and Sally McMaster.

"May I be excused, please?" she asked.

Her mother looked up and smiled.

"Yes, dear. But why don't you introduce us to your new friend?"

"Mother and Father, this is Julia Browne," Violet said, flushing with pleasure.

"How do you do?" Julia said, extending a hand first to Violet's mother, then to her father.

"How do you do?" said Maggie.

"Good to meet you, Julia," Clive replied. "Thank you for keeping Violet company."

"It's my pleasure," she said. "She's in safe hands with me."

As the pair headed off together, Julia whispered, "Your father's very attractive. He has sex appeal."

Again, this was something none of the other girls Violet's age would ever say out loud.

"I know that," said Violet, unsure whether to be scandalized or proud. Julia, it seemed, had the ability to elicit both reactions in her effortlessly.

IN THE KITCHEN, Violet watched as Julia went over to one of the counters and grasped a tin bucket by the handle. It was filled with table scraps.

"Cook collects them for me," she said. "Now we can go."

Violet followed her out of the hotel and down the lane leading around back.

"Those two at dinner — what sort of game were they playing?" Violet asked as they walked along side by side.

"Adult games," Julia said breezily, swinging the bucket in her hand.

Violet thought this over. Bridge came to mind. So did chess, though she preferred Old Maid and Crazy Eights.

She shrugged dismissively. "Oh, *those* games. They're boring."

"Yes, aren't they?"

Julia gave her an amused look. She was pretty when she smiled. The sadness seemed to leave her face for a moment. They wandered for another minute till they reached the end of the grounds.

"Nearly there," Julia said, striding up the path and under some trees.

A shed loomed up ahead. To the left of it stood a fenced-in compound.

"Wait," said the older girl, putting up a hand.

They stopped. In the half-light, Violet could make out the shapes of several dogs moving restlessly inside a kennel. She heard quiet whimpers, but nothing more. Suddenly, as if they'd been cued, the dogs began to howl. A few seconds later, faint and faraway, the grandfather clock in the lobby chimed eight times.

Julia clapped her hands and the hounds stopped howling.

"Did you hear that? They always know what time it is," she said proudly. "If I'm not here right on the dot, there's hell to pay!"

She opened a slot in the fence and tipped the scraps into a trough as the dogs whimpered impatiently. Setting the bucket on the ground, Julia pointed out a large reddish hound, the only one to approach the food.

"That's Homer, the pack leader. He eats first, then the others get fed."

They crouched and watched. Homer looked up, turning his baleful eyes on Violet. He let out a long, mournful howl, as though greeting the newcomer. Violet held out a hand and let him lick it through the fence.

"Hello, Homer," she said softly.

"He likes you," Julia declared.

Homer ate quickly, growling softly if either of the other dogs approached. Once he finished, the other two took their turns. They were smaller and watchful of their leader.

"They're beautiful," Violet said.

"Tomorrow, if you like, we'll take them out for a long walk," Julia promised. "Just us."

"Yes, please!" Violet exclaimed, thinking of all the adventures she and Julia were going to have.

-8-

THE SHERSTON ARMS

DESPITE A FEW moments of turbulence, the flight is very comfortable. The meal is served hot and tasty. The flight attendants find Violet charming as she compliments them on their efficient service and thanks them for their patient handling of so many demanding passengers. Time passes a good deal faster than she expects. In fact, she wonders if they've cut the trip short to land in Winnipeg instead, when the pilot's voice informs them of their descent into the airport at Hamilton. She will definitely have things to report to the Silver Swans over drinks on her return.

It's raining lightly as they get off the plane, but the afternoon is warm. Claire pulls her aunt's oversized carrier bag along on its tipsy wheels, her own smaller bag slung over her shoulder. They hail a cab and soon find themselves outside the Sherston Arms Hotel in nearby Dundas. The name brings to mind a book Violet once taught, *Memoirs of a Fox-Hunting Man*. It featured a character named Sherston and was the work of the war poet and author Siegfried Sassoon, who was said to resemble her father so long ago. Sassoon is largely forgotten now, though Violet felt him to be an admirable author with progressive social values, not to mention a bit of a misfit like her. Definitely a man she would like to have met, given the chance. She hadn't been surprised to learn he was gay. People on the fringes were usually more interesting than the run-of-the-mill people one met.

From outside, the Sherston Arms is charming. An elegant Victorian three-storey walk-up with a turret and gables, it's suggestive of the image of the proper hotel Violet has in her mind. As the cabbie drives off, the two women make their way up the walk. Violet rings the bell and stands back in anticipation. Her favourable first impression of the establishment is altered somewhat when the door opens and they are greeted by the proprietress, a Mrs. Clarice Palmerston, who is neither charming nor elegant in Violet's estimation. A thick layer of powder coats her features, putting Violet in mind of a large pink marshmallow. Her breezy manner and puffy face further suggest that Mrs. Palmerston has a close personal relationship with alcohol, though there will be no finger pointing in that regard for obvious reasons. In keeping with whatever libations Mrs. Palmerston may have poured for herself behind closed doors, she has likewise poured herself into a dress two sizes too small, showing a good deal more cleavage than she ought. Worse, the woman has airs about running her establishment.

"Visitors are strictly prohibited in the rooms after eleven p.m. And I'm sure I need not point out that all hotel rules must be obeyed."

She says this with overly precise enunciation on ushering them in, as though she thinks she may be speaking to barely literate foreigners.

"I guarantee you won't have to worry about me," Violet says. "I'll be in bed long before that. As for my niece, Claire, I think you will find her behaviour quite exemplary."

Mrs. Palmerston acknowledges the remark with a grimace that might be meant for a smile. For a moment, Violet thinks the woman has Bell's palsy. The lecture continues as she gets them to sign the register and runs Violet's credit card through a machine.

"Breakfast is served promptly at eight thirty, lunch at noon, and dinner at six thirty, for the duration of one hour each. Regrettably, dining hours cannot be extended for latecomers."

She eyes them as though anticipating insurrection.

"We stand warned," Violet says, with a wink to Claire.

Their proprietress hands them the keys to their rooms, pointing down a long corridor to a set of wooden stairs.

"I've put you on the second floor, but I'm afraid there's no elevator."

"We'll manage," Violet says, taking one last look at that cleavage before attempting the climb.

Claire carries the luggage, their footsteps grumbling on the stairs. Violet waits till they're upstairs before relaying her disapproval.

"The older one gets," she says, "I feel the less one's 'assets' should be exposed in public."

"Oh, thank goodness," says Claire. "I thought it was just me being prim and proper, but that certainly was a horrendous getup she had on."

They share a quiet laugh.

Their rooms are adjacent and prove to be quite pleasant, outfitted in cheery colours and plain but tasteful furniture. The beds are comfy. Violet experiences an unexpected moment of appreciation for the no-nonsense atmosphere both the rooms and their haughty proprietress exude. At the very least, it assures her there won't be any unexpected surprises during their stay.

As they part, Violet reminds Claire that she will have a taxi pick them up shortly. She fully intends to seize the day and not waste any time hanging around in hotel rooms, however pleasant they may be. She unpacks with a leisurely hand and lies down for a few minutes before ringing to ask Mrs. Palmerston to call a cab. She half expects to be given a lecture about the inappropriateness of asking hotel owners to perform such menial tasks, but instead their hostess says, "Very good, my dear. Be downstairs in ten minutes. It shall be done."

Violet considers wearing her red hat and matching calfskin gloves to the spa, but decides against it. This is to be an exploratory trip. No need for formalities. There's no telling what they'll find when they arrive at the grounds. Instead, she dons a casual outfit and a pair of sensible walking shoes. Chances are the trails will be no less treacherous now than they were seventy years ago.

When Claire knocks at her door a few minutes later, Violet is pleased to see she has had the same thought about wearing practical clothing. Elizabeth would be proud of her daughter, Violet thinks. There are no ninnies in this family.

The same might not be said for the cabbie who greets them as they emerge from the hotel. His flak jacket and camouflage trousers seem entirely inappropriate, even if he is just operating a rundown cab in the countryside. She's tempted to ask if he belongs to a paramilitary operation of some sort, but then thinks better of it. If he does, she'd rather not know.

At least his manners extend to opening the door for the elderly and closing it behind her once she is comfortably settled. He doesn't hide his surprise, however, when she tells him their destination.

"You won't find much left there nowadays," he says, eyeing her in the rear-view mirror as the car lurches down the tree-lined roadway. "You can take my word for it, there's nothing there." He turns to them and affects a friendlier tone, one Violet senses is totally devoid of sincerity. "Why not let me take youse shopping somewhere instead, eh? We got some nice craft stores nearby. I could show you the best of the best, ladies. What do you say?"

"No, thank you," says Violet, hoping the man won't turn out to be a total chatterbox. She dislikes unnecessary conversation from people who pretend to be polite or knowledgeable, when in reality they're just being nosy or using others as an excuse to hear themselves talk.

The driver takes a moment to digest her refusal before turning the car around and heading for a road that runs through the centre of the valley. He continues with his chatty, offhand remarks, though the conversation is not returned.

Violet gazes out the window as the road winds gently down the valley basin. Here are the stands of tall, slender poplars with their yellow, crown-like leaves she remembers so well. Over there are white-slippered birches, their silvery branches turning in the wind. Farther off are massive bur oaks and maples. Robust wands of goldenrod have taken over the sides of the road. Violet is intent on trying to recall it all. When she last saw it, this strip of road had been little more than an overgrown cow path. In fact, she's unclear whether it's even the same route. Nevertheless, as she eyes the horizon, things begin to acquire a vague familiarity.

"Not much left out there now," the driver remarks, still trying to convince them of the futility of their expedition. "Yous're just wasting your time, I can tell you."

Hopeless, Violet thinks. The man is beginning to annoy her. What if Queen Isabella had had the same mindset when Columbus came calling?

"I'm sure my niece and I will find what we need to find," she says firmly.

The driver's brows knit together. Violet can tell he wants to ask what they're hoping to find — buried treasure, perhaps — but her eyebrows arched at him in the mirror quell the thought.

"Were you brought up around here?" asks Claire, ever the diplomat.

"Born and bred here all my life," the man replies.

And it shows, Violet thinks, trying to stifle the snobbery brewing in her breast. If she's not careful, it will come out. She's always despised people who let themselves be conditioned by their fore-shortened intellects and appallingly unimaginative upbringings. Small-mindedness is everywhere, she believes, in men as well as women, in all races and social classes, in every majority and minority. It's the rule, not the exception. She has seen enough of the world to know this to be true.

"Then you'll know all about the sulphur springs and the hotel that were here once," she remarks.

The driver coughs. "I heard tell of them. Excellent for whatever ails you," he says, seizing on the remark. "It's long gone now, the hotel is. Though you might be able to find someone selling the sulphur water at a road stand or two. Is it that you're after?"

Violet ignores his question. "And you'll know all about the murder too, I suppose," she says.

He smiles. "Everyone's heard about the murder," he replies, feeling himself on solid ground now. "Young society gentleman killed his wealthy fiancée here right after the war."

"That's entirely incorrect. The young man you refer to was a soldier, not a society gentleman. And the young lady was not his fiancée—nor anyone else's for that matter. She was also far from wealthy. Moreover, the murder happened *before* the war, not after."

"Of course — I knew that. Just seeing how much you were acquainted with it, is all." He grins at her in the mirror, absurdly assured of his modest charms.

"And you'll of course know what ended the hotel's prosperity, no doubt?" Violet follows, wondering just how far the man's oafish ego will take him.

"The murder killed it off, I suppose," he says, seemingly unconscious of the irony in his words.

"On the contrary," Violet says. "The murder proved to be great publicity for the spa. Crowds thronged to partake of the famous sulphuretted water for a considerable time afterwards, with the curiosity for murder growing even when all the hubbub and publicity died down. Even the murder couldn't 'kill it off,' as you say. It was the fire six years later that finally finished things not long after the end of the war."

"Right you are! I'd forgotten that. The owners were out to cash in on the insurance policy. Burned it to the ground. Happens all the time," he says, with what Violet suspects might be personal experience talking.

A deplorable mentality, she thinks. "Again, you are mistaken. There was no insurance policy, which is why the estate was never rebuilt."

"Oh, yeah? That's rough," he says, taking in the news of the missed opportunity. "Say, you certainly seem to know a great deal about it."

Violet harrumphs without answering.

They drive in silence for the rest of the ride, which isn't long, thankfully. She and Claire marvel at the scenery flashing by outside the car windows. With all British Columbia's abundant greenery, this valley could easily rival Vancouver Island for its beauty. Violet is pleased to see it looking as majestic as ever.

The cab slows as they approach their destination. Violet feels her heart quicken when they round a bend in the road and pass a sign pointing to the Sulphur Springs turn-off. The hotel may be long gone, but its fame has left a mark on the surrounding landscape. Within minutes they come to a halt outside a padlocked gate leading to the grounds.

This, Violet remembers, is the precise spot where the cab entered when she and her parents arrived seventy years earlier. How strange to see it all still here. And that ramshackle rock wall is the same one that knotted and wound around the estate. Somewhere there will be a crevice with a flat stone to hide it from prying eyes. It looks little different now than it did then. Extraordinary how time stands still when we persist in believing that it moves inexorably onward, she thinks. Nothing could be more false.

The driver slows to a halt and glances at Violet in the mirror. "We're here," he announces.

"Go on," she says. "Go closer. We don't want to have to traipse across the field."

"This is it, though, ma'am," he says. "We can't go any farther. That gate don't open nowadays."

"How do you know? Have you tried it?" she demands.

The driver glances at her again. He starts to speak, then realizes it will have no effect on her.

They watch as he steps out of the car and heads over to the gate. He looks doubtfully at the lock, then tentatively puts his hands on it. Nothing happens. He turns to them with a know-it-all look, giving the lock a shake for good measure, just to show he's tried his best. Suddenly, it seems to spring open of its own accord. He glances back at the car, his mouth gaping in surprise.

"Come on!" Violet calls, before he wastes the rest of the day looking deranged.

As he gets back in, he turns to look at her. "Lady, you must be a wi—"

"Watch it!" she cuts him off.

"I was going to say a 'wizard,'" he tells her with a grin.

"You're right. I am," says Violet. "And I've turned more than a few talkative cab drivers into toads in my day. Permanently, in case you were wondering."

The car drives through onto the estate grounds.

-9-

THE HERMITAGE

AS THEY PASS a copse of trees, Violet's breath escapes her. She knows the hotel burned down years ago, but she isn't prepared to see the ruins of those same walls jutting up on the very spot where she and so many guests once walked and slept and dined. The limestone, greyed by fire and age, stands as a bleak reminder of what time brings to all. It's as if in some way she'd believed it had still been standing here, undiminished by rain or shine, until she set eyes on it again. Only from this moment, in her mind, has it gone into a permanent decline.

"Dear me," Violet says at last.

"I told you there's not much left to it now," says the driver in a triumphant tone. "I could drive you right back now, if youse'd like —"

"Don't even dream of it," Violet says, shooting him a glance that stops his chatter. She reaches for the door handle. "What we are looking for is going to be right here."

"Yes, ma'am. If you say so."

Violet steps from the cab and checks her watch. She taps on the roof of the car. "If you would be so kind, please meet us back here in an hour. And promptly, mind," she orders.

The driver gives them a grim look before he slowly reverses and heads back down the lane.

The two women stand facing the ruins.

"Obviously that man is not used to being given orders by women," Claire says, with a look of amusement.

"Obviously," says Violet. "If he has a wife — which I very much doubt — then she hasn't figured out yet how to get the better of him."

She takes a few steps forward. Grass has grown up inside what was once the perimeter of the hotel. Pieces of foundation jut up like the ribs of a giant animal carcass. Violet picks up her stride, moving forward. The whiteness of her hair is a beacon in the sunlight, a wisp of dandelion fluff in the breeze.

Only when she gets closer does she see the obvious intrusion of human hands. The smell of sulphur has been replaced by the stinging aroma of urine. The place has become a camping ground for vagrants and other visitors. Empty tins and bottles lie on the other side of a wall, evidence of a few meals having taken place at some time in the recent past. She hates litterers. Have fun, she thinks, but why spoil it for others?

There had always been vagrants and tramps in the days before the war. The Depression was rife with them, men and women both, moving about the country in search of a chance to make a new life that might bring an end to their collective misery. For the most part, Violet had thought them harmless, though after the murder the police tried to convince everyone otherwise. She isn't one to believe everything the police say, however. Not then and certainly not now.

She surveys the land, taking a moment to get her bearings. Claire watches as she stops beside the remnants of a chimney.

"The library was right here," Violet says, spreading her arms wide as if to encompass it. "I spent a good many hours in it. This fireplace was nearly big enough to stand up in. And over here was the Hermitage."

She recalls the portrait of Judge Emond Browne, whose cold eyes gave him a menacing appearance. She can still hear Julia's description of him as a "nasty old bugger."

"Yes, this was it."

She remembers his precious chapel — brown, brown everywhere, with thick curtains to keep the sunshine out and the dullness in, as though he'd purposely cultivated that dismal atmosphere. Even out in the countryside, the sanctimonious were always there to remind you of their pious claims on the dark and dreary.

She closes her eyes and tries to recollect. It had been a fine building once, with leaded windows and a steep sloping roof. There had been three wings encompassing an inner courtyard and, at the back, a large kitchen facing the forest. Pacing it out, she arrives at what was conceivably the front entrance. Here was where Willoughby greeted the guests on their arrival before depositing them in front of Enid Browne's unsmiling countenance as she stared out from behind her oversized reception desk. To the right had been the grand stairwell curving upward. Just before that, you passed one of the wonders of the place: a floor-to-ceiling gilded cage with canaries flitting and fluttering from one level to another. All long gone.

Proceeding up the stairwell, nooks and ledges held various treasures: stone statuary and clay crockery, piles of books, leather-bound and ancient. Brass jars and copper vessels gleamed in the sunlight that streamed bountifully through the windows. Amazingly, she can still recall the wallpaper's curvaceous vines that slid ceilingward between window wells and landings.

On each floor, when the rooms were open for cleaning, you caught sight of vivid colours — poppy red, emerald green, and canary yellow. Enid Browne may have been a drab individual with a dour view of life — even Violet had thought so at the age of fourteen — but the suites had been spectacular. Enid had inherited her father's gloomy outlook on life, but with one exception: her sense of décor included a palette of highly colourful whimsy. Warm hues filled the spa, room after sumptuous room, as though somewhere deep inside she had dared to hope for more from life than that backwater retreat for the broken and invalided.

At the time, Violet thought it an odd quirk of personality, all that vividness from such a blur of a woman. Later, Julia revealed her mother's inspiration: a single visit to France before her marriage. There, she'd been inspired by colours and ornamentation, so foreign to her Scottish Presbyterian upbringing, where frivolity was frowned upon when it wasn't outright forbidden. If anyone other than a judge's daughter had decorated in such a fashion it would have been viewed as heresy by the locals.

It's all coming back to her. Her room had been on the ground floor in the north wing. Julia's had been on the south, beside her mother's. Ned's room ... she tries to place it, but it eludes her. Then suddenly, she has a vision of Ned's brilliant smile flashing at her from one of the windows that gave way onto the courtyard as she explored the gardens. Yes, his room had been on the east wing, along with the other staff.

She still remembers his forget-me-not blue eyes. You wanted to trust him, she thinks. You wanted to be on his side, but those eyes said you would be wrong to trust him completely. His sudden appearance on that long-ago day had unnerved her. She'd been examining a line of ants emerging from a crack in the hotel's facade when she looked up to see him leaning from the window of his room. He'd exhaled, watching her through a cloud of cigarette smoke.

"You are a pretty young lady."

She still recalls the blush that spread over her cheeks.

"Oh! There now — I've embarrassed you," Ned said. "No need to blush!"

Violet had turned as red as raspberry jam. She wanted to run, but it was too late. Besides, part of her wanted to hear his flattery.

"I believe your mother is the lady with the sprained ankle, is she not?"

Violet nodded. It didn't surprise her that Ned should know about her mother's condition. Adults seemed to know many things about one another, even more so when it came to children. When they weren't reporting you for climbing someone's crabapple tree or cutting through their backyards, they seemed to know everything that had gone on at school even before you arrived home, breathless, to tell of the day's events.

"My mother says you're a soldier," she told him.

"Your mother is very observant," Ned replied with that winning smile of his. "It's true, but don't tell the others." He reached down with his hand. "I'm Ned," he said, engulfing her small hand in his own.

"I know. We met when we arrived. I'm Violet."

"Pleased to meet you again, Violet."

At that moment, Violet heard a giggle from somewhere behind him.

"Stop playing with little girls," said a woman's voice.

Ned looked over his shoulder. "Shush! You'll get us in trouble." He turned to Violet, flicking his cigarette over the sill. "It's just a friend. Don't tell anyone, okay?"

"Okay."

"I'd better get going. Maybe I'll see you at supper tonight?"

"Yes," said Violet.

She wanted to tell him she sat with her parents every night at supper just two tables apart from his, but the window had already closed. She turned away, wondering whose voice she had just heard coming from behind him.

Watching the ghost of her fourteen-year-old self, Violet takes a few tentative steps to where the north wing once stood. She remembers the smell of the dull red carpet and the gleaming wooden stairs with the thick banister that twisted and wound its way to the top. There had been chandeliers and an impressive dance floor in the dining room, not to mention oil paintings in the halls. They'd looked ancient even then, the paint dark and cracking with age. It would all have gone in the fire. A shame to think of the loss. Suddenly an image surfaces, something that has been hidden in the recesses of her mind for decades. She stops and looks around. Had it been here or over there? She turns her head and then it hits her. Yes, it was right here on this very spot that Julia's sombre grandfather clock had stood, the one she wound each morning with a big, brass key.

It's all coming back to her. Not far off is the valley where the sulphur water spilled freely from the hillside, along with its dreadful odour. It was also the place where a murder had been committed seventy years ago. A murder that, as far as Violet is concerned, has never been properly investigated. And that, she believes, was the fault of the law enforcement officers of the day. They had been little more than incompetent bumblers, despite the air of authority they exuded trying to impress everyone: bloodied clothing held up to the light, a woman's personal items paraded for public inspection. Forget about justice. A show was what had been wanted and a show was what had been given.

It was obscene, the lengths they went to in order to satisfy the public appetite for scandal and bloodshed, as if they were dealing with some cheap melodrama peopled with film stars instead of a real-life murder and flesh-and-blood human beings. During the investigation, one of the officers even posed for a snapshot with some of the guests — his little moment of glory — all puffed up with importance, as Violet looked on.

In the end, it hadn't seemed to matter much, as long as they could point fingers and say they knew who had done it, though when all was said and done the culprit was never even tried in court. A perversion of justice is what it had been. Who were they trying to protect? What had made them wary of accusing the one person who could have been responsible?

Violet sighs. How astonishing to think a lifetime has passed and here she is, returning to the scene of one of the most momentous events of her life. Despite her memory of the tragedy, it gives her a belated sense of joy to be back here after all these years. Yet there's a strange sense of loss at the centre of it; the feeling is hollow somehow. Her heart is full and empty at the same time.

She is at last beginning to feel the effects of travel. Her feet are aching. Claire has been standing off to one side, not wanting to disturb her aunt's thoughts as she stares out over a grove of beech trees, lost in her memories. Now she advises her to rest and take it easy.

By the time the cab comes back, they are ready to return to the hotel. The driver is bursting with curiosity. He is still wearing his military fatigues. If Violet hadn't seen him drive off earlier, she might think he'd stayed behind, watching to see what they were looking for.

"Hello, ladies!" he says with exaggerated cheer. "Find what you were after?"

"Not exactly," says Violet.

"Well, that's too bad then," he sympathizes. "Though I'm not surprised."

"Not at all," Violet says, annoyed by his nosiness. "In fact, we found far more than we were looking for."

She is amused when his brow furrows at her reply. What, she wonders, does he think they might be looking for amid these ruins? What else could there be here but memories?

"Well, that's good then, isn't it?" he says heartily, his voice animated. He opens the door to his cab. "Ready to return to civilization?"

"For now," Violet says, as she steps in and he closes the door behind her. "But we'll be back, that's for sure."

At the hotel, he seems almost relieved to be rid of them, yet he stops and considers a moment before handing them a card.

"If you need another ride to the old ruins, ladies, be sure to call the dispatcher and ask for Wally. I can show you a thing or two. I'm an excellent tour guide. The very best, in fact. Youse don't want to get lost wandering around in those woods, I can tell you that."

"No, indeed," says Violet, handing over the fare and a considerable tip, as though to compensate for her impatience, but really just wanting to be done with him.

"There are swamps back there," Wally intones direly. "Maybe even a few bears."

Violet is only half-listening to his silly prattle. She turns to Claire. "Come, Claire — supper awaits. Goodbye, Wally. Thank you. We may call you in future."

"Anytime, ladies," he says, as they turn and enter the hotel.

AH, SWEET MYSTERY OF LIFE!

IT WASN'T UNTIL her second day at the spa that Violet saw the sulphur springs. Julia had suggested a hike and Violet, taken with the older girl, readily agreed. Julia seemed far surer of herself than most girls her age. So much so, in fact, that she seemed daunting. Violet was happy to let her take the lead.

They followed a path that wound along the edge of the grounds, wandering across fields and skirting a stream that rippled nearby, sometimes in clear sight and sometimes disappearing in the undergrowth, but never straying far from the footpath.

"Look!" Julia exclaimed, pointing out a long-legged bird flying overhead.

"It's a snowy egret!" Violet cried.

They watched as the creature winged silently over the treetops and disappeared from sight.

"You're so lucky to live here," Violet said.

Julia's expression darkened. "If you lived here, you might not think so. I'll bet you wouldn't want to put up with those tiresome old women night and day. 'Oh, my poor legs!' 'Oh, my poor hips!'"

Violet giggled.

"Just be glad your mother doesn't spend her entire day moaning and groaning the way they do." Julia cast a sharp glance around. "My mother hates this place. She says it ruined her life."

Violet was taken aback. "How can a spa ruin someone's life? I thought it was supposed to be good for people."

"It's because she's stuck here, when she wishes she could be leading a glamorous life in town."

Violet nearly laughed. She couldn't imagine the dour Mrs. Browne being in any way glamorous, but perhaps that was precisely because she'd been stuck at the spa and hating it for all these years.

The farther they roamed from the hotel, the more freely Julia talked. She and her mother had always lived on the estate. They'd been forced to open it as a spa after the death of Julia's father, who had died on a business trip to Bangkok. A travelling salesman, he sold cigarettes for the Rothmans Company and was opening new territory in Asia when he got caught up in a revolution. As Julia told it, his death sounded like a three-act tragedy involving war, travel disruptions, jealous business associates, and angry natives. It would have made a good adventure story.

Violet wondered whether his body had been shipped back to Canada for burial. She envisioned a coffin strapped in the bottom of an ocean liner, curious to know if his remains had been preserved. She had once put a frog in formaldehyde for a school project. The smells had been revolting, but oddly satisfying. Perhaps it was her father's death that made Julia look so unhappy at times.

A thought struck her: "Why is your last name Browne? I mean, why is it the same as your grandfather's? Shouldn't your mother have taken your father's name?"

Julia looked impressed.

"You are a sly boots, aren't you? You're right. We used to be called Clancey. But after my father died, my mother took her maiden name back. She said it made it simpler to manage the business, among other things."

Their path took them past a stand of cedar. Shafts of sunlight dappled the ground. Julia paused at the edge of the grove.

"You have to be careful walking here," she said. "There's poison ivy all through this area. You won't know it till you've got covered in rashes. I had it for nearly two months one summer. It was terrible."

"I know what it looks like," Violet said breezily.

She hunted around till she spied the telltale leaves.

"That's poison ivy. You can always tell because it has three leaves together. *Leaves of three, leave them be*," she chanted.

"How exceptionally clever you are," said Julia.

"I told you — my father's a botanist. He teaches me. There are other dangerous plants in these woods as well, in case you're interested. I saw some poisonous mushrooms on our way here. You must never eat them."

Julia's eyebrows rose. "Everyone knows not to eat mushrooms you find in the wild."

"Yet people do. And they die. It's their own fault, of course."

As they wandered farther into the woods, layers of rotting evergreen needles made for slippery walking. The atmosphere changed starkly as overhead branches blotted out the sun. Here, the rocks were moss-covered and fungus grew from the trunks of the trees. From a mystical, elfin forest they suddenly found themselves in a land of trolls and gremlins. The overall effect was gloomy and threatening.

A breeze gusted toward them as a sickening odour caught Violet's attention.

"What's that terrible smell?" she gasped, suspecting something dead lay in the bushes nearby.

"That's the spring!" Julia replied with a laugh. "Haven't you smelled the sulphur before?"

"Not up close like this. It's not as strong by the hotel. This smells like eggs gone off!"

"That describes it perfectly!"

They passed out of the trees and joined the road where a milky-grey fluid gurgled out of a rock crevice and ran along a narrow gorge. It pooled at the foot of a hill where a pipe siphoned off the emissions. Julia pointed to a concrete bunker up ahead.

"That's the bathing pavilion," she said.

Inside, Violet knew, her mother and the other bathers were at that moment sitting up to their necks in the noxious waters. As they drew closer, the hum of an engine channelling the water through the structure grew louder, drowning out all other sounds. Blue-and-white reclining chairs had been set up on a concrete platform outside the pavilion. A large woman sat smoking a cigarette and turning the pages of a magazine beside the front door.

"Hello, young ladies," she called out. "Come for your baths, have you?"

Julia shook her head. "Violet wants to take a look. Her mother's inside."

"That's no problem," said the attendant, waving her cigarette about. "The changeover's about to happen, but you can have a quick look."

"What's the changeover?" Violet asked.

"That's when they all come out for the massage and stretching portion of the therapy." She pointed at the reclining chairs. "Good for what ails 'em. Go on — have a look."

A sign hung over the door: No Unsupervised Use of This Bathing Station. Through the doorway, Violet saw shadowy figures reclining in a shallow pool. A large fan turned gently, blowing across the floor. Sunlight filtered in from a window high up, lightening up the shadows, though the overall effect was of a gloomy, subterranean cavern.

"Creepy, isn't it?" said Julia.

As her eyes adjusted, Violet could make out her mother among the group. She waved and her mother waved back. Violet wondered whether she would reek of sulphur when she returned to the hotel.

"I wouldn't bathe in that if you paid me!" she said, as they made their way back to the road.

"Well, we're not going to pay *you*, silly! People pay *us* to bathe in the waters. They come here from all over the world. The doctors say it's the miracle cure of the century."

"Does it really do all they say?"

Julia laughed.

"I don't know. I've never tried it. You won't catch me bathing in it, either." She made a face. "Mother certainly seems to believe in the springs. My grandfather swore by them. He called them the Gift of Life. And he lived to ninety."

"How many people come here to take the cure?"

"Oh, loads!"

"Dozens?"

"Thousands!"

"And do they all get better after?"

Julia shrugged. "You tell me at the end of your mother's stay. The proof is in the pudding. Isn't that what they say? Speaking of pudding, have you thought of a way to catch the brownie thief?"

Violet had thought about it since the previous afternoon. "I have a few ideas that should work, but I'd like to see the kitchen again. Can we take a look this afternoon?"

Julia stopped to face her.

"Tell! What are they?"

Violet smirked. "You'll have to wait and see. I'm a smarty-pants, remember?"

"All right," said Julia. "If you're sure they're going to work."

"I am. We just need a list of suspects."

As they continued walking, Julia glanced at Violet.

"Who do you think it is?"

"Well, I don't think it's poor Miss McMaster in her wheelchair."

Julia laughed. "Or Frank Larsen. He's stiff as a board and skinny as a rake. But then again, I suppose it could be him if he's so hungry all the time. Maybe his condition makes him desperate enough to steal."

"Exactly!" Violet pronounced. "It's the psychology we have to think of."

"Ooh — psychology," Julia taunted, making a face.

"Words are important," said Violet huffily. "What about that soldier?"

"What soldier?"

"Ned. The one who came in late to supper last night."

Julia looked at her queerly. "Ned's not a soldier. He's just the gardener. Sometimes he wheels people around the grounds in their wheelchairs."

"He *is* a soldier. He told me so himself. He just doesn't want anyone to know."

Julia crossed her arms. A looked of amusement passed over her face. "Oh — I see. You like him too."

"I do not!"

"Then you tell me if he's a likely suspect, since you know everything about him."

"I don't know everything about him," Violet said. "I just talked to him once. He told me he was a soldier."

"Well, I know a few things about him too."

"For instance?"

"For instance, he came from out west. He worked in the public gardens in Vancouver."

"Is that why he has that strange accent?"

"Probably. He was practically penniless when he got here. Mother hired him because she felt sorry for him."

"Does he like brownies?" She giggled. "That would be an important clue."

Julia shrugged. "Doesn't everyone?"

"Okay, then does he seem like a thief to you?"

"Hard to say, really. There was money missing from the front desk last month. Mother won't say who she suspects, but it could have been him. And I know he has secrets." Her eyes narrowed. "I don't trust him for a second."

THEY TURNED A corner and found themselves back at the hotel. Julia pointed to a window surrounded by ivy.

"That's the pantry," she said.

Violet regarded it from different angles. The sill was nearly six feet off the ground.

"We can't watch from here," she said, shaking her head. "We'd need a ladder. And even then, we would be seen by anyone inside. How many entrances are there to the kitchen?"

"Three," Julia said. "Two from the dining room and one leading to the hallway."

"Well, there are only two of us, so we can't guard all three entrances."

"And Cook gets annoyed if anyone hangs around her kitchen. That's part of the problem. She sets the tea out for the ladies and they come through one at a time, helping themselves to milk and sugar. It's while they're helping themselves that things disappear. Sometimes, it's cookies cooling on the racks. Once, someone pinched a whole lemon pound cake."

"Do they all come in at once?"

"No. People come and go. Tea lasts an hour."

Violet shook her head. "That's too long. We can't stay inside the whole time just to watch."

Julia nodded. "And it would be way too obvious if we went in to check after every single person. Mother won't like it if we annoy the guests. There has to be another way to solve this."

"Let's look!"

The lobby was silent except for the ticking of the grandfather clock. Dark and sombre, it seemed to brood over them as they entered and filed past. The canaries had fallen asleep in their cage. In the kitchen, a surly-looking cook ambulated back and forth between the sink and stove.

"Afternoon, misses," she said gruffly.

"Afternoon, Cook," Julia replied.

"Good afternoon," said Violet.

"They've been at it again, miss," the cook said, shaking her head.

"More brownies?"

"Yes, miss. Tea time's just begun and someone's been in and done it again. Brazen, I calls it."

She turned huffily and went about her work.

Julia signalled to Violet to head to the back of the kitchen. Urns had been set out for tea alongside cups and saucers. Milk and sugar and lemon wedges were off to the side. In the pantry, a scattering of crumbs lay on the counter beside a ravaged brownie tray.

"I wish I had a kit to take fingerprints," Violet said, scrutinizing a knife abandoned beside the pilfered dessert. She looked around and snatched up a pile of napkins. "I know! This is what we'll do. Come on."

In the sitting room, a dozen women sat chatting. Violet recognized Mrs. Hutchins, the lady with the ermine collar at dinner the previous night, as well as her companion, Miss Turner, and Miss McMaster, the woman with palsy who had shared the McPhersons' table.

"Good afternoon," Violet said, going up to each in turn, offering napkins.

"How thoughtful," said Mrs. Hutchins, accepting the linen.

Having distributed the napkins, Violet left.

"Now we just have to remember who sat where," she whispered to Julia as they retreated to the kitchen.

They helped themselves to scones as they waited till the end of tea time, returning to the sitting room once everyone had gone.

"Now what?" Julia asked, looking around at the used plates.

"Now we gather the evidence," Violet said. "Whoever took the brownies will have left a trace on the napkins."

They examined the cloths one at a time; not a single napkin showed chocolate stains.

"What about the teacups?" Julia asked.

Again, on examining the cups, they found no evidence of chocolate smudges anywhere.

"Well, that's frustrating," Violet said. "On the other hand, it may mean that none of these ladies is the thief."

"Or maybe she ate them with a fork," Julia said, with a withering look. "So much for your bright idea, Violet McPherson."

"Never mind. I have another plan, but we have to wait until supper."

AT SUPPER THAT evening, Julia sat with her mother at her usual table at the head of the room. She waved when Violet entered with her parents. All through the meal, Violet barely paid attention to her food. Her parents were engaged in conversation with the other guests, comparing therapies and discussing their improvements. She hardly heard a word they said.

Once the meal was over and the dishes cleared away, the maid brought out coffee. Everyone looked around expectantly, but there was no dessert to go with it.

"Maybe it's going to be something special," Miss McMaster murmured hopefully.

Julia stood and walked to the middle of the dining room, calling for everyone's attention.

"On behalf of my mother, I'm very sorry to tell you that tonight there will be no dessert," she announced.

There were audible sighs of disappointment.

"Unfortunately," Julia went on, "Cook was to have made brownies this afternoon, but she seems to have forgot."

A voice rang out over the clamour. "Nonsense! There were some in the pantry on the lower shelf. I had one not two hours ago."

The declaration came from Miss Turner, the thin, demure woman who had laughed at the maid with Mrs. Hutchins the previous evening. All eyes turned to her. Suddenly realizing what she had said, her face flushed. "That is, I *saw* them in the pantry," she corrected. "Anyway, they were just sitting there!"

"Perhaps I was mistaken," Julia said brightly. "I'll have another look." Within minutes she returned with a platter of brownies. Addressing the room again, she said, "There aren't as many as we would have liked, but if we cut them in half and serve them with ice cream, there will be just enough to go around."

This elicited a sprinkle of applause. Dessert was served with ice cream, as promised. Miss Turner declined, protesting that she didn't care for brownies anyway.

Afterwards, Julia came up to Violet, eyes flashing.

"I hereby declare that Violet McPherson can get to the bottom of anything. An admission of guilt and everything! Mother said if there are any more missing brownies, she'll put them on Miss Turner's bill."

Clive turned to his daughter. "What's this? You've been sleuthing, have you?"

"You have a very clever daughter, Mr. McPherson," Julia said.

"We call her Nancy Drew at home. She's very good at solving things."

Violet grinned. "Mysteries solved — by request. Let me know if there's anything else you need me to solve."

"Come with me," Julia said, taking her by the hand. "There's a surprise in the kitchen for you."

In the pantry, Julia brought out a bowl of trifle.

"I had Cook make it specially for you. I couldn't serve it in front of the others," she said as she handed it to Violet. "It's for being such a good sleuth."

"What if my trick hadn't worked?"

"I still would have given it to you for trying, just because it was such a good idea."

Had it been anyone else, Violet might have thought she was being flattered. As it was Julia, however, she accepted her answer without hesitation.

DINNER WAS OVER by the time they returned to the dining room. As they entered, Violet saw Ned unscrew the top from a small green bottle beneath the table. Curious, she watched as he surreptitiously poured the contents into his water glass. She looked at Julia, but the older girl seemed not to have noticed.

Once again, the dance floor was cleared. Enid Browne brought in the Victrola. She cranked the machine and lowered the needle onto a record. After a scratchy start, a Viennese waltz emerged from the horn. Ned came over to her, one arm extended.

"Would you do me the honour, madam?"

Enid looked startled. Violet thought she might refuse, but to her surprise she took Ned's arm and allowed him to lead her onto the dance floor. His steps were ungainly as they waltzed around the room, but she smiled through it. Other diners rose and joined them. When the song ended, Enid nodded her thanks and went back to the Victrola.

Ned sat and lit a cigarette as the maid came out to clear the dishes. She glanced over at him from time to time. He ignored her as he sat chatting with two of the older women. Some of the diners slowly began to make their way back to their rooms. When Violet looked again, Ned had gone.

"Don't bother. He slips away without anyone noticing."

Violet turned to see Julia standing beside her

"That could be your next assignment," Julia told her. "Every evening he lights up a cigarette and disappears right after supper."

"Where does he go?"

"It's a mystery. I dare you to follow him."

"Leave it to me," Violet said.

-11-

MAD ABOUT THE BOY

IN THE MORNING, Violet and Claire leave for the springs after a nicely prepared breakfast of crepes, croissants, yoghurt, and fresh fruit. While she was serving them, Mrs. Palmerston even smiled once. Violet is beginning to think they might be in good hands after all.

Although they haven't specifically requested him, Wally, the cabbie from the previous day, answers their call. Violet wonders if he's the only driver in this part of town. Once again, he drives them to the springs, but this time with considerably less conversation. On being dropped off, Violet instructs him to return in two hours. He gives her a look as though to ask if he's heard her correctly. She simply has to nod for him to understand that she meant what she said. He seems to have learned that it is better to acquiesce than argue. Maybe he's smarter than she gives him credit for.

They have arrived much earlier today. The sun is just cutting through the treetops. As before, Violet plants herself in the midst of the ruins, surveying the grounds as far as she can see. She looks like a shaman searching out the vibrations of the land, though what she is really doing is comparing what is with what was, the way people can sometimes see things distilled over the years, knowing at a glance what had been important and what hadn't of all the many experiences they'd had down through the decades.

Although the buildings are largely gone, mere outlines where walls once stood, the site has not been completely left to run wild. Remnants of the gardens survive, including the *vinca minor* she had named on first seeing it, now running unimpeded through cracks and crevices. She has long had battles of her own with the invasive weed, considering it more of a menace to the well-being of other plants than something to admire. The roses have not been as resilient, their thorny branches now scraggly and unkempt, like some village beauty gone to seed, although here and there a bud has burst into flower as a reminder of the glory that once was.

She thinks of calling on Julia's daughter, Brenda, and her grandson Bryson. As much as she'd like to, she doubts she'll have time for a visit. It's a shame, really. For all she knows, the estate may still belong to the Browne family. Perhaps some distant cousin of Julia's drops by to see that things are taken care of, if only to forestall local gossip. And we all know what that can be like, she reminds herself, putting her in mind of the sharp-tongued Mrs. Hutchins from all those years ago.

Apart from the burned-out shell of the main building, Violet is pleased to see the grounds looking not so very different from what they were in those last few months of tranquillity before the war. The paths running through the estate have been kept clear. A young couple with a toddler walks a hundred yards up ahead. A nearby parking lot allows visitors to leave their cars and explore the area. The stream still runs freely through the valley and the forest floors have been cleared of trees felled by winter storms. From a distance, it seems a breathless wonderland of nature existing in harmony with civilization, although, not surprisingly, nature seems to be on the ascendant.

High above, the wind sighs through the branches. Oak, maple, and beech trees coexist nicely. Violet turns to face the forest, her back to the ruins. It's a trick of the eye, but for just a second it all manages to look exactly the same. Even time hasn't been able to erase the past. She can still hear Julia congratulating her for having exposed the brownie thief that long-ago night. If only Julia hadn't told her about Ned's habit of disappearing after dinner. Then, all that happened afterwards might never have occurred. But the challenge had been too great for her inquisitive young self to resist.

As usual, Ned arrived late the following night. He'd dressed in a shirt and tie, but soon removed his jacket. His sleeves were rolled to the elbows, exposing tanned, well-developed forearms. It gave him a rough, almost brutish quality.

Violet bolted her food, keeping one eye on Ned while answering her parents' questions about her afternoon's activities. The moment Ned pushed his plate aside, Violet was alert. She signalled to Julia, who nodded. The Victrola had just come out when Ned laid down his napkin and headed for the door.

Violet turned to her parents. Her father was engaged in conversation with Frank Larsen. Her mother was discussing sports with Miss McMaster, who had turned out to be a tennis fan. Maggie nodded distractedly when Violet asked to be excused, adding a reminder not to stray off the grounds with darkness coming on. Violet felt a surge of energy, the sort of release a bird would feel on taking flight.

Unfortunately, Enid Browne had prevented Julia from leaving at the last moment. Julia looked resignedly at Violet and nodded toward the kitchen: dish duty. Rashly, Violet had gone off on her own.

Outside, she set off down the path behind Ned, scarcely stopping to think about what she was doing. If her mother had known her intentions, she'd never have been allowed to go off on her own. Regrettably, Maggie hadn't known.

Ned was a quick walker. She found it hard to keep up with him as he struck out along the lane leading away from the hotel, his jacket slung over his shoulder. On the other hand, she had no problem keeping him in sight. It was past sunset and the grounds were growing dark, but even in the shadows beneath the trees, Ned's white shirt was easy to keep in view.

He seemed headed in no particular direction, as if he were just out for an evening stroll. Every so often, he paused and stared off into the forest before striking out along the path again. The smell of sulphur grew stronger. Violet knew where they were heading. Just before reaching the bathing pavilion, Ned left the trail and went up to the stone wall that circled the estate.

Pressing herself against a tree trunk, she watched, curious, as he lit a cigarette and stood with his back to the wall. A minute passed, maybe more. Then, seemingly satisfied that he was alone, he turned to the wall. What Ned did next remains etched in her memory after all these years. He pushed aside a rock, then reached down and retrieved a slip of paper. Violet held her breath.

Shaking his head, as if he had read something that annoyed or amused him, he turned and wandered over to the bathhouse with Violet trailing twenty yards behind. When he reached the bathing pavilion, he sat on one of the porch chairs and smoked another cigarette. There, he reread the note, then balled it up and tossed it into the stream. After a few minutes, he stood and headed back in the direction he had come.

Violet crouched in the shadows until he passed her and continued on out of sight. She raced over to the spring where the note floated just out of reach. Searching the ground, she found a branch and used it to fish the ball of paper from the water. She had just managed to bring it within reach when her foot slipped.

"Ugh!"

Her shoe sank in silver-grey slime right up to the buckle. Appalled, she stepped back. The earth emitted a sucking sound as she pulled. At last, her foot came free, but her shoe remained stuck in the mud. Hopping on one foot, she reached down to pull it out. After considerable effort, it came unstuck.

She tossed the shoe onto the bank behind her. Still hobbling on one foot, she grasped at the ball of paper. It melted at her touch, sending little wispy pieces twirling down the stream.

"Some sleuth you are, Violet McPherson," she told herself.

Both her shoe and sock were now thoroughly soaked and covered in grime. She removed her sock and rinsed it in the pool, then went over and sat on the edge of the pavilion, wiping the shoe on the grass. When she put them back on, her sock was the same murky grey as the water. Worse, it reeked of sulphur. She dreaded to think what her mother would say when she came back with one white sock and one grey one. But that would soon be the least of her worries.

The memory fades. Standing there in the ruins seventy years later, Violet shudders to think of that day and its aftermath. If only she hadn't followed Ned. If only she hadn't let her curiosity get the better of her. Why did fate make fools of the curious? Because we let it, she decides.

Claire watches the shifting emotions on her aunt's face.

"What was he up to?" she asks.

"It took me a little while to figure out," Violet replies. "You see, he was a very clever man. I don't think he knew then that I was following him, but he soon figured it out. Once he realized what I was doing, he played things out to see if he could get the better of me."

"Why would he do that?"

"Ned was a great game player and a tease. He also had a knack for getting whatever he wanted."

Claire nods. "My ex-husband is much the same," she says.

It's the first time Claire has spoken of Michael directly.

"Knowing that is half the battle of figuring out what is really going on in their devious minds," Violet says.

"I've learned that much," Claire replies.

Violet waits, but nothing more is forthcoming.

"We can talk about it anytime you like, my dear. This is just my little fascination at present. I can always work it out on my own. You are far more important to me."

"Thank you, Aunt Vi. I ... I'm not ready to talk about it. Please go on."

"As you wish. In any case, I knew Ned wasn't going to give himself away. I knew I had to outsmart him to find out what was really going on behind the scenes, as they say."

"And did you?"

Violet gives her a piercing glance. "What do you think?"

Claire smiles. "I'm sure you did."

She nods ruefully. "And I've wished ever since that I hadn't been such a smarty-pants."

"He must have been very dashing," Claire prompts.

"To me, he was terribly handsome. We called them 'matinee idols' back then. They were very sleek and suave, like Gary Cooper and Ramon Novarro. There was a song, 'Mad About the Boy'. That was about Cooper. We were all a little crazy when it came to Ned, too." She pauses. "I think that actor George Clooney has matinee idol looks these days, but hardly anyone else. It's not the style anymore. They're all rough-and-tumble nowadays — Sean Penn and Russell Crowe and whatnot. A face like the back end of a horse, we would have said. And more's the pity."

She clucks and turns to the ruins. "The gardens extended to right about here," she says, measuring the space with her feet. "Enid Browne kept the most beautiful roses you ever saw. She would have us believe it was Ned who did the gardening. But I found him out after a while."

Claire watches as her aunt reconstructs it from memory, pointing out everything as though it all still lay right before her eyes and not buried beneath a pile of rubble. If her brothers and sisters believed their aunt to be a doddering, absent-minded old woman, it would change their minds in an instant to see her now.

"This is where the pantry was. Right here!" Violet declares with a note of triumph. She looks down, as if she expected to find the remnants of a stove, maybe a cooking pot or two. There's nothing here now, though she is convinced this is the very spot where the pantry stood all those years ago, conjuring memories of stolen brownies and the irascible cook before heading off again.

She's exhilarated, Claire thinks, watching her aunt zigzag around the ruins. For a moment, she holds out hope that Violet might somehow make sense of a tragic event from seventy years ago. But that would be asking too much. Even if her aunt's memory holds, as it appears to be doing, there's little chance that some long-overlooked clue will still be lying around waiting to be discovered. Not here, amid these ruins.

Violet makes a beeline across the property like a rogue gnome sailing through the garden, her hair a white flag. Claire has no idea where she's headed. She only knows her aunt is moving faster than she's ever seen her move before. She follows her along the property line and through the woods, where Violet circumvents the stream and comes to a halt beside a rock wall.

Perplexed, Claire watches as she reaches out and touches first one stone, then another, before she hears her cry out, "Here! This is the one!"

With considerable effort, Violet shoves the rock aside. She peers into the cavity and shakes her head. It has to be empty, Claire thinks. Surely she can't have fooled herself into thinking a scrap of paper could survive unscathed for seventy years. She watches, scarcely believing, as Violet dips her hand into the crevice and pulls out a small colourful square from the hiding place.

"What is it?" Claire asks breathlessly, coming up behind her.

"Condoms!" Violet says, laughing and holding out the packet. "What else would be hidden here?"

Her laughter echoes through the woods. Claire finds herself laughing along with her aunt.

"Oh, dear," says Violet. "We've come halfway across the country to find a packet of condoms."

She holds them out to Claire. "Would you like them, my dear? I have no use for such things."

Claire flushes, but it only takes a moment to regain her equanimity. "Not at the moment," she says, "but thanks for the offer."

Violet pats the back of her hand. "Sensible girl."

She drops the package back down into the hole. Somehow, she thinks, Ned would have found all this quite amusing. But perhaps she's being presumptuous.

She starts off through the woods again, surging ahead of Claire. "Come along," she calls over her shoulder. "We're almost there."

THE DARKNESS UNDER the trees is deceptive. It's as if they've entered another world, one overlaid by a huge canopy, though it's just midday and the sun hangs directly overhead. In this false twilight, the glen surrounding the spring looks no less forbidding now than when Violet first set eyes on it in that summer of 1939. The water no longer tumbles freely from the hillside but is channelled through a concrete monument the size of a small oven. The township has erected a plaque citing Judge Emond Browne with the discovery of the sulphur springs. On reading it, you would be forgiven for thinking him a paragon of virtue and industry. There is no hint of his brooding presence or his lack of human kindness that prompted Julia to declare him a "nasty old bugger."

"I see what you mean about the smell, Aunt Vi," Claire says. "It's rather off-putting, isn't it?"

"That was the price of a cure, apparently. When it wasn't murder."

"Oh!" Claire gasps.

"Sorry, my dear — just being colourful. I still can't believe what women used to put up with in those days. Of course, I'm referring to the men as much as the mud baths."

Claire glances around. "It's not really the most pleasant part of the grounds, is it? There's something quite malevolent about it."

It's hard to imagine this as an appealing spot for a bit of conversation and whiling away the hours, but for a moment Violet envisions her mother sitting with the other women, chatting and soaking up the cure in hopes it would bring them some relief from their various ailments. From what she remembers, there had been fans gently wafting the odours away.

Apart from what exists in her memories, there is little left today. The bathing pavilion has long since been dismantled. Or maybe it, too, burned to the ground. The only trace of it is a ragged concrete foundation and a small groove cut into the rock where the pipeline once ran. Time and neglect are to blame somewhat, but perhaps the land itself conspired to make everything disappear, as though feeling a revulsion for the evil that occurred here, erasing every trace of the crime.

"Did anyone other than you know about the affair between Ned and the maid?" Claire asks.

"I told Julia about the notes, of course. We had become accomplices by then."

"What about Willoughby or Mrs. Browne? It must have created a good deal of animosity among the staff, possibly even jealousy. Or maybe one of the ladies he seduced fell in love with him."

Violet gives a short laugh. "Everyone fell in love with Ned — even me. He must have felt it as much a curse as a blessing. Willoughby? Yes, Willoughby knew."

The word *sinister* always came to mind when she thought of the hotel's humourless director. She recalls how his eyes were hooded. They reminded her of the deadly monkshood flower. Though she couldn't prove it, she suspected he had been the éminence grise, the presence hiding behind the curtains covering the fateful events of that long ago summer. To her he was, and always would remain, a shadow. She knew nothing of his past and nothing of what must eventually have become his future, if he had one. She had seen him every day for nearly a month, but he'd long been relegated to the role of a minor character in a novel, someone who came and went in the space of a single chapter.

"As for Enid Browne, she was a frustrated woman who had little happiness or pleasure in her life. She was a single mother with a child to raise during one of the worst economic crises in modern history. I have no doubt that she was susceptible to Ned's charms. And yes — she knew what he had been doing too."

It explained a lot, Violet thinks. Somehow, even then, she suspected Julia's father had not died in Bangkok, as she'd claimed. Despite Julia's colourful stories, Violet eventually learned the truth — he may have started out a businessman, but gambling and alcohol got the better of him, leading him to abandon Enid when Julia was still a child. His promise of love everlasting had got him as far as the altar, but all Enid ended up with was a few postcards from distant places before the horizon swallowed him forever.

"I'm sure it must have galled Enid to see Ned carrying on under her nose, but the truth is, she needed him. In fact, she hired him to chat up the ladies and add further enticement to the spa to give it a little bit of spice beyond the rather dubious miracles promised by its waters."

"Was he a gigolo?" Claire asks, matter-of-factly.

"Well, he certainly knew how to use his looks. I'll say that much for him. The way they talked about Ned afterwards, you would have thought him capable of just about anything — rape, treason, incest, arson, the lot. As for the girl, they didn't find out anything much about her afterwards, except that she'd come from a poor family. You have to remember those were hard times back then. There were thousands of girls just like her, all looking for a place to belong."

A man in a red hunting jacket passes them carrying a rifle. He gives them a long stare. His face is hard and weathered, like some of the tramps Violet remembered as a girl.

"Good afternoon," Violet says, wondering for a second if he is going to try to rob them, his expression is that harsh.

"Afternoon, ladies," he says gruffly, before turning and heading down another path.

Claire takes a breath once he is out of earshot. "Is it just me or did that man seem a little menacing?"

Violet nods. "He was indeed a dubious-looking individual. Though my mother would have said I was being uncharitable for saying so."

Claire checks her wristwatch. They've been on the grounds for almost an hour and a half. It's as though time dissolves into nothingness here. She reminds Violet they should head back if they are to catch their ride to the hotel, though they're both sorely tempted to stay. After a bit more exploring, they dutifully tromp back across the grounds to find Wally smoking a cigarette and waiting for them.

He looks up curiously at their approach, flicking his butt onto the grass. "Did youse find a gold mine or something? You ladies sure seem interested in this old place."

"Yes, well, there's quite a lot to be found if you look closely enough," is all Violet says.

12

GYPSIES, TRAMPS, AND THIEVES

IT'S JUST GOING on six o'clock when they sit down for supper. There are three other guests at the Sherston Arms this evening, including a retired army captain named George Luscombe. The captain is a jolly sort with a pleasant face. He wears a dinner jacket but has not put on a tie. It's not really a formal occasion, after all. He is nearly Violet's age, judging by his looks, and professes to have grown up around Dundas, having recently returned to Canada after living most of his life abroad in Indonesia and other places.

"I see we've all heeded Mrs. Palmerston's warning to arrive on time for dinner," the captain says mischievously.

"Oh, yes!" says Lucy, a young Indian woman seated across from him. She is dressed in a light-blue cotton dress. "She scared me half to death. I was terrified to be even a minute late."

Beside her is her fiancé, an attractive man named Bart. He sports a preppie look and a goatee. "Nothing wrong with rules and good manners," he teases.

"Oh, yes. You would say that," Lucy chides. To the others, she says. "Bart is in international banking. It's all about rules."

"And the dress code," he adds.

As if on cue, the curtain parts. Lucy gasps as Mrs. Palmerston enters. Tonight, she is wearing a pink Chanel suit. The colour seems to shock everyone to attention. At least the outfit is a suitable size,

Violet thinks. Their hostess's cleavage is well hidden and the other bulges seem in proportion to the rest of her.

They're all surprised to learn that, along with her other duties, Mrs. Palmerston cooks and serves the meals as well.

"Cook and chief bottle washer," she tells them.

Violet has ordered the garlic chicken. "Don't spare the garlic!" she instructed on being asked whether she preferred it mild. "I won't be kissing anyone."

Claire has opted for grilled salmon and watercress soup. The food is top-notch. Mrs. Palmerston may not be one for fashion sense, but she clearly knows her cuisine.

Over dinner, conversation turns to Violet and Claire's expedition to the hotel ruins and their fabled springs. The younger couple have not heard of the spa, but the captain dredges his memory and comes up with a surprise recollection.

"Had an aunt who claimed to have been cured of some terrible affliction there," he announces. "Rheumatism, I think. She swore by those waters."

"My mother came for the cure," Violet says. "This was in the summer of 1939. She was a tennis player and had hoped to recuperate from a turned ankle," she informs them, avoiding any mention of what turned out to be the more serious nature of her mother's illness.

"Did it help her?" asks Lucy.

"It's impossible to say whether it would have helped her or not. She was booked for a month, but the murder cut her stay short."

A hush falls over the room.

"Was there really a murder there?" asks Lucy, eyes wide.

"Oh, yes!" the captain exclaims. "It was talked about for years afterwards. Some local woman was poisoned, I think. Or possibly shot. I can't recall now," he says.

Before Violet can correct him, Bart breaks in. "Did they ever catch the killer? I have an interest in amateur sleuthing."

"No. They never did," says a voice from behind.

They turn to see their hostess standing in the doorway, bearing a platter of grilled vegetables. She sets it down before them and departs without another word.

"It was shocking," Violet says, turning back to the table at large. "There was one very obvious suspect, but the killer got off scot-free. No one was ever convicted."

The talk shifts to a litany of unsolved crimes, murders and lesser offences trotted out side by side with equal keenness. These stories figure large in the minds of everyone at the table and it turns into a lively discussion. Dinner is long over by the time the conversation ends and the guests excuse themselves and retire to their rooms.

"An entertaining lot, if a trifle gruesome," Violet tells Claire. "I've never really stopped to consider how long it would take for someone to bleed to death or how to fake a drowning."

"Or how to steal a million gallons of maple syrup. That was intriguing."

"Indeed. Perhaps our amateur sleuths would like to accompany us on the expedition tomorrow. It might excite them to find a few bones to dig up and bring home with them."

Claire gives her a sly smile. "I'll let you do the inviting, Aunt Vi."

"What we need is a rental car," Violet declares, as they make their way up the stairs. "That way we can avoid nosy cab drivers and all these excessive fares."

"I'm with you there," Claire says. "A car is certainly a bonus when you're travelling."

"Can you order a car on the Internet too?"

"You'd be surprised what you can get on the Internet. I doubt there's anything worth having that you can't find online."

"What about single men?" Violet asks. "I'm thinking of you, of course."

Claire smiles. "In fact, there are dating sites where you can meet people. There's also something called Facebook where you can make new friends."

"Goodness, what a useful thing the Internet is. Why wasn't it invented earlier?"

They pause on reaching the top of the stairs. Violet looks at her niece a moment then says, "Red, I should think."

Claire gives her a curious look. Is this odd remark a sign of senility or of some impending seizure?

"Red?"

"Yes," says Violet. "I think a red car will match my outfit nicely, don't you? I'll leave the model up to you — as long as it has at least two seats."

Claire gives a little laugh. "Of course. I'll go online tonight and get something we can pick up tomorrow morning."

"Very good, my dear. I'm glad I can depend on you. I don't know what I'd do otherwise."

Claire shakes her head. "You know you would do very well on your own, no matter what. You are the most capable octogenarian I've ever met."

Violet winks. "You ain't seen nothing yet!"

"I don't doubt that, somehow."

"Well, don't let it worry you needlessly."

AT NINE P.M. they rendezvous in the library for a nightcap, supplied with a knowing look from Mrs. Palmerston who, fortunately, is not stinting with her gin. She gives them a conspiratorial smile

— drink pouring is apparently something she approves of — and picks up the tray. She has just turned to leave, when Violet stops her at the door.

"Mrs. Palmerston?"

She turns. "Yes?"

"If you don't mind my asking, how did you come to learn about the Sulphur Springs murder?"

For a second, their proprietress looks trapped. She hesitates only a moment, then says simply, "My mother used to speak of it. She was acquainted with the crime."

"Did she grow up around here?" Violet asks.

"No. She moved here as a young woman."

"Did she ever venture a guess as to who was responsible?"

"I believe she sided with the police, who concluded that the murderer was a tramp. Their conclusion was based on certain unidentified footsteps around the crime scene at the time."

"Yes, that's so," Violet says.

Clarice nods and goes out the door.

Claire looks at her aunt. "A tramp?"

Violet sips her drink and settles into the chair. "It was ridiculous, really. It's the sort of thing people used to believe in cases like this. Pah! When you can't figure something out, blame it on strangers. Gypsies, tramps, and thieves, as the song says. Almost everyone will believe you. And if they're foreign strangers, even better, since we all know foreigners can't be trusted."

Claire giggles.

"There — you see? You know what I mean."

"Yes, I guess I do."

It was a sign of the times, Violet remembers. It wasn't unusual to have people show up on your doorstep at all hours, some begging for food and others for work — whatever you could spare. The only problem was, there was precious little to spare. It had all gone up in smoke during the Depression.

"They were different times back then. It wasn't just the failing economy, though that was a great part of it. Everything was changing. There were entirely new ways of doing things. The old ways were passing quickly. Some of the changes were good. Women secured the right to vote by the end of the First World War. Young girls went off to marry, sometimes without family consent, or even to live alone if they could support themselves." She gives Claire a knowing look. "Still others became tennis champions or far worse."

Claire smiles. "Still, it can't have been easy."

"Not really, no, apart from a privileged few. In those days, there were many people without homes, transients of all sorts. People lost their jobs and were forced to keep moving until they found a place where they could put down roots. Entire families were torn apart. It was quite terrible and far more common than you might imagine. There was no welfare system back then, no unemployment insurance. No health insurance either. Some of the girls were very young, though they quickly learned to act older. Many turned to dubious forms of employment."

Despite her position at the spa, Violet knew, the maid, Celeste Holmes, was that sort of girl. There had been others like her at school. Unless they got into trouble, however, no one paid much attention to them. They were the kind of girls you might not even notice had gone missing if they stopped coming to school one day. Violet recalls a girl named Renata who'd shown up in the middle of the semester and always came to school wearing second-hand clothes. Nobody made much of an effort to be friendly with her. Violet had said hello once or twice, but Renata rebuffed her approaches. The following year, when she didn't return, no one asked about her. Violet knows now she was probably afraid to make friends, no doubt having learned she would lose them the next time she and her family moved. Once she left school for good, she was quickly forgotten. You might never know what happened to her. Celeste had been of that type. She was just someone who was around, mostly unseen. If Ned hadn't noticed her, no one would have paid her any attention.

Later, during the war, people came and went just as mysteriously — sometimes entire families disappeared overnight. Once the true nature of Violet's mother's illness became apparent, the doctors advised her to move to a more moderate clime. The war was on by then. The McPhersons took their doctor's suggestion and moved to British Columbia where they hoped life would be easier.

The house Violet and her family moved into had been recently vacated. The upper floors were empty when they arrived, but Violet discovered a leather suitcase in the basement tucked behind the furnace. It was packed as though someone had intended to take it and then forgot. Inside, she found a compact of face powder and a silk scarf. Beneath these were a handful of stiff-backed wedding photographs bound in string. A proud-looking young Asian woman stood at the centre of a gathering next to a handsome man. Violet suspected she was the owner of the case, though she never learned for sure. Whatever else it signified, the case resolutely refused to yield up its secrets other than the one Violet surmised — that the couple had been detained and dispossessed of their home by the government, sent to an internment camp for the duration of the war, never to return.

She finishes her drink and sets the glass on the sideboard. She hasn't thought of this sad event in years — the detainment of Japanese Canadians under the War Measures Act. Once the war was over, no one wanted to look back. They'd been too anxious to forge ahead with better times, better memories. Before the war, of course, few knew what it would end up costing in human terms, but something priceless was about to be taken away from all of them. Many would lose their lives in the war; others lost homes and family members. Still others would lose something far less easily defined, even those who never experienced the war firsthand. You could only measure the loss afterwards, often in the most intangible ways.

13

ALONE AND PALELY LOITERING

RUMOURS OF WAR persisted, but to Violet they seemed distant and far-off enough not to be real. The mornings dawned sticky and hot. By mid-afternoon, the air crackled and the heat pooled in the valley. Men and women alike shed extra layers of clothing like children warming before a fire. The day Violet's father left, the spa received warning that a forest fire had broken out in the next county, though it too was far enough away that it was not considered an immediate concern.

"I'm sure it will be fine," Clive told his wife as they parted. "But don't take any chances. I can be back here on the next train, if you need me." To Violet, he said, "Be a help to your mother. She's going to need you."

And then he was gone.

All that week, Maggie McPherson divided her days between physiotherapy and sessions at the springs. She was redoubling her efforts, determined more than ever to get better. Violet moved in with her mother following her father's departure, giving up her room with the magical walls.

Julia had work duties most days, so Violet was left on her own. Afternoons she spent watching Ned from a distance while he puttered around the grounds. At no point did he go anywhere near the rock wall where she had seen him read the mysterious message.

It was mid-week when Julia summoned Violet for a meeting. They were sitting in the gazebo near one of the rose arbours. Julia twisted the tendrils of a vine with her fingers as she spoke.

"Mother's in a tizzy. There's more money missing. She says it's serious, this time. Nearly a hundred dollars."

"Has she called the police?"

"She won't. She doesn't trust them, and she thinks it will upset the guests."

"She must have some idea who's doing it," Violet insisted.

Julia shook her head while her hands kept up their twisting motions. "She won't say. My guess is that it's one of the staff."

"Ned!" Violet practically shrieked.

Julia shushed her. "Keep your voice down. Ned's been here for nearly a year, so why would he start stealing now? Anyway, it's not like we're making pots of money."

"I thought your family was rich."

Julia snorted. "You're such an imaginative girl."

"First I'm a smarty-pants and now I'm an imaginative girl. Which is it?"

Julia gave her a sobering look. "If you must know, Mother and I are practically slaves to the spa. We barely make enough to keep living here ourselves."

"I didn't know that," Violet said contritely. It was the first time she considered that maybe Julia, and not just her mother, might be desperate to escape the spa. "What about Celeste? Or one of the bathhouse attendants?"

"I don't know. It's hard to say. Most of them are day labourers. Only a handful stay here overnight. Ned does. So does Celeste. Speaking of, has there been anything else on the Ned front?"

Violet shook her head. "He hasn't gone near the wall once. Not since the time I followed him."

"Good grief," Julia exclaimed. "What could be so secret that he needs to hide notes in a hole in a wall?"

Violet's opinion of Ned had changed drastically over the past few days. The previous evening, he'd arrived at dinner with a black eye. When the others *oohed* and *aahed* over it, he laughed and made a joke of it.

"Stepped on my own hoe," he said.

But the next morning Violet overheard Mrs. Hutchins talking about him.

"Carl Mathers punched him for flirting with his wife," she said. "Can you believe it, a boy like that flirting with such an old bat?"

"Is that really what happened?" exclaimed the other, a new arrival.

Mrs. Hutchins nodded. "Apparently. But mark my words, it won't happen again. Mathers dragged his wife off in a huff. They left yesterday."

Julia nodded when Violet repeated this bit of gossip to her. "It's true," the older girl said.

"He said he stepped on a hoe!" Violet protested.

"Don't be so naïve."

But Violet had already come to a conclusion of her own.

"I think he's a spy," she declared. "Why else would he be leaving secret messages in that wall?"

Julia gave her a scornful look. "How can he be a spy? There isn't even a war on."

"Yet!" Violet crowed, as Julia shushed her once more. "My father says it's nearly started in Europe and once it does it's only a matter of time before it's here."

A sharp rapping came from behind. Julia started, as if she'd been caught doing something wrong. They looked up. Enid Browne stood inside at the chapel window.

"At her prayers again, no doubt," Julia said. "Pious old bag."

Violet's mouth gaped in surprise.

"I have to go," Julia said. She held up a vine bracelet, the ends of which she'd knotted in a loop. "Hold out your arm."

Violet watched as Julia slipped the wreath over her wrist.

"There. Now we're sisters." She looked Violet in the eye. "That's forever."

IN THE AFTERNOON, Violet saw Ned working on one of the garden beds. She watched as he pulled up a row of summer phlox that had gone dormant, tossing the stalks into a wheelbarrow. He looked up at her and wiped an arm across his forehead.

"Weeds, eh? It's hard work."

"Actually, that was a flower," Violet said, looking disapprovingly at the plants he'd uprooted.

Ned pursed his lips, but made no reply.

"They're called 'phlox,' if you want to know."

"I know that," he said.

"Then why'd you pull them up?"

"They were in the way." He paused and scratched his head then said, "Do they all have names?"

Violet gave him a scornful look. "Of course. Don't you know anything? I thought you were a gardener."

"Sure, I am, but I don't worry about the names of everything. All I care about is if they're healthy."

"Well," said Violet, "you should know a little more about them or you could get in trouble."

Ned laughed. "Trouble? How can a plant get you in trouble?"

Violet pointed to the monkshood. "You see that dark blue flower behind the roses?"

"Yeah."

"Well, you shouldn't touch it without wearing gloves."

"Why?"

"Because it's poisonous. If you even touch it and you have a cut on your hand, the sap could get into your blood and kill you. If you're a gardener, you should know that."

"Maybe I do." He seemed to contemplate the plant with greater respect. "You mean you don't even need to eat it to get sick? Even if you just touch it?"

"That's right," Violet said. "Even if you just touch it."

After a moment, Ned grinned. "Could put that to some use, eh? Maybe cause a little trouble of my own."

Violet's eyes widened. "You better not!"

Ned winked. "Just joking. I would never do such a thing."

THAT EVENING AFTER supper, Violet joined Julia at her table when Enid left the room. She looked around to be sure no one was listening.

"I've got something important to tell you," she said. "Ned isn't really a gardener."

Julia looked sceptical. "How do you know?"

Violet glanced over to where Ned sat three tables over. A butt dangled from his lip as he offered his cache of hand-rolled cigarettes to the others around him. A burst of laughter erupted from several of the women at the table next to him.

"He doesn't know a thing about plants. Not even the basics."

Julia's eyes narrowed. "If he's not a gardener, then what's he doing here?"

"Maybe you should ask your mother. Didn't she hire him?"

Violet turned to watch as Ned retrieved a piece of paper and a pencil from his pocket. He laboured over the note, writing in a slow, steady hand.

"What's he doing?" Julia asked, purposely avoiding looking at him.

"He's writing a note," said Violet.

Just then, Julia's mother returned with the Victrola and a handful of phonograph records in paper sleeves.

"Hello, Violet," she said, smiling her sour smile.

"Hello, Mrs. Browne."

Enid turned to her daughter. "Julia, I'll need you in the kitchen in two minutes."

"But we were just —"

"No arguing, young lady," Enid snapped. "You can visit with Violet when you're finished."

Julia made an exasperated face at Violet when her mother turned away.

"Sorry, I have to go."

"I'll see you later."

Across the room, Ned pocketed the pencil and paper. As the music started and others began to dance, he slipped out the door. If she hadn't been watching for him to make a move, Violet wouldn't have noticed. She looked back at her table — her mother was preoccupied. She waited a moment, then followed. He headed down the lane, just as he had on the previous occasion. Once again, he took a curious meandering route through the woods, pausing now and again to look around before making his way over to the rock wall. This time, however, rather than look to see if the hole contained anything, he slipped the note he'd written at dinner inside, then replaced the stone.

He strolled slowly away, stopping once to light a cigarette. It seemed ages before he was out of sight. At last, certain he was gone, Violet went over to the wall. Her hands fumbled around as she felt to see which rock Ned had moved. It took several tries before she located the right one. She had to use both hands to shift it.

The hole was smaller than she'd expected — a few inches wide and no more than eight inches deep. She reached down and drew out the note, her hands trembling as she unfolded it. She stared at the words: *Why won't you meet me, you know you want to? I have importent stuff to tell you. That fight wasn't nothing. Don't beleave what anyone says. Ned.*

She smirked at the grammar before returning the note to the bottom of the hole and replacing the rock. She considered for a moment. This was a discovery. Should she go back and tell Julia or follow Ned? Curiosity took hold. She continued cautiously along the road in the direction Ned had gone.

There was no sign of him until she reached the pavilion. Cigarette smoke hung in the air. She crept up to the entrance. The door was ajar. Peering through the doorframe, she could make out Ned's silhouette where he sat smoking by the pool. After a moment, he stood and tossed his cigarette aside. It hit a wall, orange sparks splintering in all directions.

As he stood there, he reached up with his arms and pulled his shirt off over his head. His chest was slender, more like a boy's than a man's. He let the shirt slip to the ground, then kicked off his shoes, reaching down to unbuckle his belt. His trousers fell to the floor. Finally, he grasped his boxer shorts, pushing them down around his ankles before kicking them aside.

His skin was pale except for a mound of dark hair between his legs. From the middle of it dangled something that was not hair, but more like a white noodle. Violet remembered a drawing in one of her father's anatomy textbooks showing a naked man and a naked woman facing forward. *Completely natural*, her father had said. Still, it unsettled her to see Ned like that.

She watched as he lowered himself into the pool, resting his arms on the edge as water splashed gently over the sides. After a moment, he reached for his cigarettes and struck a match against a loose brick from a pile nearby. The light flared. In that instant, Violet saw his face clearly. The flame shrank as he drew on his cigarette and leaned back, exhaling. Smoke rose in lazy clouds toward the ceiling.

ON THE WAY back to the hotel Violet could barely keep her mind on where she was walking. Twice she stumbled and nearly fell. She had seen a naked man. Not in a textbook, but for real. And it was Ned. She wanted to dash the image from her mind, to banish it for all time, but she knew that was impossible. She was reminded of the day she'd seen her neighbour's cat run over by a car. There were things that, once seen, you could never unsee.

A few guests stood around on the porch, talking softly in the darkness. Frank Larsen turned at her approach. He called out to her.

"Hello, young lady. I hope you're not out wandering alone in the dark?"

"I ... no. I was just looking for Julia Browne."

"Well, good. Don't get lost. We'd have to send out a search party for you. I think you will find Miss Browne in the kitchen."

"Thank you, Mr. Larsen. Don't worry. I won't get lost."

She stepped around to the side of the hotel, heading for the kitchen entrance, then stopped short. Two of the ground floor windows were dark. Inside a third, she saw a shadowy movement. It was Ned's room. She remembered it from the day he had leaned out the window to tease her right before she heard a woman's voice calling from inside. How had he got back before her?

She crept closer, keeping hidden by the rose bushes. Inside the room, a figure slipped through the door and into the hallway, momentarily outlined by the light as he went. It wasn't Ned; it was Willoughby. But what was Willoughby doing in Ned's room?

Julia was in the kitchen with her hands plunged in soapy water when Violet entered. A shuffling sound came from the other side of the door. Julia placed a finger to her lips.

"Meet me at the kennel in five minutes," she whispered. In a louder voice, she said, "I'm almost done the dishes, Mother. I'll feed the dogs next."

Violet nodded and headed up the hill to the kennel. The dogs were restless as she approached. They sniffed eagerly at her hands, whimpering softly, but made no other sound. Five minutes passed. Just as she thought Enid must have kept Julia from coming, the dark-haired girl turned up. As if on cue, a long, incessant howl split the air. Seconds later, the grandfather clock gonged out the time.

Julia brought the table scraps to the fence and tipped them in. The instant they hit the tray, the howling stopped and Homer stepped up to eat.

"What did you discover?" Julia hissed.

"Another note," Violet said.

Should she tell Julia that she had seen Ned naked? She thought it was probably not a good idea. Julia might ask embarrassing questions.

"Where? In the rock wall, like last time?"

"Yes."

"What did it say? Come on — tell me!"

"It said, 'Why won't you meet me, you know you want to.' Then, a question mark, which is wrong. Then it said, 'I have important stuff to tell you. That fight wasn't nothing. Don't believe what anyone says. Ned.' His spelling was atrocious."

"I doubt he finished high school," Julia said. "We're not all so lucky, you know."

Violet was surprised to hear Julia defend him.

"Anyway, it's clear he wants to meet someone," she said, put out.

"But who? And why won't they meet him?"

Violet shrugged.

"I still think he's a spy. Why else would he have 'important stuff' to tell someone?"

Julia laughed. "There are no spies, silly. At least not in Canada. Don't you know anything?"

Violet gave Julia a reproachful look. "Well, what's your bright idea then?"

"Sorry — you're doing a good job," Julia said, softening. "Anyway, I couldn't do it without you. You know that. Tomorrow, I have to go into town to do the shopping. Will you be able to keep your eye on him then?"

"Of course. I found the note, didn't I?"

"I'll bring you treats from the store. Do you like liquorice?"

"You don't have to bribe me," Violet said huffily.

"As you wish."

The dogs had nearly finished eating. Homer was lapping at the water dish.

"We should go back," Julia said. "Mother's been keeping an eye on me lately."

ONCE THEY REACHED the hotel, Violet left Julia and made her way down the long hallway, dark now except for the chandeliers at either end. She found her mother lying on the bed with her leg suspended by a sling. Maggie looked up.

"You see what Doctor Cheavers has me doing?"

Violet stared. "It looks very uncomfortable. Isn't your ankle getting better yet?"

"It's still too soon to say. And now that both you and your father have deserted me, I'm all alone." Seeing Violet's guilty expression, she smiled. "I'm only joking. What on earth have you been up to?"

"I was helping Julia feed the dogs."

"It's nice you two have become friends. What sort of things do you talk about?"

"Many things, actually. We were discussing the war in Europe. Daddy said it was going to start any day now. Julia's not so sure."

Maggie's face darkened. "I'm afraid it is very likely. I only hope it doesn't come here. And I hope you don't start having nightmares over it. Young girls grow up far too quickly these days."

Violet flushed, thinking of having seen Ned naked. While she might have had a conversation with her father about what she had seen, she could never tell her mother.

"I don't want to be a girl forever."

"You'll always be my little girl. But life will come to you far faster than you could ever imagine. One day you may wish you hadn't grown up so quickly."

"I'm tired of being a girl and I don't want to play with dolls anymore," Violet said impatiently. "Anyway, we can't stop the war from happening."

Maggie patted the bed. Violet sat beside her.

"War is a terrible thing, Violet. I lost my brother, your Uncle Charlie, in the last war. He was just a boy, not much older than you are now. And now your cousin Herbert will be going to war, if it begins."

Violet had heard all this before, spoken in hushed tones by her grandparents and older relatives. There was a photograph of Charlie in the sitting room. He was just out of his teens when he went to war and never came back. Herbert was Charlie's son. He'd been born a few months before his father died, but couldn't remember anything about him. Violet tried to imagine Herbert carrying a gun and shooting somebody. It didn't seem real. He had won medals in school track and field events and was said to be the fastest boy his age in Ontario. He had taught her to run when she was just eight, challenging her to race him to a neighbour's barn. He'd let her win by feigning a sore leg right before he reached the finish line, though she hadn't realized it till she was older.

"Herbert's a good runner. He can get away fast if anything bad happens."

"Let's hope so. We'll all be very worried for him. I never want to have anything to do with war again."

Violet felt a twinge of remorse at having caused her mother to worry. She helped her lower her leg from the sling, then brushed her teeth and dressed for bed.

Once under the covers, she struggled to sleep. The bed seemed big enough for a giant, yet here she was, just one small girl who could do nothing about war or the terrible things that happened to other people.

She lay there listening to her mother's gentle breathing and the chirping of crickets outside. A fan stirred the air slowly in one corner. Violet got up and went to the window and stood staring out at the sky. The world seemed large and very close up. The stars were bright and clear, but distant.

As she looked, a pinprick of light appeared in the forest. It wavered a moment, then headed slowly away from the hotel. Without thinking, she threw a sweater over her pyjama top, unlatched the door, and slipped out. There was no sound in the hall save for the ticking of the grandfather clock. The canaries were asleep in their cage as she crossed the lobby and let herself out the front entrance.

The air was cool. Dew soaked her bare feet as she crossed the lawn. The orange dot was moving steadily through the trees. Before long, Violet heard water trickling in the distance. The cigarette made an arc as it flew into the air and disappeared soundlessly into the stream. After a moment, a match flared and fell to the ground. That was extremely careless given the current forest fire situation, she thought indignantly.

She could clearly see Ned by the light of the moon. Once again, he seemed to be waiting for someone as he stood there smoking. After a few minutes, he tossed the butt into the stream. An owl hooted. Violet continued to watch, but no one approached.

Eventually, Ned turned and headed back to the hotel, passing within a few feet of where she lay crouched beneath the low-hanging limbs of a cedar.

"Good night, Violet," he said.

-14-

THE LADY IN THE LAKE

IN THE MORNING, Violet went back to where she'd watched Ned smoke his cigarette the previous night. A burnt matchstick lay on the ground next to a trampled patch of grass. There was nothing to show why he'd been wandering around the woods alone at night. If he was expecting to meet someone, then he'd been disappointed. Or perhaps knowing that Violet was following him had prevented a get-together. The mystery was growing.

She went back to the hotel and looked around for Julia, but the older girl had already left for the day's shopping. From the window of her room, she could see Ned puttering around the grounds, whistling as he worked. From time to time, one of the hotel guests stopped to chat with him. Whatever he'd been up to the night before, he gave no sign of it now. Once, he looked in Violet's direction, but she was well hidden behind the curtains. He did not go near the rock wall at all that morning. Violet vacillated between thinking he was a spy and thinking it highly unlikely, when it occurred to her that she wouldn't know if anyone had replied to his note. She shouldn't have been watching Ned — she should have been watching the wall.

She slipped out the back entrance and hightailed it over to the wall, pushing aside the covering stone. There, at the bottom, was a new note. She fished it out and read: *I will meet you this evening*

at the usual spot at 7. It wasn't Ned's handwriting. At least someone knew how to spell properly.

Violet felt her heart pounding. Her childish convictions
suddenly seemed far less unlikely. Who was meeting him? The
morning newspaper had confirmed the rumours: *War in Europe
Imminent.* Her mother had telephoned her father and spoken to
him in a hushed voice for nearly a quarter of an hour at long-
distance rates.

Violet wished more than ever that her father was there. If he
had been, she might have taken her concerns to him. But he was
back home and she felt a reluctance to bother her mother with
such things. At the very least, Maggie would disapprove of her
investigations; at worst, she might prevent her from following
through with her sleuthing.

She returned the note to the hole and replaced the rock. It
wouldn't do to have Ned and whoever had written the other note
suspect that she was privy to their secrets. She decided she would
tell Julia about it at some point. Not so Julia would take her seriously — she'd already ridiculed her spy theories — but because
Julia had set her on this path. Whatever was going on, whatever
Ned was up to, one thing was clear: his actions required secrecy.
The reasons for it remained to be seen.

He was standing outside the tool shed when Violet got back.
It was too late to avoid him. He had already seen her. In the heat,
he had rolled up his sleeves past the elbows. His forearms were
tanned and glistening with sweat. He leaned on his hoe while he
talked to two women Violet had seen for the first time the previous evening.

"We must be very careful with plants," he informed them.
"Otherwise, we could get in a good deal of trouble."

"What sort of trouble?" asked one of the women.

"Do you see this plant here?" He pointed to the monkshood.

"It's highly poisonous. Why, if you even just touched it and you had a cut on your hands, it could kill you stone dead."

The women gasped. "Really!"

He winked as Violet approached.

"It's true."

Violet ignored him and headed around to the front entrance. A car drove up to the gate and stopped. The driver got out and opened it, then got back in and continued up the drive to the hotel. Julia stepped out and waved to Violet.

"I have liquorice," she proclaimed, holding out a paper bag crammed with red and black strands.

"And I have news," Violet said softly.

"You found out who the note was for?"

"Not exactly. But someone replied to it. They're meeting tonight at seven."

Julia looked impressed. "Who?"

"I still don't know."

"I'm almost beginning to believe in your spy theory. What now?"

"I'll wait till Ned finds the note, then I'll follow him."

Julia's eyes flashed. "You'll figure it out. I have the utmost faith in you, Violet McPherson!"

THE AFTERNOON PASSED slowly. Her mother was still away for her treatments. Violet lay on the bed and read, toying with the vine bracelet Julia had given her. She liked the feel of it on her arm and how it twirled when she shook her wrist. She found it hard to focus. Her attention kept straying from her book. From time to time, she got up and went to the window, peering through the curtains. Ned seemed content to putter around the gardens. If he had a plan of any sort, it consisted of looking like he wasn't doing anything. She wondered if anyone else suspected him of treachery.

It occurred to her that any of the guests could be involved as well. Most of them seemed ordinary, but a good spy was supposed to be just that. Mrs. Hutchins knew a lot about what went on around the spa, but that didn't make her a spy; it just made her nosy. Miss Turner's only interest, apart from taking the treatment, seemed to be in food. There was also Frank Larsen and Miss McMaster, as well as a number of others she'd met. Violet knew next to nothing about them apart from the basic facts of their illnesses, though she doubted any of them were faking their symptoms. Then she thought of Willoughby. What had he been doing in Ned's room while Ned was at the bathing pavilion? Leaving messages? As the hotel's director, he had the perfect opportunity to slip in and out of the rooms. But why would Ned leave notes for him in a rock wall when they could exchange information privately in his room? Or perhaps Ned was secretly passing along information from Willoughby to someone else. There'd been that mysterious woman in his room the day Ned reached out the window to shake Violet's hand. It was impossible to say.

VIOLET WOKE WITH a start. The book had fallen from her hands. When she looked out the window again, Ned was gone. She put on her shoes and went out. The afternoon was stifling. Clouds hung in a clear blue sky but did little to shelter her from the sun. She wandered around the grounds; there was no sign of him. If he'd gone to check for messages in the crevice, he'd be too far ahead to follow. In any case, she already knew what the note said.

She decided to sit in the gazebo and wait to see if he turned up. From there she could see anyone approaching the hotel. Before she reached it, however, the gardening shed caught her eye. She wandered over. The door was closed. There was no sound from within. Violet coughed, half expecting him to emerge, but when nothing happened, she pushed on the door.

Light threaded through cracks in the roof and walls and from a single window near the back. The air felt still and expectant. She breathed in the smell of peat and something leathery as she shut the door behind her. Lined up against the wall on the right were shears and rakes, two hoes and a shovel. Against the back wall were bags of fertilizer. The ball of twine she'd watched Ned use to tie up the rose bushes lay on the floor.

Overhead, a half-dozen bottles had been lined up on a bare wooden shelf. The glass was dark, mostly blues and browns. She brought one down. On the faded handwritten label, the words *Rat Poison* could just be made out. She replaced it and picked up another: *Poison. DANGER. Neem Oil. For treatment of pests on roses and other ornamental plants. Do not ingest.*

All but one of the bottles were positioned at the front of the shelf. A final bottle had been pushed to the back, as though it had been forgotten or purposely set aside. She stood on her toes to reach it, coaxing it forward with her fingers till she could grasp it firmly. As she pulled back, Julia's vine bracelet caught on a nail head, snapping and unravelling.

"Oh no!" she cried.

The strands lay scattered on the floor. She remembered how Julia had given it to her and said "forever." Surely, she hadn't meant the bracelet to last forever. Maybe Julia would make her another one.

She held the bottle up, letting it glitter in the light. *Cutty Sark — Blended Scotch Whisky.* It was like the one Ned had poured from at dinner the other night. A fly buzzed around her head. She swatted at it, nearly flinging the bottle away, but caught herself and gripped it tighter.

She stood very still. For a moment, the light outside increased in brightness, then faded as the sun passed behind a cloud. Somewhere, a cicada started up its incessant droning. A breeze sighed high up in the trees. Time seemed to stand still, as though waiting to see what she would do.

A thin pink and white seal had been affixed to the bottle's mouth. She scratched at it with her fingernail till a corner came loose. Slowly, she unpeeled it and pulled on the stopper till it slid free with a small pop. She held the bottle up to her nose and sniffed. It smelled like turpentine. Through the window, she saw Willoughby striding soundlessly across the lawn at the far end of the hotel. For a moment, the world outside the shed seemed to recede. She could stay here, safe and unseen, for as long as she wanted. What had Frank Larsen said? *Don't get lost. We'd have to send out a search party for you.* In here, she might not be found for quite a while. Everything was quiet and contained. Everything was still. No one would suspect she'd hidden inside the gardening shed, like Alice in Wonderland down her rabbit hole. The first person to check would probably be Ned. She shivered pleasantly, thinking of hiding behind the fertilizer sacks, waiting till he uncovered her with a cry of surprise.

Slowly, she lifted the bottle to her lips and tipped it forward. At first there was only the cool slither of the whiskey as it slid around her mouth. Then, suddenly, it burned as it went down her throat. Her face flushed as she coughed and spewed it on the ground.

Her father had given her a glass of sherry at Christmas. It was sweetly pleasant. But this was her first taste of what her grandfather called "yellow liquor," curling his lip in disdain when he said it. He had been an abstainer — what others called a teetotaller. His older brother, Albert, had been an alcoholic. Albert had inherited the family fortune from their father with the expectation that he would share it equally with his four brothers and sisters, but instead he secretly drank it away till there was nothing left. Her grandfather never forgave him. Not that it would have mattered.

Albert's actions brought their own punishment, biblical-style. He died in his forties from cirrhosis of the liver.

"And good riddance to him," her grandfather declared at his funeral. Ever since, he had had no patience for drinkers.

Violet understood all this, though she still wasn't sure how anyone could become addicted to something that tasted so vile. You'd have to force yourself to drink it, and what would be the point? She pushed the stopper back into the bottle, reattached the pink and white label, then pushed it to the farthest reaches of the shelf.

The door slammed behind her as she left the shed. Mrs. Hutchins and a woman Violet didn't recognize passed by as she stood there blinking in the blazing light.

"Visiting your boyfriend, Violet?" she asked.

"He's not —"

Mrs. Hutchins turned to her companion. "Let me tell you — that gardener is definitely something to write home about."

There were titters as the women shushed themselves. Violet turned and headed off, barely restraining herself from breaking into a run. Behind her, she heard Mrs. Hutchins say, "I wonder if her mother knows what she gets up to."

Up ahead, the laneway was deserted. It would soon be time for the bathers to return to the hotel. On instinct, she stopped at the hiding place in the wall. When she moved the stone and looked down, the hole was empty.

THAT EVENING, MAGGIE felt well enough to walk to the dining room on her own. It was a definite sign she was getting better, she told Violet. And indeed, she seemed more secure on her feet than when they had arrived.

They sat at the table with Frank Larsen and Miss McMaster again. It was the first time Violet had seen Frank since running into him on the porch the previous night. She stole a glance at him, wondering if he would mention their surprise meeting as she returned from the darkened woods, but he just smiled pleasantly and wished her a good evening.

Tonight was Miss McMaster's last night at the spa. She looked despondent. It seemed there had been no relief for her, as there was for Violet's mother. Frank patted her hand.

"Perhaps the improvements will come in time," he said. "It could be a delayed reaction, you know. You've got to take heart, my girl. A month from now we may both be dancing, as Dr. Cheavers said."

"Yes, I hope you're right," Miss McMaster said, but she didn't smile.

Dinner passed quickly. Desserts were brought out with tea and coffee. Ned was his usual jovial self, laughing and joking with the women at the nearby tables. When Enid Browne left to get the Victrola, Violet watched as he unscrewed his bottle and poured a dash into his water glass. If anyone else noticed, no one said anything.

Dinner was over. Celeste began clearing away the dishes as the nightly dancing began. Ned had just pulled out his cigarette case — the sign Violet had been waiting for — when her mother turned to her.

"I'm feeling a little tired. I may have overdone things a bit. I'll need help to get back to the room, so don't run off."

Violet looked around. Julia was nowhere in sight. If she left now, she'd miss her chance to follow Ned, but there was no way she could refuse.

It seemed an eternity before Maggie was ready to leave, saying goodbye to the others and offering Miss McMaster her fervent wishes for a full recovery. The strains of a waltz floated in the air as they made their way down the hall.

Getting back to their room seemed especially slow going. Violet had to restrain her impatience as they ambled along. Once in the room, she waited for her mother to get settled. Then, claiming a date with Julia, she left.

Ned was gone by the time she got back to the dining hall. She headed for the kitchen. There, inside, was Julia, standing with her hands plunged into the sink. She gave Violet a miserable look, shaking her head.

Violet hurried to the front door and stood on the porch, scanning the path ahead. It was nearing twilight. The smell of smoke stung her throat and lungs. The forest fires were getting closer. The weather had continued hot and dry all that week; the heat wave had no doubt helped them spread. All day they had seen birds winging past, huge flocks darkening the sky.

She was just about to give up when she saw Ned up ahead, his jacket slung over his shoulder and his white shirt just visible in the dying light. Without thinking, she took off after him. Once again, he seemed in no hurry to get wherever he was going. He meandered and stopped twice to smoke. It had to be close to seven, the designated meeting time. All at once, his pace quickened and he headed directly for the bathing pavilion. Of course, she thought. This was the "usual" place.

Out on the steps, he looked briefly around, then slipped inside. Violet crept closer, keeping well hidden in the underbrush. Knowing he had seen her following him the previous night made her extra cautious.

He had left the door ajar again. No lights showed from inside; no voices came from within. She waited without moving, wondering if anyone would show up. It was ten minutes or more when at last she heard footsteps coming along the road, faint at first, then growing louder.

Violet held her breath as a figure came into view around the bend in the road. For a moment, it didn't register. It was Celeste. She had taken off her apron, but was still dressed in her uniform.

Violet was confused. If anyone was an unlikely spy, it was Celeste. She watched as the maid stopped outside the pavilion and looked around briefly, then opened the door and went in.

"Well, you took your time," she heard Ned say.

"I got here as soon as I could." Celeste sounded annoyed. "The old biddy wanted me to help with the dishes. I told her I was sick."

"Come on in. The water's fine." Ned laughed. "Stinks like hell, though."

For a full minute there was only silence. A bat flitted above, its squeaks echoing in the twilight. Violet crept up onto the porch, inching her way forward, wary of creaking floorboards. There were no sounds from inside, not even the murmur of conversation. Then something unsettling reached her ears. It might have been a laugh or a cry. It was impossible to tell.

The door was closed. She turned the knob and let herself in. At first it was too dark to make anything out. The sound repeated itself, growing louder and more urgent. It was almost guttural, like a cat in heat.

As her eyes adjusted, she could see Ned and Celeste in the pool. She watched as Ned pressed himself against Celeste, raising and lowering himself repeatedly. He seemed to be crushing her, gasping a little each time he moved. At one point, Celeste gave a cry and raised her arms overhead. He pinned them against the wall.

She cried out again and Ned put a hand over her mouth.

"Shh!" he said softly.

After a moment, he groaned and shoved hard, banging Celeste's head against the wall. She winced and reached up with her hand.

"Ow! That hurt."

Ned laughed. "You should be used to it by now."

"You bastard."

"Takes one to know one."

He climbed out of the pool and shook the water from his body, brushing himself off with his hands, then reached for his clothes where they lay in a pile beside the pool.

Violet slipped out the door and down the porch to the road. She wanted to get as far away from the pavilion as possible. An understanding had dawned somewhere deep inside her: as she flew along the path back to the hotel, she knew she would never play with dolls again.

15

ANYPLACE I HANG MY HAT IS HOME

TRUE TO HER word, Claire has rented a red Audi for them. Violet wears her red hat and matching gloves, while Claire is dressed in breezy blues and greens. They spend the day driving up and down winding country roads, stopping to explore antique stores and treat themselves to ice cream at a roadside stand. The freedom is exhilarating.

It's early afternoon by the time they reach the spa. They park the car and strike out along a path leading directly into the forest. They've brought fried chicken, potato salad, and coleslaw. A veritable picnic. After a short trek, they stop beside the rock wall where it runs alongside the stream. Here, the water is clear and odourless.

Violet removes her hat and gloves and turns to survey the landscape. Everything feels peaceful and reassuring, as though that might be the normal state of things in nature, though she knows it is not. She tucks the gloves into her purse, then hangs the hat from a knot in a pine tree while Claire spreads a blanket on the ground.

Claire watches her aunt's tentative attempts to lower herself. She doesn't offer to help. If her aunt wants help, she will ask. Violet is stubborn and finally manages it, slowly crossing her legs and making herself as comfortable as she can.

"Brava!" Claire cries as Violet settles herself.

"It's all those gin and tonics. They keep me nimble."

"So I hear, Aunt Vi!"

Claire unpacks the lunch, handing over the food containers to Violet, who carefully lifts the lids and digs in with a spoon, piling mounds on their plates.

"I want to thank you for indulging a silly old woman," she says at length, biting into a chicken leg.

Claire looks over. "What do you mean?"

"I feel like I've dragged you here for nothing. I keep asking myself, what are we really doing here? What do I hope to discover? And I can't come up with anything."

"That's not entirely true." Claire smiles, settling on the blanket. "If nothing else, I enjoy spending time with you. I never had the chance as a kid."

"Yes, you're right," Violet says. It strikes her that it's time to open the shutters on family secrets, to let in some fresh air if Claire is willing. "With all my silly amateur sleuth games, I haven't given you a chance to talk about your troubles. What you've gone through this last year can't have been easy."

Claire nods knowingly. Emotions flicker across her face. It's not clear if she's going to speak about it or not. Finally, she does.

"You're right. It hasn't been easy for me. But the truth is, Mike and I weren't suited for each other. Or so Mike convinced himself. I'm not really sure I had a say in the matter. He wanted me to be something different. He wanted a career wife. Someone with ambition. I'm good at math, so he thinks I should have been an aerospace engineer or something."

"And what did you want to be?"

"Happy," Claire replies, then shrugs it off. "I wanted to be that woman on TV who smiles while she's cooking supper or packing the kids off to school. Maybe with a part-time job at a library to bring in extra money. Instead, I ended up being a very unhappy accounts manager for a large firm that isn't known for treating its employees well."

"The corporate world wasn't for you?" Violet suggests, tasting the potato salad.

"I'm a hard worker, but I found running the department was counter-conducive to having a stress-free life. That was part of the problem, but maybe the real truth was that Mike and I got married too soon. After only a few years, we seemed to have grown apart."

"Sometimes people grow apart. Other times they grow so alike they get on each another's nerves. Only they don't have the guts to admit how miserable they are or to say they've lost what once mattered to them. I don't know which is worse: to hang in there for no good reason or to part because you can't figure out why you're together."

"I think it was the latter." Claire smiles ruefully. "We discussed it and decided it was best for us to divorce. That's all it was, really. No great mystery. It just took me a while to grasp."

"I think sometimes we fail to grasp the obvious, expecting things to be far more complicated than they really are."

"After nearly a year of therapy, I think I'm okay with it."

"Good. I'm sure it helps. When I miss Edgar, I've got my girls. The Silver Swans. I think I mentioned them. They're my therapy."

"Yes, you did mention them. They sound like fun. Maybe I should join."

"We're a bit old for you, dear."

They both laugh.

"Did you ever try yoga?" Violet asks.

"As a matter of fact, I did. It was a group that met once a week for an hour. We had this round little man as a teacher. I was astonished how he could sit with his legs crossed and his large belly hanging over. He kept talking about how our minds need to be motivated by compassion because life is only an illusion. Everything is emptiness, he kept saying, and virtually meaning-less. If life is empty and nothing means anything, I thought, then what's the point? I don't think I grasped his concept of emptiness. All I could think of was the mountains of food he had to consume for his belly to get so enormous."

"The contradictions of life."

"Anyway, I wasn't very successful at it. Not only could I not imagine life as total emptiness, I also couldn't visualize pure wisdom. Apparently, that's what you need to do to succeed. But I never could."

"Most of us are failed human beings," Violet says, putting the lids back on the containers. "So few of us get to be the Buddha."

She holds out a paper cup. Claire fills it with lemonade.

"In any case," she says, "You'll be better off without Mike. You're sensible and attractive and you'll meet someone right for you. Maybe in that Facebook club. If you're looking, of course. There's no reason you should rush. And one day, years from now, you'll run into him on the street, you looking happy and him looking miserable, then he'll realize what he lost."

Claire smiles. "It's nice to think so."

There's a momentary silence. A bird trills in the bush nearby.

"What about revenge?" Violet says suddenly.

Claire looks up from the paper plate she has balanced on her knee. "I ... I don't approve of it," she says.

"Good. Neither do I. The Lord and I quibble over a lot of minor details, but when He says 'Vengeance is mine,' I'm more than happy to let Him have it." Seeing Claire's confusion, she says. "I'm talking about the murder, of course."

Claire gives her a quizzical look. "Is that what we're doing here? Is this a sort of revenge?"

"Goodness, no! There's no one left to get revenge on. This is curiosity, dear. And a healthy respect for justice, of course. What I meant was, what do you think of revenge as a motive for the killing?"

"Certainly, but revenge for what?"

"That's what I'm still not sure of. Enid Browne fired the maid when she found out what they were up to, but Ned gave his notice before she could fire him. Then there was the missing money, of course. I wasn't at all surprised to learn who stole that."

Just then, Violet looks to her left and sees a figure lurking in the underbrush. It's the man in the hunting jacket from the previous day. Once again, he's carrying his rifle.

"Don't look now, but here's our creepy friend," she says.

Before Claire can turn, the man steps off the path and disappears into the brush.

"I don't see anybody," she says.

"He was right over there behind those trees. With his gun."

"What on earth can he be doing? There's no hunting allowed here."

"Something nefarious, no doubt," Violet replies, staring after the vanished figure.

"You're not thinking of following him, I hope?"

Violet pats her niece's hand. "No, I've learned that lesson. But if I were fourteen again ..."

She leaves the rest unspoken. The man appears to have gone. The conversation turns to happier things. The two women pass a pleasant hour before packing their belongings and heading back to the car.

"I feel a storm coming on," Violet says.

"Really? I don't feel a thing."

"Trust me, dear. I feel it in my bones."

Violet finds the walk back harder; her rheumatism is bothering her. It's the change of weather.

"I wonder if Wally misses us," she says mischievously.

They wander along the path looking for a place to dispose of their garbage. They're in luck. They find a recycling container. Violet insists on separating every scrap of packaging from the food, even where the labels insist they are biodegradable.

"What is it the environmentalists say? We don't want to leave behind any dirty fingerprints where we have been?"

Claire smiles, amused by her aunt's insistence on being up to date.

"Footprints, I think it is. We want to reduce our carbon footprints."

Violet nods. "Let's reduce both, while we're at it. Many a criminal has been caught by leaving both fingerprints and footprints behind."

A dog howls forlornly in the distance. Violet turns her head to listen.

"It's odd," she says. "When I think about this place, I can still hear Julia's hounds after all these years. Dinner was served at six and the dogs ate two hours after us. It was amazing how they always knew the time. They would start howling precisely on the dot of eight — and God forbid you should be late feeding them. That was a terrible uproar. Being late with supper was out of the question."

"Mike was a bit like that too," Claire says.

They both laugh.

SURE ENOUGH, ON their way back to the hotel the radio is calling for thunderstorms even though the sky overhead is clear. The return is uneventful and Violet gives in to the temptation to snooze while Claire drives.

At dinner that evening, Violet and the captain strike up a conversation while Claire finds common ground with Lucy and Bart.

Mrs. Palmerston's food excels again. For once her outfit, blacks and greys, is surprisingly demure. All in all, it's a pleasant evening, though it ends soon enough. It's not until Violet returns to her room that she realizes her hat is missing. Thinking over the day, she knows she must have left it back at the picnic grounds. Five minutes after saying goodnight, she is knocking at Claire's door.

"Are you sure you left it there?"

"Yes, I'm quite sure," Violet says, exasperated by her forgetfulness.

"But why didn't we see it when we were leaving?"

Violet sighs. "Because I was too clever by half. I strung it up in a tree rather than set it on the ground where it might have got dirty. We looked on the ground around us to see if we'd left anything behind. I don't recall looking up."

"Neither do I," Claire says. "Do you think it can wait till tomorrow?"

Violet makes a face. "The radio is forecasting thunder showers this evening. If it gets wet, it will be ruined."

"Then we shall have to get it."

"I'm so sorry to put you to this bother. I'm usually not so forgetful."

"It's not a bother. Let's go now before it gets too late and we can't find our way."

Mrs. Palmerston gives them a wry look when they ask to borrow a flashlight.

"I won't ask why," she says.

"Good for you," Violet says. "And we won't tell."

It's already dark when they arrive back at the parking lot. Trees loom up ahead, oppressive and gloomy, like a forest in a ghost tale. Without wasting time, they head for the stream. Wind stirs all around them. The storm is not far off. A hoot owl seems to be mocking the two forlorn figures trudging about in the dark.

Somewhere in the darkness an animal cries. Tattered streaks cloud the moon, as though it's swathed in bandages. Violet points the flashlight on the ground directly ahead. It barely illumines the forest floor.

"Watch your step, dear. The last thing we need is for you to fall and sprain your ankle. I won't be much use if I have to carry you out."

In a few minutes, they reach the picnic spot. Sure enough, the hat hangs right where Violet left it earlier in the afternoon. It seems to have been waiting for them to come back and retrieve it, like a puppy leashed to a tree and left behind when the children finished their games. They are just in time. Lightning flashes in the distance. The rain is clearly not far off.

"That's a relief," Violet says, plunking it on her head. "It's my favourite hat and the very last thing Edgar bought me before he died."

"Oh, dear," says Claire. "Then I'm certainly glad we came back to fetch it. What a terrible loss it would have been if it was ruined."

They are almost back to the car when they see lights wavering on the path dead ahead, accompanied by the sound of a motor revving. Only it's not a car engine. A massive shape looms in the darkness right in front of them. Whatever it is moves slowly toward them, then stops abruptly. There are two men moving around.

Violet switches off the flashlight and clutches Claire's arm. They watch the lights in silence. For a moment they shine brightly before being suddenly extinguished. The path is dark once more. Violet recalls the night she followed Ned through the woods by the glow of his cigarette. Back then, she'd understandably put his movements down to spies and wartime intrigue. She was quite wrong, of course, but she knows there is definitely something odd going on in these woods now. And it's something that someone doesn't want to be seen.

"What do you think it is?" Claire whispers hesitantly.

"I daren't even hazard a guess," Violet answers. "But I don't think we want to get near enough to find out, if we don't need to."

"I'm with you there," Claire says. "It could be almost anything, including that creepy man with the gun."

She looks around.

"I think we passed a side path a little farther back. Shall we try that?"

"Yes," says Violet. "You lead. I'll follow."

It takes a bit of doing, but eventually they come across a path heading to the main road. Once they are a little way along, they turn the flashlight back on, but they still walk at a slower rate, taking care not to stumble over unseen roots and protruding rocks.

A streetlight up ahead tells them they are close to their car. They're nearly back at the parking lot when a flashlight shines in their faces. Two men stand directly in their path. For a moment, Violet wonders if they've been ambushed by whoever they left behind in the woods. Claire raises her hands in the air, as though they're being held up. It's a tad dramatic, Violet thinks.

"Dundas Conservation Authority," a voice booms. "Who are you?"

"My name is Violet McAdams and this is my niece, Claire Thomas."

"What are you doing out here in the dead of night, Mrs. McAdams?"

"I was about to ask you the same question."

"We're looking for poachers, if you must know. Please answer my question."

"Very well. We have come to retrieve my hat," she says with mild indignation, as though it were quite natural for an eighty-four-year-old and her niece to be wandering around the woods in the dark. She holds the hat up as if for proof. "While you may note there is a feather in the headband, I dare say it was put there legally. We're not your poachers."

The second officer snorts. "There is a bylaw against poaching just as there is against traipsing about on park property after sundown."

Violet gives an exasperated snort. "We weren't traipsing about, as you put it. We were rescuing a lost hat."

"Whatever you want to call it …"

"That is precisely what I want to call it." Violet points to the car up ahead. "That's us right up there. The red car. You will note that it matches my hat, if you require further proof. We'll be off now, unless you intend to arrest us for hat-napping."

"That won't be necessary," the first officer says. "Please be careful on your way out." He points his flashlight beam on the ground ahead of them.

Violet is about to continue when she stops and turns.

"You might want to know that while we were rescuing my hat, we observed strange lights and some rather suspicious activity here in the woods tonight."

"Is that a fact?" says the officer. "Do you have any idea what it was?"

Violet gives him a stern look. "Why do you suppose I'm telling you?"

"We should probably take a look," he says to his partner. He aims his flashlight at a nasty-looking metal foot-trap dangling from his hand. "That's the sort of danger you're in wandering around here in the dark."

Claire gasps.

"It wasn't just lights," Violet continues undeterred. "There were strange noises and people driving about in the dark in a very unusual-looking vehicle."

"What sort of noises?"

Violet hesitates. "A gurgling sound. Like a giant dishwasher, I should say."

"You think there is a giant dishwasher out here in the woods?"

"No, I said it sounded like one. I had to think about it for a moment, because I still wash my dishes by hand."

The other officer snickers. "Sounds like the space aliens are making illegal visits to the valley again, Charlie."

Violet isn't put off by his sarcasm. "Laugh if you will, but don't you think you should do something about it?"

"Thank you. We will, Mrs. McAdams. But please don't let us catch the two of you here again after dark."

"I guarantee you, officer, if you find us back here in future it's because we have good reason to be here. Perhaps lost knickers next time."

He shakes his head. "Please be careful, ladies."

As he heads off down the path, Violet calls to him.

"Sergeant …"

"I'm only a park warden," he says, turning.

"No matter. You're a smart lad, I'm sure you'll soon make sergeant. What I'm wondering is, what else would people be doing here in the dead of night? Besides poaching, I mean."

"I don't have a clue, Mrs. McAdams."

"Why I'm asking," Violet continues, "is because in my experience people often know far more than they think they know."

He gives her a look that's half-amused and half-curious. "What is it you think I might know?"

"I'm not sure, but just keep it under your cap." She reaches up and taps her hat. "You can never tell what might turn up."

Back in the car, Claire turns to her. "I think you've put a bee in his bonnet. He'll be more observant from now on."

Violet looks knowingly at her niece. "Or else he'll think we're two batty women wandering around the forest tempting fate in the middle of the night."

Claire smiles. "Do you think whatever is going on out there is somehow connected with the murder?"

"No, not seventy years on. But it's getting my wheels spinning. Sometimes I need that before I can get down to figuring things out. It lights my fire, so to speak. For instance, when Julia and I solved the mystery of the disappearing brownies, we weren't able to catch the thief in action, so I needed to think of a way to get her to admit her guilt. We had to flush her out. And I could only do that by having Julia tell a bold-faced lie. Which is really the best kind, if you think about it. Half-lies are too easy to spot. Anyway, she told everyone that there was no dessert that evening because Cook had neglected to make it, even though there was. Then the culprit contradicted Julia and ended up framing herself," she says, still amused by her ingenuity all those years ago.

"And you were absolutely right with your reasoning."

"Sometimes these things just solve themselves, given enough time. But time is the one thing I don't have too much left of. As they say, 'It's now or never.'" She sits looking off in the distance. "I have a feeling it will come to me."

Claire turns the key and puts the car in gear.

"You said earlier that you were surprised when you discovered who had stolen money from the hotel till. Do you mean to say it wasn't Ned, after all?"

"Ah, I was just getting around to that."

16

VENGEANCE IS MINE

FEAR HAD GIVEN her one wing; confusion lent her the other. Instinctively, Violet had broken into a run after seeing Ned and Celeste in the bathing pavilion together. She stopped at last and stood in the middle of the path, trying to catch her breath and listen for footsteps from behind. If they caught up with her, she would simply say that she'd been passing by and ... and what? And heard a strange noise, perhaps. But then they might guess what she had seen. Easier to lie. She couldn't risk saying she had purposely set out to spy on Ned.

There was no sound coming from behind her, nothing to say she was being pursued. Her brain was still trying to make sense of what she had seen, to sort it into some semblance of meaning. She knew it was sex, of course. It had to be, though she was still not completely sure about all that that entailed. It made her feel queasy.

Julia was in the kitchen drying the dishes. She looked up with curiosity. On seeing Violet's face, her hands stopped their work.

"Did you find him?"

"He was at the bathing pavilion."

"And?"

Till that moment, Violet hadn't been sure what she was going to tell Julia. Suddenly, her mind was made up.

"He was with Celeste. That's who he was waiting for. They were in the water together." She paused. "They were naked."

Julia's face was expressionless.

"He banged her head and put his hand over her mouth to stop her from crying."

Julia put the plate down. "Did they see you?"

"I don't know."

"Think, Violet," Julia said commandingly. "Did they see you?"

"No. I'm pretty sure they didn't."

When she ran off, Ned had been dressing. Celeste was still in the pool. If they had known she was there, they would have chased after her. At least, that's what she would have done.

Violet picked up a towel and began to help Julia dry the dishes. They'd been standing there less than a minute when the door opened at the back of the kitchen and Celeste slipped in. The maid's hair was still damp and her clothes dishevelled. Her eyes caught Violet's for a second. There was something in them: fear, embarrassment, shame. Impossible to say what. She passed them by without a word and headed down the hall to her room.

Once she had gone, Julia turned to Violet. The intensity of her expression was frightening.

"You must promise never to tell anyone what you saw."

"Why?"

"When a girl has been interfered with, she will keep it to herself."

Violet stared at her blankly.

"You know what that means, don't you?"

"Of course," Violet said, though she wasn't at all sure.

"It's how babies are made."

"You mean sex."

"Exactly. We need to stop Ned from meeting Celeste again," Julia said. "We need to make sure he doesn't hurt her again."

"But how can we —?"

"Don't worry about how. We'll think of something." Julia attempted a smile; the effect was unconvincing. She reminded Violet of Enid Browne. "That's my clever little sleuth."

Violet did not feel clever. She felt more like a criminal, though she couldn't have said why. If these were more adult games, then they were very confusing.

She suddenly thought of her mother.

"I'd better get back before my mother starts to wonder where I've been."

"All right," Julia said. "I'll see you tomorrow."

She put down her dish towel and gave Violet a hug.

"Not a word — remember."

VIOLET FOUND HER mother in bed. Maggie had her leg elevated in the sling again. With a stab of guilt, Violet remembered her sudden bout of exhaustion after dinner. She could hear her father reminding her that once he was gone she would need to help her mother more.

"There you are, darling. I was worried. You were gone so long."

"I went with Julia to feed the dogs."

The lie was effortless. It was out before she could stop it.

Magazines lay scattered on the bedspread within Maggie's reach. Violet had never noticed before how slender her mother's hands were. Despite their strength, there was a fragility to them. She suddenly felt fearful on seeing her lying there. They'd been at the spa for two weeks and her mother was not improving noticeably. Violet recalled an evening at home, right before the trip, when she'd overheard her parents talking upstairs in stifled tones.

"But what *if*, honey? What if it is? It doesn't seem to be getting any better."

"Don't worry," Clive had said. "The possibility is very remote. You heard the doctor say so."

Afterwards, her father had come downstairs looking glum. Violet wasn't sure what the unspoken *if* suggested, but it left her worried. What was the worst thing that could happen? She remembered the minister at her church delivering an Old-World doom-and-gloom sermon: *Vengeance is Mine, sayeth the Lord.* With its fire and brimstone prognostications, it had been one of the few sermons Violet had enjoyed. Now she wasn't so sure. Why would God avenge Himself on her mother? Far from being safe and predictable, the world suddenly seemed precarious and out of control, as though life itself might be no more than a series of random occurrences strung together in one long line from birth to death. If that were true, then no matter how hard you tried or how good you were, you still could never be certain that things would turn out all right. For all your efforts and for all God's supposed love of justice and righteousness, life still might not turn out the way you hoped. Things could change overnight with an unexpected illness or a forest fire or with the world going to war. Something in the natural order seemed set against safety and predictability.

"Violet? Did you hear me?"

Violet looked over. Her mother was watching her.

"I'm sorry. What did you say?"

"Could you help me with the pillows?"

Maggie winced as Violet helped shift her onto her side. It seemed a sign of weakness, almost a betrayal of her mother's strength. Once the pillows were settled, Maggie asked her to read to her. Violet picked up one of the magazines and began. It was a mother-daughter routine they usually enjoyed, but tonight Violet could barely keep her mind on what she was reading. Her mother looked over as she stumbled for the fourth time.

"Are you all right, darling?"

Violet wondered if her guilt showed on her face. She suddenly wanted to confess how she had caught Ned and the maid together, and to apologize for her lies, but the urge quickly passed. It would just be more worry for her mother.

"I'm tired," she said.

"Don't worry then. I can read for myself. I just thought you looked as though you wanted company."

Violet handed her the magazine. Her mother closed it and put it aside.

"I have some news. I've been saving it for a mother-daughter talk. I'm pregnant," she announced with a smile. "You're going to have a little sister or brother. We'd almost given up hope."

Violet thought of Ned and the maid in the bathing pavilion. The strange cries she had heard were running in her head, over and over again. She remembered how Ned had covered Celeste's mouth with his hand to stop her from crying out. That was how babies were made, Julia had said. Was that what her parents had done? The queasy feeling returned.

"Isn't that good?" her mother asked.

"I'm happy for you," Violet said at last.

IN THE MORNING, Violet accompanied her mother to her therapy session, then made her way back to the room. With most of the guests away, the hotel was quiet apart from Celeste going from room to room one floor above. From outside came the buzzing of insects and the occasional bird call. Her mind strayed to what she had witnessed in the pavilion the previous night — Ned and Celeste clinging to one another in the pool. A feeling of light-headedness stole over her. She went to the bathroom and stood in the door-way. She could see herself clearly in the mirror. As she stepped forward, her body vanished in the gloom. She fumbled for the switch and flicked it on. She was flesh and blood once more. The outside world melted away as she closed the door behind her.

Staring at her reflection, she reached up and grasped her blouse by the shoulders, pulling it overhead. Turning from side to side, she observed the changing perspectives in the mirror. Her breasts were small, but firm. For some time, she had been aware of the swelling where once they had been flat, as well as the occasional ache as they grew. Her nipples were the soft pinky-brown of chestnuts before they got hard and dry in the fall, though the shape and texture reminded her of the crinkly surface of rosebuds right before they opened.

Slowly, she unfastened her skirt and let it fall to her ankles. She hesitated, then grasped the waistband of her panties and pushed them down, kicking them aside. There, in the mirror, she saw the beginning of the same mysterious growth of hair between her legs that she had seen on Ned's body. Holding her breath, she reached down to the crease between her legs. It felt soft and strangely moist. Her eyelids fluttered to a close as she concentrated to get the details just right.

She remembered how Ned had pressed himself up against the maid and felt a sudden warmth flooding through her. Celeste's breasts were much larger than Violet's, even when they were bound tightly inside her uniform. While she watched, Ned had bitten one of them, making Celeste gasp. Violet could feel it now as he did that to her. It didn't matter. It was only a matter of time before he would leave the maid for her. Soon, he would realize she was the only one for him.

She opened her eyes. In the mirror, Ned stood before her. She smiled as he turned away from Celeste and came toward her, taking her in his arms. She leaned back until her head hit the wall.

"Ouch, not so hard," she said softly.

Oh, my darling, I'm sorry, I didn't mean to. You know I would never hurt you that way. He didn't clamp his hand over her mouth or try to stop her from calling out. Instead, he kissed the top of her head before kissing her gently on the lips and moving down her throat.

She shivered.

"It's all right," she said. "You can interfere with me. I don't mind."

They were lost in the darkness of the pavilion. The blue of his eyes gleamed. *I love you, Violet,* he said. She knew he meant it. Theirs would be a long-lasting marriage, like her parents'. They would be envied by many. They would have children as soon as he returned from the war with a medal for gallantry and they would live in the country in a large house with a garden and dogs. Eventually, over time, they would become pillars of the community. Everyone would know and look up to them.

Her breathing quickened as her fingers probed, gently at first then more vigorously, until she felt herself shuddering, flashes of heat and cold coursing through her body. It went on and on before finally dying out altogether. Afterwards, she dressed and brushed her hair quietly and calmly, then turned out the light on her secret world, the one she would be anxious to return to, before re-entering the normal, everyday world.

THE FOLLOWING DAY was Sunday. A sign in the lobby announced a prayer service to be held in the Hermitage after breakfast. *All Welcome*, it read. Violet hoped her mother wouldn't want her to attend, but she was quickly disappointed. *Just to be polite*, Maggie said. The Reverend Ettinger was a personal friend of Enid Browne, who gushed when describing him to the guests. He had started as a street-corner evangelist, she said, preaching at county fairs and anywhere people would listen to him deliver the Word, and quickly gained a solid following. He'd been to Russia and thereabouts, places where they were crying for the religion now that it was banned. He talked tough, but he told it straight. She claimed his voice had the power to convert through the strength of his conviction alone.

Willoughby greeted them at the door to the chapel. Violet's mother sat up front near Mrs. Browne. On their right were Miss Turner and two other women. Frank Larsen was to their left. Mrs. Hutchins entered and made her way to the front, wearing her ermine and wafting a scent that filled the room. Violet sat with Julia two rows from the back. As they waited for the service to begin, someone coughed. They turned to see Ned sitting behind them.

"What are you doing here?" Julia asked, her voice cool.

"I've come to sort out my heathen soul," he said. "I hope he talks about temptation. They usually do. I wouldn't want to miss out."

Julia glanced at Violet, then turned to face the front. All in all, there were a dozen people seated when Reverend Ettinger walked in. He was tall and thin, a man in need of nourishment. His greying temples said he was fifty or more. He was followed by a woman in a long, purple dress that swept the floor and who turned out to be his accompanist. He waited till she sat at the piano and spread her music sheets.

"A blessed good morning," he said to the room. "And welcome, brothers and sisters. We are gathered here in these troubled times to take a moral stand in the name of our Lord Jesus Christ." He paused to look around, engaging them with his eyes. "Why do we do this? Why do we take this stand? We do it in order that we may live a godly life, despite the unbelievers in our midst, the sowers of war and dissension."

He swayed gently as he spoke, moving his hands, caught up in his words. His voice was sonorous and smooth, but Violet didn't think it powerful. Nor did she find him charismatic, as Enid Browne had claimed. By comparison, she'd heard her father deliver a lecture on arboreal forests to a roomful of scientists. His voice had been far more engaging. Judging by the interest and enthusiasm of the listeners who had congratulated him afterwards, his fellow scientists felt the same. Maybe Enid found Reverend Ettinger attractive for reasons other than his preaching abilities.

The woman in purple sat listening to him with her hands clasped on her lap. He nodded and she turned to face the piano.

"Let us sing 'A Mighty Fortress Is Our God,'" the reverend said. "Those of you who can, please stand. The others may remain seated."

The piano rang out around them as the hymn began. *Our helper He, amid the flood of mortal ills prevailing …* Violet mouthed the words and looked down at the hymnbook, hoping that would satisfy anyone watching. *For still our ancient foe doth seek to work us woe … armed with cruel hate, on earth is not his equal.*

The hymn was soon over. They sat again. The reverend moved in front of the dais and began speaking. Gently at first, then with gathering strength, his voice filled the room as he talked about love and charity and sin and death. His manner was exaggerated and theatrical. Violet found her interest waning the more he went on. In her mind, she was back at the pavilion, trying to decide whether Ned knew she had seen him with Celeste. She decided she didn't care one way or the other. He would soon forget all about the maid.

Her attention was wrenched away from her daydream. The reverend was pointing a bony finger at the gathering. It seemed to be aimed directly at her.

"And now we come to a story about a woman named Delilah," he proclaimed. "One of the most beautiful and sinful women of all time."

Violet knew the story, how Delilah destroyed the great Israelite warrior Samson by cutting off his hair. Rather than feel indignation on his behalf, she felt it served him right for being so gullible.

"And then Satan came to her in the form of an angel and offered her a choice. He would grant her most fervent wish: to know this man Samson."

Julia leaned in and nudged her in the ribs. "They always blame the woman."

"What's so bad about knowing a man?" Violet whispered, her voice low.

"Not that kind of knowing, silly."

"Then what?"

"Do you remember what we were talking about?"

"You mean when men interfere?"

"Yes."

The reverend continued, while staring out at the gathering. Behind him, the portrait of Judge Emond Browne glowered with grim satisfaction.

"To the young among us, I say that you must beware temptation. You must resist it at all times lest you find yourselves among the fallen, down among the sinners, unable to rise."

"Amen!" Ned cried behind them.

Julia lowered her head and stifled a laugh.

"Amen," echoed the unsuspecting reverend. "We must resist temptations. The temptations of the flesh, the temptation to be morally weak. And we must resist the temptation to be fearful when it comes to war. War is coming to this land and each of us will be asked to do our part. We must not turn away or fear the evil that men do. It is only obedience to God's will that can protect us from the storms of life."

As his voice rose and fell, Violet felt he was staring at her and her alone. She fanned herself with her hand and looked to see if others were bothered by the heat. No one else seemed to notice as he decried the war mongers and Delilahs in their midst, the heathens and the profligates, with Sodom and Gomorrah thrown in for good measure. It was not the great and mighty who would inherit the kingdom of earth, he reminded them, but the meek and the mild. His voice raged and thundered, tossing a net thrown wide enough to ensnare just about any sinner. "And most of all, be not afraid of death or troubled times, for on the Day of Judgment the dead shall walk again and we shall all heed His call!"

The piano gave a mighty crash, punctuating his words like a blast from above. His voice lowered till it was barely audible, drawing them in close. The whole time, Violet felt his eyes on her. "But the most sinful deeds in the cities of this world are nothing to match the sinful deeds in the heart. Know this! Know that your conscience is vile. Your lust is depraved! God will have vengeance!"

The room tilted. Violet's mouth was dry; her heart beat wildly. She was choking with the overpowering scent of Mrs. Hutchins's perfume. The image of Ned's naked body rose before her; the memory of her own naked body in the mirror swam before her eyes. From the corner of her eye, she saw Julia turn to look at her. She wanted to stand and run, but she was paralyzed. A stranger, a man of God, had seen through her. She had no doubt he was speaking directly to her. But there was no escaping. He had found her out.

"*Amen!*" he thundered, as the piano crashed again.

"*Amen!*" the faithful cried in return.

17

DULL SUBLUNARY LOVERS' LOVE

AS SOON AS she felt no one was looking, Violet slipped from the chapel, convinced Reverend Ettinger had been addressing her directly with his sermon. For all her disbelief, she felt he had looked right into her heart and mind. His words stayed with her; his thundering tone and the crashing piano had got under her skin and unsettled her.

Outside in the courtyard, she watched as her mother exited and stopped to chat with the reverend and Enid Browne. They seemed totally unaware of her torment.

"It was a lovely sermon," Maggie said. "Very stirring. I'm glad you were able to address the war."

But he was calling out for war, Violet wanted to say. Don't be a hypocrite!

Ned had left as soon as the last chord on the piano sounded, doing his disappearing act. Others followed and were standing in the bright sunshine. Now Julia came and stood beside her.

"What happened in there?" Julia asked.

"I don't know."

"I thought you were sick."

"Maybe I am. I was sweating."

"Did he scare you? The reverend?"

"Don't be ridiculous."

"I thought he was horrible," Julia huffed, glaring at him across the courtyard.

"He *is* horrible. He puts things in your mind."

Mrs. Hutchins emerged and shook hands with the reverend, then continued on down the walk. She stopped and smiled at Violet and Julia.

"It's so nice the two of you came." Her gaze fell on Violet. "You're looking a bit flushed, dear. Are you not feeling well?"

"I'm fine, thank you, Mrs. Hutchins."

"You want to be careful you don't catch a chill wandering around at night."

She turned and went off.

"Speaking of horrible," Julia said.

"I hate her," Violet said. "What was Ned doing there? He's the last person I would have thought would come to a church sermon."

"Just being his usual stupid self." Julia said. "Did you find any more notes?"

"I haven't checked today." A thought occurred to her, a chance of escape. "Do you want to see where I found them?"

"Yes!"

"May I be excused?" Violet called out to her mother. "Julia and I are going for a walk."

Maggie looked over with a distracted expression. "Yes, of course."

"Remember it's Sunday, Julia," Enid Browne called out. "Try to behave like a young lady."

"Of course, Mother."

They turned and went off around the corner. Julia snickered.

"Young lady indeed!"

The pathway was deserted. There were no Sunday sessions at the bathing pavilion. They soon reached the wall where Ned hid his messages.

"It's right here," Violet said, pointing to the stone and pushing it aside.

There was another note. Violet fished it out. It was in Ned's ragged handwriting: *Meet me tonite at 7 in the ushual place.*

"He's asking her to meet him again!" Julia said.

"Why would she go back? He'll only hurt her again."

"You still don't understand, do you?"

"Understand what?"

"She has no choice. She goes to him because she can't help herself."

Violet stared at her.

"Rape."

The word was harsh and unfamiliar.

"How can we stop her?"

"Like this," Julia said.

She grabbed the note in both hands and ripped it in half and then again, letting the pieces fall to the ground. Violet looked down in annoyance.

"We can't put it back now!"

"It's the only way to protect her."

"But they'll know it was me who took the note."

"They won't know it was you," Julia declared. "It could have been anyone. You said they didn't see you at the bathing pavilion, so they can't possibly know it was you."

Julia sounded certain, but Violet was far less sure.

"Let's get out of here before anyone shows up," Julia said.

ALL THROUGH LUNCH Violet watched Ned for signs that he knew the note had been taken. Even though Julia had ripped it in pieces, she felt responsible. If he suspected anything, he gave no indication.

Celeste did her rounds, clearing the dishes and serving coffee. To the casual observer, there was no hint of anything between

184 / JEFFREY ROUND

them. Ned didn't look at Celeste, even when she went over to pick up his empty plate. It was as if she wasn't there. To Violet, however, each small glance by Celeste in Ned's direction spoke volumes. So these were the adult games Julia had spoken of.

At the end of lunch there was talk of the fire. The smell of smoke was now more overpowering than the sulphur fumes hanging about the valley. Willoughby addressed the issue briefly, saying they were "keeping an eye on the situation." In the meantime, he said, there was no need to panic. The fire was still north of the valley. There were plenty of evacuation routes open to the west and south, if it got to that, but he didn't think it would.

After lunch Julia went off to help her mother with the dishes. Maggie announced her intention of spending the afternoon playing cards with some of the other guests.

"Will you find something to do?" she asked Violet.

"I might read," she said.

As she passed through the lobby, the canaries were singing. The male sat on the top perch giving a jubilant trill. She headed down the hall to the library. Peering in, she saw that the drapes had been drawn. The room lay in gloom, the door to the chapel shut.

She let herself in and, after a quick search, found a large *Oxford Dictionary* with a navy-blue cover. It had been prominently placed on a wooden dais. The edges of the pages were dyed red, like a Bible, with gilt indents for each letter of the alphabet. Her fingers turned them softly till she found an entry for *rape*. Under *noun*, it read: 1. *Oilseed rape, rapeseed; a plant with yellow flowers.* 2. *Destruction of the natural world, often for profit.* 3. *To damage or destroy something in an unsuitable way.* Then below, under *verb*, it read, 4. *To engage in unlawful sexual activity.*

She closed the dictionary and sat on a chair with a plush velvet covering, trying to make sense of what she had just read. Had Ned and Celeste been engaged in an unlawful activity? Was sex illegal? It didn't make sense. Her father would have explained it better, if he were there.

From down the hall came the sound of voices, distant at first but drawing closer. The words were indistinguishable, but the tone sounded rancorous. Someone turned the doorknob. Violet instinctively slipped behind one of the heavy drapes as the door opened and closed again.

"I am well aware of what's been going on under my nose here," Enid Browne said. "I want you to leave that girl alone."

"That silly bitch means nothing to me."

It was Ned's voice. Violet was confused. If Mrs. Browne knew what was going on between Ned and Celeste, why hadn't she stopped it earlier?

"Don't use that language with me," she said.

"Come on, Enid. I know you don't disapprove of a little bit of fun now and then."

There was a murmur followed by the sound of a slap.

"Don't think you can charm me the way you charm these silly old dames who come here for the waters."

When he spoke at last, Ned's voice was changed. He sounded angry.

"Well, in that case, don't forget that it's me who brings them here. You would have lost this place long ago without me."

"You heard me," Enid continued. "Leave the maid alone. If you don't, I'll fire you both."

"Is that right? Well, for your information, I'm reporting for active duty with the army in two weeks. So, it's me giving *you* notice."

Violet felt vindicated. Ned really was a soldier. She peered out cautiously from the curtains.

"And by the way …" He put a hand in his pocket and drew out an envelope. "Tell Willoughby to stay out of my room. Here's the money missing from your till. If you count it, I think you'll find it's exactly the right amount."

"Willoughby?" Enid looked startled. "But he wouldn't —"

"He's the only one who would have had access to my room. Apart from you."

Ned tossed the envelope on a side table and headed for the door, leaving Enid standing there. For a moment, nothing happened. Footsteps, a door opening, then the sound of notes being picked out hesitantly on the piano. Violet craned her head. Enid sat in the chapel, softly touching the keys. After a moment she began to sing. Her voice was sad and faraway:

> *Every evening when shadows grow tall*
> *That's when my heart yearns most of all*
> *The breezes sigh and so do I*
> *I miss you so much I hope to …*

Her voice broke. The playing stopped.

THE RAIN STARTED just after supper and continued overnight. By morning, the fires that blackened the hillsides and threatened communities in the adjacent county were in check. The ground was rutted with tracks from passing cars and buggies. Everywhere they went, people seemed to leave a trace of their passing as the landscape turned to mud. By afternoon, the sun emerged and the temperature rose until the thousand and one puddles and tire tracks dried and hardened. The smell of smoke was gone. News came from nearby towns that the forest fires were completely extinguished.

Violet wheeled her mother along the path to the pavilion.

Today Maggie had a full regimen: two bathing sessions and a course of stretching, to be followed by a lengthy massage. She seemed more cheerful and was looking forward to returning home at the end of the week.

"We have to get back to make sure your father's eating properly. I hate to think what he might be up to in our absence."

"And are you really getting better?"

"Yes — at last. I'm sure of it."

Violet left her with the attendant at the springs and headed back to the hotel. The route was now so familiar she could have walked it blindfolded. She stopped by the stream near the wall. When no one was watching, she pushed the rock covering aside. There had been no messages since the one Julia had torn to pieces. That morning, there was a new note in Ned's handwriting: *Whare were you last nite? Meet me tonite at 7. It's importent.*

It seemed Ned still hadn't figured out that anyone was tampering with the notes. Violet stashed the slip of paper in her pocket, then raced back to the hotel. Julia was with her mother at the reception desk. Mrs. Browne looked up. Her expression was distant.

"Hello, Violet. How is your mother feeling today?"

"She's fine, thank you. I believe she is feeling much better."

"That's wonderful. Please tell her I said so."

Violet wanted to ask how Mrs. Browne was feeling, but didn't dare reveal she had seen her looking sad and vulnerable after her argument with Ned yesterday.

Mrs. Hutchins came down the stairs. She cast a quick glance at Violet, then turned to Enid. "There you are, Mrs. Browne. If I could just have a quick word with you?"

"Certainly, Mrs. Hutchins. What can I do for you?"

There followed a discussion about fresh sheets and pillowcases. While Mrs. Browne's attention was distracted, Violet passed the note to Julia, who read it and shrugged. There was nothing to be done, she seemed to be saying. She returned the note. Mrs. Hutchins left and Enid came back to the desk.

"You will have to excuse us, Violet. We are very busy today. Julia will see you later this afternoon, when we've finished."

"Yes, Mrs. Browne."

Violet crossed the lobby and headed down the hall. She knew what she needed to do. In her room, she retrieved a pencil from her school bag. With a steady hand, she drew a line from the top of the 7 diagonally down through the middle and across the bottom so that it looked like an eccentric 8. She sat back and examined her handiwork. It wasn't perfect, but then Ned's penmanship was nothing to write home about. She hoped Celeste wouldn't look too carefully if she found the note. At the very least, it would confuse her as to when they were to meet. By then, Violet hoped she would have come up with a better idea.

She hurried back to the wall. The bathers would be occupied. She knew the regimen well enough by now, how they sat in the water for up to an hour at a time, then got out and stretched, followed by a massage. Then, after a break, the routine was repeated. Sometimes they came outside to smoke or walk around. There was no one in sight as she pushed the stone aside and dropped the note in. Julia's words were ringing in her head. *She goes to him because she can't help herself.* Then all the better not to let the maid be tempted, Violet thought, recalling Reverend Ettinger's sermon.

Julia was still at reception with her mother when Violet got back. There was no chance to tell her what she'd done.

"You're still busy," Violet said. "I'll see you at supper."

Julia nodded. "Yes, see you then."

She had nearly reached her room. Up ahead, the library door stood ajar. For the second time in two days, Violet heard someone crying inside. She looked and saw Celeste sitting with a hanky in her hands. The maid had wedged herself between the fireplace and a wall of books.

"Excuse me. Are you all right?" Violet asked, thinking guiltily of the terrible thing she had done.

Celeste looked up with a startled expression. She straightened her clothes, then wiped a hand across her face.

"Yes, I'm fine, miss."

Violet wanted to warn her against meeting up with Ned again. She wanted to warn her about the feelings that made her go to him, but she didn't dare admit knowing anything about the notes or how she had seen them together in the pavilion. In any case, it was too late. She'd already seen to it that the meeting would never happen. If Celeste found the note, she would arrive at the pavilion at eight o'clock expecting to meet him, but Ned wouldn't be there.

THE REST OF the day was a blur. The heat was unbearable. It was the hottest day of the season so far. People went around as if they were in a stupor. Everyone seemed to have lost track of time. The bathers returned late from their session. When the bell was rung, the dining room hadn't been set, dinner wasn't ready, and Cook was in a tizzy. Even Julia stayed out of her way.

Violet was back in their room when her mother returned. As they dressed for dinner, Maggie asked Violet how her day had gone.

"I was mostly here studying," Violet answered, thinking the rest was better left unsaid.

That evening, for the first time since their arrival at the spa, Celeste was not on hand to serve dinner. In a surprise turn, Mr. Willoughby served in her absence. He was no better at the job than Celeste, Violet noted, watching as he scurried about the room handing out plates. She remembered how Ned had said he was responsible for leaving the missing money in his room. She wanted to tell Ned he was correct, that she had seen Willoughby there the night she spied on him at the pavilion. But, of course, she couldn't do that either.

The windows were open, but there was no breeze and the air was close. A sombre atmosphere pervaded the room. With the fires out, the talk returned to the likelihood of war. To everyone's surprise, Ned showed up wearing a soldier's uniform. Despite the heat, he kept it on for the entire meal. Having given his notice, Violet realized, he was letting them all know that he was a real soldier.

Dinner that evening was roast pork with Brussels sprouts and mashed potatoes. Normally it was one of Violet's favourites, but tonight she was barely able to concentrate on eating. When the meal concluded, Ned stood and left without having his customary cigarette. Violet tried to make eye contact with Julia, but the other girl kept her head down. She wanted to say all was well, that she had taken care of the problem, but there was a ball of tension in her stomach.

When Enid stood to bring in the Victrola, Maggie asked Violet to take her back to their room. She'd been feeling better earlier, but now claimed to feel unsteady. The walk seemed to take forever, with Violet willing each step forward.

In the room, she waited till her mother was seated comfortably on the bed.

"May I be excused, please?"

Maggie looked up with surprise.

"Oh! I thought we might read together."

"I promised Julia to help with the dogs. She practically begged me." More lies. "I think she'll feel neglected if I don't go."

"All right. We can read together when you get back."

"Thank you!"

Outside, she raced along the path, taking the shortcut through the woods. Ned would be expecting the maid at seven o'clock, but Celeste would have found the altered note saying to meet him at eight o'clock instead. Would he be angry when she didn't show up? She slowed her pace as she approached the pavilion, trying to think of what she would say if he caught her there. Or what she would do.

At first, there was silence as she walked onto the porch, then Ned's voice came to her from inside, loud and jaunty. A few seconds later, she heard a giggle. Celeste had shown up after all. Either she hadn't found the doctored note or else Ned had somehow convinced her to come regardless. If she chose to go to him, what could anyone do about it?

The voices grew subdued. Through a crack in the door, Violet could make out their silhouettes embracing, just as they had the previous time. Well then, Celeste was on her own. Whatever happened, she had let herself in for it. It had all been a waste of time. Violet turned and headed back down the road to the hotel.

She had just reached the edge of the forest when she heard a cry from behind. This was different from the cries she'd heard the previous night. There was something frightening about it. She stopped to listen, but nothing more came to her. Suddenly, she was afraid. For a moment she felt paralyzed with indecision, then turned and started back to the pavilion. She half expected Ned and Celeste to emerge, but the door remained closed. All was silent inside. She turned the knob and let herself in.

At first, she could see nothing in the darkness. The only sound was the trickle of water and the shushing of the pumps.

"Hello?" she called.

There was no answer. She waited a moment then flicked the switch. The room flooded with light. From where she stood, she could make out someone lying face down in the pool, a bare back and arms bobbing lightly as a dark stain seeped through the milky-grey water. She knelt, hoping someone was playing a joke on her, grasping the body by the shoulders and turning it over.

In the days to come, Violet would feel that something irreplaceable had been stolen from her in that moment, though she did not yet know what it was. For the first time in her life she was aware of the presence of God, not as some tyrannical authority figure who could mete out punishments for telling lies or assign extra chores if you were lazy around the home, but as an implacable force that could give and take, that could shake and break everything around you, bringing the tallest mountains crashing down into the seas with a resounding blast of trumpets. As she knelt there at the edge of the pool, she heard Reverend Ettinger's voice declaiming how the meek and mild would inherit the earth. Violet had not been meek or mild. Rather, she had been stubborn and wilful, and it had brought her to this. Her screams matched the howling of the dogs outside as she stared into Ned Barker's lightless eyes.

-18-

A LITTLE SEPARATION

WHEN THEY HAD a potential diagnosis to explain the pains that had been coming on strong for some time, Violet took Edgar for all the tests. Once the tests, which were really little more than a formality, had confirmed the doctor's suspicions, she sat through the treatments with him, but they both knew it was an inevitability. In the meantime, there were the practical things that needed doing, like a prelude to the grief that would set in. That was inevitable too, they said. Other than that, there was nothing more to be done for him. Or for me, thought Violet.

"It's only for a little while," he'd said one day as she helped him arrange the pillows around him.

She looked over at him. "What is?"

He reached out and put his hand over hers. "This phase. You know I will never leave you. It's just a little separation and then we'll be together again."

"I know, dear," she said softly, though she didn't really believe it.

He'd had the faith she lacked. As his illness progressed, she told no one but her nieces and nephews. There was no one else to tell, her sister Elizabeth having died the previous year. And so, she and Edgar prepared for the end together, mostly alone, only it had come sooner than either of them expected. She'd hoped he would hold on for a while, but he went far more quickly than the doctors had predicted he would. Odd that he should have gone first, Violet remembered thinking, because he'd always been the more patient of the two of them.

When it was over, she closed his eyes and drew the sheet over his body, covering up what she felt was the better part of herself. He had been in many ways kinder and gentler, especially with the sort of people Violet had always had little time for. He'd been far more forgiving, too. And so, he was gone, taking the best of her with him.

She sat beside him in the upstairs bedroom for an hour, barely moving, watching the window as it grew dark outside and the light vanished altogether. She wouldn't exactly have called it praying, what she did then, though that is by and large what it was, as her thoughts went round and round: If you exist, dear God, please be kind to my Edgar, the sanest, gentlest, most loving man I've ever known. Apart from my father, of course. And I know you'd be good to him too if you met him. Well, if you're really out there, of course. And forgive me if I prefer the Buddhist version of the hereafter. It's just a bit more logical.

When she was ready and had thought all the things she felt she needed to, she kissed his lips and went downstairs to call the doctor. There was really no one else to call. And that was when it struck her how alone she was. They were all of them gone: her father and mother and Elizabeth, and now Edgar, her one true companion for all those years that were just over. Only the nieces and nephews were left. Life would be lonely from now on. It was the end of everything that meant anything to her.

THE FOLLOWING DAY she put a notice in the papers and got the word out to some of his former work colleagues, many of them as old as Edgar had been if they weren't already gone too. She didn't really expect to see any of them, but it was only proper to say goodbye for him since he couldn't do it himself, and because she knew he would have wanted her to.

On the day of the funeral, Violet was surprised by all the impressive flower arrangements that awaited her when she arrived at the funeral home. A number of them were from those same former work colleagues, a few were from neighbours. Julia's was a stunning bouquet of white lilies. She nearly cried when she read the card on the largest and most beautiful of them all:

Dear Violet,

We know how much you will miss Edgar after all those years, but you still had them. Good years. You will always have that. And us.

With love, your Silver Swans

She hadn't told them. Someone, most likely Sheila the self-appointed dogsbody, had no doubt seen the notice in the paper and commandeered the rest of them to make arrangements. It was a lovely gesture and it warmed her heart.

She had never stopped to consider before how many of the group's members were actual widows, as opposed to how many were divorcées or separated from their partners and husbands. Nor had it occurred to her before that swans mated for life. And clearly they were, most of them, bereft of their mates before their "life sentences" — as they jokingly referred to them — had been lifted.

Violet was surprised again when, at the appointed hour, they had all trooped into the chapel. And moreover, all of them had worn hats, even Kaye, who, for once, came without her sombrero.

Inspired by Violet's collection, they were determined to give Edgar a memorable send-off, and they had done just that, all of them sitting at the back, upright, hats on their heads. Afterwards, Violet cried a little to think that they had never even met Edgar and that she had been so thoughtless as to deny him a chance to join the group on grounds of arbitrary rules. Humans were such an ignorant, cruelly insensitive species, denying people on the basis of race, creed, or gender. Heartless, really. What did it matter so long as you just wanted the best for everyone?

After the ceremony, which was brief, they had hugged her and cried with her outside on the steps in the blinding sunshine.

"We don't want you to feel defeated and displaced," Sheila said.

"Yes," Meena echoed. "You can always count on us, Violet. We're here for you."

She was moved by their declaration. True to her word, the day following the funeral Sheila stopped by with lasagne and salad and offered to help her sort out Edgar's possessions. What to keep, what to give away. There were places, she said. Value Village, for instance. She stopped herself. Violet would know that. There was no need to spell it out for her.

But when she thought about it, Violet wasn't prepared to see his boots missing from the front hall or his hat gone from the peg beside the wardrobe. Next week, maybe. Not now.

"Thank you, but no," she said. There were limits to what she could allow to intrude on the reality that had been their life together before it vanished forever. "I prefer to do it myself."

"Of course," Sheila said. "You just let us know when you're ready to come back to join us again."

"I will," Violet reassured her, waving as she went down the walk.

FALL CAME AND went, but Violet did not return to the YMCA. Sheila called from time to time. Just checking in, she'd say. In case you want company. But Violet always found a way to put her off. Nursing herself back to strength, she'd called it, but the truth was she was just avoiding life. She wondered, not for the first time, if it had felt that way to her mother, losing first her mobility, followed by the man she loved and depended on more than anyone else. He had never deserted her till the day he died, Violet thought. And neither did Edgar desert me. In that, we were lucky.

For a while Violet took in a lodger, a young student. She was a little on the dull side, but their conversations were pleasant enough. It helped at first to have someone to fuss over, but when the girl left at the end of term, Violet did not renew the ad. Nor did she return to the YMCA and the Silver Swans, though she spoke with some of them on the phone every now and then to relieve the boredom.

One day, as the anniversary of his death approached, she opened Edgar's armoire and saw all his shirts hanging there: short- and long-sleeved, some striped, most of them plain. She broke down. There was really no need for that, she reminded herself when she had recovered. It was only temporary. *A little separation*, as Edgar had said.

She wandered through the house with a dust rag. In the living room, it struck her that she couldn't remember the last time she'd turned on the TV. Books had been more than a companion to her, but still — she'd have liked to hear a human voice once in a while. She spent the afternoon cleaning out closets, nooks and crannies that had slowly accumulated their treasures over decades without ever quite exhausting their capacity to retain.

She stared at the telephone off and on. Nothing happened. What did she expect — that it would ring on command?

Finally, she picked up the phone and dialled.

Sheila's voice leapt out of the receiver.

"I need a gin and tonic," Violet said.

"About time! Come back to us, Violet McAdams. We miss you!"

After they made their plans, Violet hung up the phone. She went to the hall closet and picked out a hat, donned a coat, and left the house for the first time in more than a week. As she later told Claire, and anyone else who would listen, the helping hands of her dear friends, for that is what they had become, reached out when she most needed them. With time, sadness was exorcised, loneliness banished. Edgar's death would have been the start of her decline but for the friendship of those kind women. Her Silver Swans. As long as she had them, Violet knew she would never be hopeless.

19

BLOOD WILL OUT

WILLOUGHBY HAD ARRIVED quickly at the pavilion after hearing Violet's screams. No one else came. She stood and watched as he pulled Ned's body out of the water then turned to her.

"The police will have to be called," he said.

Violet nodded dumbly.

"Did you see what happened, Violet?" he asked in a gentle voice.

He was watching her carefully. She shook her head.

"Were you just passing by?"

Again, she nodded. Instinct made her keep her answers to herself until she could sort out what to say. Lies were all well and good, and often necessary when dealing with adults, but you couldn't take them back once they were out.

"I'm sorry you had to see this, my dear. Perhaps we should go back to the hotel now. It's probably best if I do the talking."

Six police officers showed up to investigate the murder. They seemed to Violet to be puffed up with self-importance, like cartoon cops in the funny papers. They tromped through the hotel and scoured the grounds looking for whatever they could find. The last thing they seemed to be interested in was Ned.

When they arrived, Willoughby took over the conversation. A crowd had gathered on the porch. Violet kept waiting for him to say that she had discovered the body, but he didn't mention her part in what had occurred.

A team of dogs was brought in to help with the search. Violet watched them tear through the gardens and the shrubbery with the air of a circus come to town. When one of the officers started grubbing around the monkshood, Violet warned him they were poisonous. He jumped from the garden onto the path, sputtering obscenities. The officer in charge spent a good deal of time writing everything down on a pad of yellow paper. She wanted to tell him to get over to the pavilion before anyone could tamper with whatever evidence there might be. It was as though he'd never read a popular detective novel in his life.

Hotel staff and guests were lined up to be interviewed one at a time. The process seemed to take forever as Violet stood and waited impatiently with them, ready to report everything she had seen and heard. But when it came to her turn, the officer simply glanced at her and moved on to the next person.

"Don't you want to hear what I have to say?" she asked.

"It's okay, kid," he said. "You run along to your mother."

Violet was torn between declaring that she knew everything and saying nothing. Let them figure it out. She knew she could get away with acting like a child. No one would challenge her. People ascribed innocence to children without a second thought. In truth, she liked the disguise it afforded her.

"Something to say, miss?" the officer asked.

"No."

Already she was slipping away along the path. She had seen the other officers heading down to the springs. She followed at a discreet distance, going as far as the wall, then took the shortcut through the woods. Her feet flew along, nearly tripping and falling over a tree root jutting up blackly from the path. Gone were all her inhibitions. They'd been replaced by a terror that something she had done might have set the stage for a tragedy and she now must be prepared to face the consequences.

One of the officers was busy measuring footprints outside the pavilion, while others combed the woods with lanterns. Violet crept closer. No one paid attention to her. When she saw that no one was looking, she slipped into the pavilion. Arc lights were being hastily strung up overhead. Ned lay beside the pool, eyes still open, his body covered with a sheet up to his chest. The blood came from a gash on his forehead, she now saw. A single brick lay on the ground, set apart from the pile that he had struck his match on the night before. Clearly, he'd been hit with it from the front. His uniform lay folded beside him. Violet wished she could comfort him, but there was nothing she could do.

The officers spoke in hushed voices. One of them glanced in Ned's direction from time to time. His complexion was a little greenish. He looked as if he'd never encountered a dead body before. Apart from the gash on the forehead, Violet thought, this one wasn't even particularly gruesome. How would he have reacted to a stabbing? As far as she was concerned, the police didn't have a clue what they were doing or what they should be looking for. She thought of telling them about the secret crevice in the wall, but then she would have to explain how she'd tampered with the notes. She wasn't prepared to do that.

She left, feeling a growing impatience as other officers looked under bushes and swept the ground outside the pavilion with their flashlights. All well and good, but who was chasing Celeste? Once more, she wished her father were here. He'd set them straight. His level-headed thinking was exactly what this investigation needed. Then she thought of her mother. Guiltily, she turned and headed back to the hotel.

THE HEAT OF the day was quickly cooling. There was a sighing in the trees overhead. The questioning was still on-going. Some of the guests had returned to their rooms, but others remained outside on the lawn, clutching sweaters and shawls. Violet spied her mother among them. She ran to her.

"Mom!"

"Where have you been?" Maggie cried.

"I was at the pavilion," she replied, for once not in the least tempted to lie.

Her mother regarded her gravely. "Sweetheart, did you see anything?"

Violet nodded, burying her head in her mother's arms. "I saw Ned."

"Oh, darling!" Mrs. McPherson gasped. "It's not right for a little girl like you to see such things."

I'm *not* little, Violet thought.

Willoughby had brought out a tea service and was busy passing around cups and saucers. He was doing his best to assure the guests that they were in no immediate danger, but he was drowned out by voices wanting information and reassurance.

The chief investigating officer put up his hands to quiet the crowd.

"Folks, if you'll just hear me out," he began.

No one paid any attention. He said it louder. Finally, they all turned to him.

"Thank you," he said. "I know you're all worried, so I want to take a minute to reassure you that you are in absolutely no danger. Now, I don't want to keep you here longer than necessary, but I can tell you —"

"Who did it?" interjected Miss Turner, no longer concerned about getting her fair share of dessert.

"I can't say for certain just yet, ma'am, but we are on top of it and we have our suspicions."

"Then how do you know we're not in danger?" someone else demanded.

Suddenly, Julia was at Violet's side, hissing over her shoulder.

"You have to tell them," she said, her eyes blazing.

"Tell them what?"

"You have to tell them about the notes. I'll come with you and we can tell them he was meeting her tonight. Were you there? Did you see anything?"

"They were in the pavilion. I saw Ned and Celeste together before she —"

Julia pulled Violet by the arm over to the police. "You have to tell them."

An officer at last seemed to take notice of the two teenagers standing in front of him. It was a different officer conducting the interviews now. This one was a sergeant. He looked sharper than the others.

"What is it, miss? Did you see something?" He winked at one of the other officers, who smiled.

"I saw Ned — the dead man — with the maid Celeste."

His expression changed. All of a sudden, he began to take her seriously. "What's your name, miss?"

"Violet McPherson."

Maggie had come up and put an arm around Violet's shoulders. "This is my daughter," she said.

The policeman nodded, then turned back to Violet. "Go on then, Violet. Your mom's here now. Tell us what happened," he said, putting his pencil to a pad of paper.

"I was over by the pavilion when I heard voices inside."

"When was this, miss? Do you remember?"

"It was after dinner. It was seven. I ... I went for a walk."

"Are you sure of the time?"

"Yes."

"Go on," he said encouragingly.

"I was walking past the pavilion. I heard voices. I looked inside and I saw them together, Ned and Celeste. I went away, but then I heard someone cry and I came back again. When I went inside it was dark. I turned on the lights and saw him lying in the water."

He was busy writing all this down in his notebook, occasionally glancing up at Violet.

"Who did you see lying in the water, Miss?"

"Ned. The gardener."

"Good." He paused to watch her. "Is there anything else you remember?"

"He was bleeding. Then I screamed."

She felt her mother's arm tighten around her.

"Is there anything else you can remember? Was this Celeste person still there?"

"No."

Willoughby stepped forward.

"They were having an affair."

The police officer turned to him.

"Is that right, Mr. Willoughby, sir? You say that this Ned fellow — the one who's dead inside the pavilion — was having an affair with her?"

"Yes, that is correct. She was a maid here at the spa. Her name is Celeste Holmes. *Miss* Holmes."

"I'd like to speak to her. Is she around, sir?"

"No, I'm afraid not. She left earlier this evening."

"Run away, has she, sir?"

Willoughby hesitated. The officer looked at him.

"You said she left. Why did she leave, sir?" he asked.

"Because I fired her," said a voice from behind. They all turned to see Enid Browne standing there. "I fired her this afternoon — I found out she was having an affair with that man. I told her that her behaviour was inappropriate for someone in her position and that she would have to leave."

There were stifled gasps from the crowd. The officer was having a hard time keeping up his notes with everyone talking at once.

"And you are who, ma'am?"

"Enid Browne. E-n-i-d. Browne with an 'e'. I am the owner of the Sulphur Springs Hotel."

"Thank you, Mrs. Browne. And when did you last see Miss Holmes, ma'am?" the police officer asked.

"I didn't see her again after I fired her. That was around four o'clock this afternoon."

Violet recalled seeing Celeste crying in the library. It would have been around the same time.

"Thank you, ma'am."

The officer turned back to Willoughby.

"And you, sir? Can you recall the last time you saw Miss Holmes?"

"I last saw her coming down those stairs." He turned and pointed to the stairwell. "She had a suitcase with her. I believe she was catching a cab to the train station. It would have been some-time around five thirty. I didn't see her again after that."

"Do you know if she caught the cab?"

He hesitated. "No, I can't say for certain."

"Thank you." The officer turned to the collection of guests assembled on the porch. "Can anyone remember seeing Miss Celeste Holmes at any point this evening?"

There were no affirmative answers. It explained why Celeste had not served dinner, Violet realized. But where had she been between the time she saw her crying in the library and when she'd gone to meet Ned at the pavilion?

"That poor man," murmured one of the guests.

"He was a monster," Enid said quietly.

The sergeant turned to one of his men.

"I need you to check the trains, Derek. See if anything left Dundas Station after five thirty."

"I can tell you, sir," said Willoughby. "There would be an evening train leaving Dundas for Hamilton and Toronto at seven o'clock. It's the only regularly scheduled run."

The officer looked at Mrs. Browne. "If you don't mind, ma'am, I'd like to have my constable use your telephone so we can alert the Hamilton and Toronto police to look for this Celeste Holmes when the train arrives at their stations."

"This way, constable," she said, heading to the lobby. "There's a private line in my office."

The sergeant turned to Willoughby. "Sir, perhaps you could give me a description of Miss Holmes."

"Yes, I can help you there," Willoughby replied, giving what Violet thought was a fairly accurate description of Celeste. He waited till the officer had written it down, then said, "I find it difficult to believe the girl would be capable of violence. Despite everything, she was a hard worker and someone who could be trusted to do her job."

The policeman tipped his hat. "You'd be surprised what people are capable of, sir," he said. "Especially when you get to know them."

For once, Violet did not disagree.

20

TO FIND THE MORTAL WORLD ENOUGH

HAVING FINALLY SATISFIED themselves that the missing maid was their chief suspect, Dundas Police alerted police stations in Hamilton and Toronto to be on the lookout for a woman with red hair in her early twenties, answering to the name of Celeste Holmes. Just after nine o'clock, she was rounded up at Union Station and questioned about the death of Private Ned Barker.

The following day, the Toronto *Evening Telegram* reported how, on being informed of the murder, Miss Holmes fainted and a policeman caught her in his arms. One witness claimed that she had appeared distraught on hearing of her lover's death, while another thought she merely looked surprised that they had captured her after she believed she had escaped.

She spent the night in custody. Following a brief arraignment, she was brought back to Dundas. Word got out of her return. By the time the train arrived, a crowd had gathered at the station, Violet and Julia among them, having used the pretext of a shopping trip to get away. They waited impatiently for a glimpse of the accused murderess as the wheels ground to a halt. After a few moments, the door swung slowly open. People gasped when Celeste appeared flanked by two detectives.

Violet was surprised to see that her hands weren't cuffed. Wasn't that tempting fate if she tried to escape a second time? As she stepped down from the car, Celeste appeared dazed. She paused and looked over the crowd of onlookers. For a second, her gaze seemed to fasten on Violet, much as the Reverend Ettinger's had. Her expression was accusatory, as though she believed Violet had been directly to blame for her arrest.

At the hotel, she was asked to retrace her actions of the previous afternoon. According to her statement, the last time she saw Ned was the afternoon of the day he died, when he told her he'd enlisted and would soon be going off to war. She had argued with him, trying to get him to change his mind, but he wouldn't listen. An hour later, she was unexpectedly fired by Mrs. Browne and claimed to have left the spa without seeing him again.

She admitted to having had sexual relations with Ned. The affair had been conducted mostly in the bathing pavilion in the evenings. When asked how they had been in the habit of communicating, she said Ned would leave notes in a crevice in a rock wall, and she would answer them in the same manner. She claimed not to have received a note on the day of his death. If there had been one, she hadn't seen it due to her being fired. No mention was made of any tampering or changes of times made to any of their notes. Violet felt only a slight relief on learning this.

CLIVE MCPHERSON ARRIVED the following day to accompany his wife and daughter home once the investigation was concluded and witnesses were allowed to leave. He spoke with Violet briefly about what she had seen. Again, she made no mention of the notes. When she was done giving her account, he asked how she felt about what had happened to Ned. Was she scared? Not particularly, Violet said. Then what did she feel? he wondered.

"Sad. I liked him," was all she said.

He ruffled her hair and told her to try not to think about it.

"You'll forget all about it in time," he said. Violet did not think it likely. He also told her not to volunteer any further information unless the police asked her specifically about what had happened. It was better, he said, not to get involved.

"Can you do that?" he asked.

He stood before her waiting for an answer. Now was the time to speak up, to admit what she had done. At first, she hadn't been allowed to speak. Now she was being told not to. Thinking it over, she felt angry. But these were her parents, she reminded herself. They had never wronged her in any way. Feelings of confusion and guilt were mixed in with the anger.

She looked from one to the other of them. It was as if they comprised a single unit, always together, whereas she was alone, without even a sister or brother to share her thoughts. There was Julia, of course, but even she could be confusing at times. Besides, how long could she rely on the friendship to last? It was clear her mother wanted her to stay a child, and, although her father knew her better than anyone, even he did not suspect the degree to which she kept things hidden from him. She felt stifled by their expectations. How much longer would she have to pretend to be the little girl they wanted her to be?

"Yes, I can do it," she said at last, not knowing how the decision would haunt her for years to come.

ON RETURNING HOME, Violet followed the case in the papers. An inquest was held. She was surprised to learn the police had released Celeste due to a lack of evidence. According to the papers, the maid's alibi was solid. A cabbie testified that he had picked her up at the hotel just before six thirty. That was an hour later than

Willoughby had claimed, but the dispatch records corroborated his statement. He then dropped her off at the station in Dundas in time to catch the seven o'clock train to Toronto.

The crown argued that the ride from the hotel to the station was only ten minutes, giving Celeste Holmes the opportunity to return secretly to the hotel, then kill Ned Barker and catch another cab back. It was entirely possible. But not likely, the judge concluded, granting Celeste her freedom. As far as he was concerned, she could not have done it.

Except I saw them together, thought Violet. But only Julia believed her.

"I think she paid the cab driver to say that he dropped her off at Dundas station," Julia wrote in a long letter to Violet the following month. "In reality, I think she killed Ned, then took a cab all the way to Hamilton and got on the train there."

Visions of Celeste sneaking on board the train in Hamilton flashed through Violet's mind. Would it be possible to get all the way to Hamilton in time? The more she thought about it, the more likely it seemed. But no one came forward to say he had driven the suspected murderess to the train station in Hamilton. A flurry of letters followed between Violet and Julia. In each letter, the crime was discussed. There was no mention of spies now, just the murder.

"Perhaps it was a tramp, as the police have said," Julia wrote a month later. "Better to let it lie."

Violet frowned on reading that. Now Julia was siding with the adults. Violet's father had said the same thing: it was better not to get involved.

In the end, it made little difference. There wasn't enough evidence to try Celeste Holmes for the murder of Private Ned Barker. The police made a lot of hoopla about a set of unidentified footprints they found in the area around the sulphur springs, concluding that Ned had been killed by an unknown person who happened by at the time. But all eyes were on the troublesome events unfolding on other shores by then, and everyone soon forgot about handsome Ned.

Everyone except Violet. She spent many hours reproaching herself for having changed the time on the note, wondering what had really happened in those final hours between the time she saw Celeste crying in the library and later saw them together in the bathing pavilion. If Celeste had killed him, how had she managed to catch the train in time? Violet couldn't figure that one out either, though she knew in her heart of hearts that the murder had not been committed by a tramp who happened to be passing by.

For one thing, she reasoned, the police hadn't taken into consideration the fact that it had rained heavily overnight. Anyone walking around the grounds that morning would have left prints. There were quite a few sets of tracks near the pavilion when it came down to it, possibly even hers. But by evening on the day of Ned's death it had been hot and bone dry — footprints would not have set in the dusty ground. Anything the police found would have to have been left the night before or earlier in the day.

As well, the officers seemed not to realize that most murders were perpetrated for a reason rather than on some spur-of-the-moment impulse. But the judge ruled on the evidence presented and the matter was put down to wanton violence on the part of an unknown person or persons who had been in the vicinity of the springs.

Hogwash! thought Violet. There was no tramp. There was only Ned and a murderous young woman named Celeste Holmes who killed him in a rage when she learned he was going to leave her for the army. After being fired by Mrs. Browne, she would have been even more desperate by the time they met that evening. *That silly bitch means nothing to me,* Ned had told Enid the day

Violet overheard them in the library. Even more reason then. She had killed him for revenge.

She recalled Ned's black eye and the rumours that he'd been punched by the husband of one of the wives at the spa. It could just as easily have been Celeste. Rather than Ned hurting her, it could have been her hurting him. It didn't really make a lot of sense, but now that he was dead, Violet felt it necessary to take his side.

She began to dream of him. He always appeared tormented, as she expected he would. On one occasion she dreamed she was back at the hotel. He came toward her through the rose bushes and leaned right up against her window, his arms crossed on the sill. *I love you, Violet*, he said. In her dream, she knew he meant it.

The next time she dreamed of him he was shivering outside in the snow, pleading for her to let him in, only her parents didn't want him in the house.

"He'd have to sleep on the mat like a dog," her father said. "Better to leave him outside."

She woke in tears.

That month, Germany invaded Poland. The long-feared war had begun. Britain and France declared war on Germany in retaliation. Violet and her parents listened to the news on the radio, a large wooden box with *Marconi* embossed on the front in gold letters, only recently purchased. It had smooth wooden knobs and a light that glowed behind a screen showing where the stations were to be found, with lots of hissing and scratching as you dialled from one station to another until you found the one you wanted. The king made a speech. Not the king who had abdicated a year and a half earlier, but the new one with two lovely daughters, Elizabeth and Margaret. A week later, Prime Minister Mackenzie King announced that Canada would join in the war effort. Interest in Ned's murder waned as the war began in earnest.

News coming from the frontlines in Europe escalated as other countries were drawn into the conflict. Violet's cousin Herbert was sent overseas and quickly came back wounded. When he recuperated, he was discharged on medical grounds. As it turned out, he'd been luckier than most.

There had been no letters from Julia for weeks. Then, out of the blue, she wrote to say she was marrying a boy she'd been dating casually throughout the summer. Perry was a soldier, a local lad. He was off to the war soon and desperate to marry her before he left, knowing he might never come back. She had accepted his proposal. Violet couldn't recall such a boy while she was at Sulphur Springs. Nevertheless, Julia was getting married. What's more, she asked Violet to be her bridesmaid. The date was set right before Perry went off to war. Violet took the train in for the ceremony and came back a few days later. It had all been very quick.

The following summer, one more surprise was added to the growing number when Violet received a photograph of their newborn daughter, Brenda. Julia had a family now. Violet's baby sister, Elizabeth, had been born just one month earlier. There was no more talk of Ned. It was as though he had never existed.

21

A FINE AND PRIVATE PLACE

VIOLET CAN'T REMEMBER when the idea came to her, but she knows she must go through with it. First, she has to lie to get away from Claire. She doesn't like deceiving her niece, but this is something best done on her own. She'd thought briefly of asking the captain to join her — there was safety in numbers, her mother always said — but in the end she decided to see it through without involving anyone else.

She feels a bit like a criminal as she slips the car keys from the hook where Claire has hung them, pocketing them after sending her niece on a wild goose chase to look for something on the Internet. When Claire's search, predictably, yields no results, Violet thanks her and bids her goodnight before returning to her own room. She waits precisely fifteen minutes, just long enough for Claire to get settled again, then puts on her gloves and exits her room, locking the door behind her.

At first the stiffness in her hands gives her trouble as she puts the car in neutral, releases the brake and rolls silently down the slope of the driveway. Only when she is on the street does she start the engine, hoping Claire won't recognize the sound of the Audi among the other passing cars. Violet doesn't fancy having to make a run for it should Claire lift the curtains and look out to see their rental car retreating down the street.

In less than twenty minutes, Violet finds herself back at the ruins. She glances up at what remains of the hotel. It had been built as a family dwelling for the Brownes, yet it seems to her now that it had served another purpose: as a monument to a man who felt himself important, a decisive statement against the vastness of the new world and the ruinous reach of time. There's always a touch of Ozymandias in such efforts, she thinks: *Look on my works, ye Mighty, and despair!* Few things apart from stone could resist such ravages, and yet, of all the varieties out of which it might have been built, the hotel was made of one of the softest: limestone, a stone weakened and worn away by something as gentle as water.

She kills the lights just up the road from the springs and edges into the parking lot, thankful to find it empty. Tonight, there are no lovers stealing a private moment together. She gets out, pocketing the flashlight. She won't use it unless she absolutely has to. With the moon as big and round as it is, it shouldn't be necessary. There's nothing like a light bobbing through the woods to give you away.

She takes the shortcut through the trees and heads over to the springs. Her instincts for stealth haven't abandoned her after all these years. She's able to find her way through the glen and along the darkened path with barely a sound. Her sensible shoes have turned out to be good for something.

She feels guilty about leaving Claire behind, but her niece tends to be a bit of a nuisance in situations requiring stealth. Too easily panicked. She'll tell her afterwards what she's been up to in the woods on her own. She'll just have to forgive her. For now, she has a job to do.

An owl hoots nearby. The sound is magnified in the night air. From farther off comes the shushing of cars passing on the highway. The air is so still it seems as though she can hear everything for miles around. When she comes to the top of a rise, she stops to catch her breath. Her heart is thudding inside its cage. She waits till it slows. The last thing she needs is to have a coronary out here alone in the woods.

Something scurries past in the underbrush. For a moment she thinks she's being ambushed, but the sound quickly dies as the creature scampers off. Presumably, it was more frightened of her than she was of it. A male, no doubt. She resumes her pace, softly placing one foot ahead of the other. She senses the ghosts gathering around her. The older she gets, the thinner the veil between the two worlds becomes. Her mother and father are here, as well as Julia and Enid Browne, Ned and Celeste, and all the others. She feels them crowding in on her, as though they're trying to warn her of something. Well, let them try. She was never very good at taking advice.

She recalls a snapshot of her mother as a young girl standing on a tennis court, having just won a match. Her expression isn't triumphant, but inexplicably bewildered. To Violet, she seems to be looking out at the oncoming future and whatever it might hold — a brother dead in one war and, later, her body slowly devoured by a wasting disease that was as tiresome as it was gruesome, with yet another war looming. Had she seen all the tragedy coming toward her? The legs that would no longer walk for her, the men who would go to war and not return? It must have seemed overwhelmingly frightening at times. Then again, there had still been good things ahead: a husband who loved her dearly, as well as two daughters born fifteen years apart. Remember that, Violet, she would say. Not everything is bad. Not everything is disappointing.

She turns onto the trail that leads to the springs — the same trail she'd followed seventy years ago the night Ned Barker was killed. History, she thinks, is repeating itself. She hopes it doesn't include another murder.

Before she reaches the springs, she sees the van parked in the clearing up ahead. It gleams bone white in the moonlight. She feels a grave satisfaction, along with a tremor of nerves, knowing she was right. Now the mystery will unravel. Whoever it is can't be very smart if they haven't thought of using a dark-coloured vehicle. Then again, most criminals aren't that smart in her estimation. Otherwise, they wouldn't be criminals.

She can make out movement in the darkness up ahead. Two men are going back and forth between the spring and the van. A low gurgling sound comes from the back of the vehicle. It's the sound she described to the conservation officers as coming from a giant dishwasher.

She creeps forward a few inches at a time. The smell of sulphur is overpowering. How well she remembers it. She has to make an effort not to gag. As she takes another step, she stumbles over a tree root, barely catching herself from falling.

What's a tree root doing in the middle of the road?

Only it's not a root — it's a hose leading into the back of the van. They're stealing the water, she realizes. It's why they come here in the middle of the night: to steal the sulphuretted water in the dark when no one is around to see. Presumably there is a market for it somewhere.

She suddenly feels an incredible annoyance with herself. Here she was thinking it was some deep, dark secret she had stumbled upon, possibly even something related to Ned's murder, however unlikely that might be, when in reality it's just a couple of lowly thieves trying to take something that doesn't belong to them.

From up ahead comes a familiar-sounding voice. How can a voice be familiar to her here? She doesn't know anyone in this area. She peers around the van and stops dead. But, of course! It's Wally, the cab driver, for heavens' sakes. And with him is the creepy-looking man who's been following her and Claire around the grounds. She should have known.

In her annoyance, she wants to confront them and tell them she will report them if they don't stop. But no — she isn't foolish enough to put herself in jeopardy. The only thing for it is to go back to the hotel and inform the police. The men will likely be long gone by then, but the authorities can follow up if they choose.

Her mother was right. Violet never knew when to leave well enough alone. *Don't borrow trouble*, was how Maggie put it. It isn't even her problem, yet here she is smack dab in the middle of it all once again. Julia always said she had a knack for getting to the bottom of things. She couldn't have been more right.

She ducks behind a tree as the men head toward the spring. In her haste, she steps on a twig. The sound is like a gunshot in the still air.

"Who's there?"

A flashlight beam cuts across the trail a few metres away. Violet turns and heads for the brush.

"I see someone!" one of the men cries. "Over there!"

The light picks up Violet's retreating form. One of the men curses. She hurries along, trying to reach the denser brush where she hopes they'll have a harder time finding her. From somewhere nearby comes the trickle of running water.

She is nearly at the top of a rise when she feels the earth slipping beneath her. Her foot slides to the right and she goes down with a cry. Reaching out to steady her fall, she feels the cool dampness of moss beneath her fingers for a second, then suddenly pitches down the hill in utter darkness.

Is this how it ends? she thinks. Falling to my death at Sulphur Springs? And fall she does, landing with a thud before blacking out.

WHEN SHE COMES to, there's a sharp pain in her ribs. Panicking, she feels herself gasping for breath. She's choking on something cold and revoltingly smelly. It's the water. Her fall has landed her in the sulphur springs. She has no idea how long she's been lying here unconscious, but she's completely soaked and chilled to the bone.

Through the haze comes a voice: "Nervy old bitch!"

It's Wally.

She hears a second voice now, as a flashlight beam plays over her body. "Serve her right if we left her here. No one would find her for days."

She wants to cry out for help, but she knows they won't feel any pity for her. Not after she has spied on them and found them out. It's a lifelong habit, and one she wishes she could give up. She doubts she will.

Everything goes black again. When she next opens her eyes, her mother is walking toward her quite capably despite her bad ankle.

"It doesn't hurt a bit, Violet," she says. "In fact, it's easy once you get used to it."

Violet wonders if she's referring to her ankle or being dead. Next, her father comes up to her and smiles, reaching out to help her to her feet. She's overjoyed to see him, but before she can take hold of his hand he vanishes. Now Julia appears. She shakes her head and bends down to look at her.

"Violet McPherson," she says. "You can't keep your nose out of anything, can you? Well, I always said you'd get to the bottom of it!"

As she lies there, Julia says, "Did you ever get my letter?"

"What letter?" Violet asks.

"The one with the photograph of my grandson."

She doesn't recall receiving a photograph of her grandson.

"I don't think I got it."

Julia smirks. "You will."

In an instant, everyone disappears. She is fourteen again and running through the undergrowth, scratching her arms and legs on brambles, heedless of poison ivy and other dangers, large and small. At last, she breaks through into a clearing. The bathing pavilion lies dead ahead. The door is ajar. She makes her way inside and stands there in the gloom. A sound catches her ears. She looks over and sees Ned standing knee deep in water. There's a deep gash on his forehead. Blood pours down and discolours the stream.

"You're bleeding!" Violet exclaims.

"Really?" He shakes his head. "Can't feel a thing."

All at once, the grandfather clock begins to strike, the pure tones ringing out in the air. At the seventh and last stroke, the dogs begin to howl. But that's wrong, Violet thinks. The dogs never howl for their supper before eight o'clock. Julia has taught them that trick.

Nevertheless, the dogs are howling like mad.

"They always know the time," Ned tells her, shaking his head. "It's ironic. You may never know how much I envied your dullness."

But those are Julia's words, Violet thinks. What a mad, crazy world it is where nothing is what it appears and no one can be trusted to be who they seem.

Just then, Homer comes up and licks her hand.

"Good boy," she says.

Now someone is at her side, stroking her hand.

"It's all right, Aunt Vi. You've had a fall, but you're going to be fine," Claire says.

Violet's eyelids flicker. Does this mean she hasn't drowned in the springs? Because if she has, where is the white light everyone talks about? Where is the big-deal introduction to the so-called Other Side? Strangely, she feels cheated. Life has few enough compensations as it is, so why should she be robbed of one of the more colourful ones?

She mumbles something, but barely gets the word out.

"What did you say?" Claire asks.

"Dogs!"

Violet feels herself lurching fully back into consciousness.

"There are no dogs here," Claire assures her.

"Yes! There were dogs!"

She opens her eyes fully and takes a deep breath. There is another woman in the room watching them. She's a nurse, judging by her uniform. No use looking for sympathy from her.

"Where am I?" she demands.

"In the hospital," Claire tells her.

"I was just in the forest." She shakes her head and tries to remember. "I was on my way to the sulphur springs when I saw Ned and my mother and all the others."

"You're in the McMaster University Medical Centre, Mrs. McAdams," the nurse tells her. "You had a bit of a fall back in the valley. Some local fellows brought you in. They had to fish you out of that spring."

"It's okay, Aunt Vi," Claire says softly. "You're safe now."

"No, it's not okay!" Violet exclaims, trying to raise herself up. "The dogs were howling!"

"Try to keep calm, Mrs. McAdams," says the nurse, rolling up Violet's sleeve and slipping in a needle.

WHEN SHE WAKES again, she can tell by the cool, clear light coming through the window that it's morning. She pauses to wonder how many more such mornings await her before there are none left at all. But, for now at least, she is alive and feeling remarkably refreshed.

She looks around the room. She is alone. Claire has gone. Hopefully back to the hotel to get some sleep. There is a bustling out in the hallway followed by a knock. It's a nurse, but it's not the one from last night who slipped her the knockout drugs.

Lucky for her, because she'd be hearing about it. This one enters pushing a trolley. There is a breakfast tray on it.

"Good morning, Mrs. McAdams. I thought you might be hungry."

"You thought right."

"You had quite a spill last night. How do you feel?"

"Pretty good, all things considered."

"I'll just leave this here with you," she says, swinging the movable arm around so that the breakfast tray sits in front of Violet. "By the way, you're going to have a visitor in about fifteen minutes. A police officer wants to ask you a few questions."

Violet gives her a stern look. "He wants to interrogate me, you mean. Let him try."

The nurse smiles and pushes the trolley out of the room. Violet turns to the breakfast. A plastic film covers the little squares and corners of a plastic tray. What will the food taste like? Plastic too? She peels back the edges. There is a ham and cheese omelette with a little mound of green beans off to one side. It smells not bad. She takes a bite. Actually, pretty good. There's even a fruit cup. Not exactly exciting fare, but it will fill the need.

She has just finished when there's a knock at the door.

"Come in," she calls out reluctantly.

Would he go away if she told him to? Not likely.

The door opens. A well-built man looks in and nods. He gives her a hesitant smile and removes his policeman's hat. His eyes are startling: forget-me-not blue. Violet catches her breath. For a moment that seems to stretch on to infinity there is no space inside her left to breathe. Because for the first time in her very long life, Violet McAdams is seeing a ghost in the flesh.

Here before her stands Ned Barker. He has grown up, but not old. Not in the slightest. Adding to that impression, when he speaks, she hears Ned's voice.

"Good morning, Mrs. McAdams. I'm Detective Sergeant Bryson Browne of the Hamilton Police Force."

"Dear god!" she exclaims.

"Please don't be alarmed. You're not in any trouble."

"Would that be Browne with an 'e'?" is all she can manage.

He gives her an odd look. "Do we know one another?"

"In a way, yes. Your mother's name is Brenda?"

He stares with his mouth open.

"Yes," he says at last. "How do you —?"

"Don't be afraid, dear. I knew your grandmother, Julia."

He laughs.

"Do you still live with your mother?"

"Yes, we live at ..."

"Seventy-five Bridlewood Drive," they finish together.

He sits back and studies her. "I see you know nearly everything about me."

"Not quite everything, but your grandmother always said I got to the bottom of things eventually."

As much as he would like to sit and chat, he tells her, he is here on police matters. He's just checking to see how she is getting along since her fall and wonders if she can add anything to what he already knows. She is not surprised to learn that a cab driver named Wally and his friend were the ones who brought her to the hospital after fishing her out of the springs. He has already interviewed them.

She looks him in the eye. "Did you ask them what they were doing there in the middle of the night?"

"No, I didn't. And you will note that I haven't asked you either," he replies.

"Fair enough," she says.

"After all, they saved your life, Mrs. McAdams," he reminds her. "If they ever find themselves back in the park at night again, however, I might be tempted to push the issue just a bit."

As promised, he does not overstay his welcome. Replacing his hat, he makes his way to the door, then turns and looks at her.

"Are you staying in Dundas long?"

"Unfortunately not. I'm leaving tomorrow. And I'll be leaving here as soon as I can today."

He gives her that hesitant smile again. "Would you by any chance be interested in dropping by for tea this afternoon? That is, if you're up to it. I think my mother would love to see you."

"Yes. I'd like that very much." She pauses. "Would you mind not telling your mother where we met exactly?"

He smiles. "Of course."

ONCE HE HAS gone, Violet gets up from her bed. After a quick search, she finds her clothes in a closet. Within five minutes, she is dressed and making her way down the hall to the front desk.

A nurse looks up in surprise as she approaches.

"I'm checking out," Violet announces. "You can't stop me."

"Mrs. McAdams ..."

"Don't mess with me," she warns. "I know my rights."

She consents to wait as long it takes for them to call Claire and inform her of her aunt's decision. Her niece is at the hospital in fifteen minutes, but Violet will not be talked out of leaving. She waits till they are outside to tell Claire what she has discovered. Not about Sergeant Bryson Browne — that will take some thinking — but about the other.

She sits on a bench outside the hospital and pats the seat beside her. Claire sits.

"I'm still not sure I understand," her niece says.

"Don't you see? It was the wrong time. The dogs always got fed at eight p.m. Not a minute before and not a minute after. So why were they howling at seven p.m.?"

Claire shakes her head. It's beyond her comprehension. "I don't know, Aunt Vi."

"Because someone changed the clock. Someone set the time back to make it look like it was earlier than it actually was."

"But why?"

"Think! Why would someone want to make everyone else believe it was seven o'clock when it was really eight?"

I'm in charge of clocks, Julia had told her the first day they met. Ned hadn't realized it, but he would keep his date with someone other than the person he expected.

"Wouldn't people just check their watches ...?" Claire starts to say, then realizes what Violet is saying. "But they couldn't, could they? All the watches had been collected, so everyone would have been fooled by the time change."

"Precisely!" Violet crows. "Which means that when I thought I saw Ned with Celeste at seven o'clock, it was actually eight. She couldn't possibly have been there. Because she left on the seven o'clock train, as she claimed to have done all those years ago. That was proved beyond the shadow of a doubt. But I saw them!"

"But how?"

"Ah! That's the trick of it. You've heard of Alice and her six impossible things before breakfast?"

"Yes, of course," said Claire. "It's from *Alice in Wonderland.*"

"Come on," Violet says, snatching up her purse and gloves. "I need you to drive me somewhere. I've got an appointment to keep. And believe me, it's long overdue."

22

LA BELLE DAME SANS MERCI

NOT LONG AFTER the end of the war, Violet was shocked to open a letter from Julia and read that the Sulphur Springs Hotel had burned down. Even more tragically, Enid Browne had died in the blaze one cold winter's night. The spa had been closed for holidays and no one else was there at the time. Julia didn't elaborate and Violet had not thought it polite to ask. She simply sent her condolences and left it at that. Ironically, the hotel had been doing well, having prospered all through the war years. Despite her lack of fondness for Enid, Violet felt grief on hearing the news. She had been a harsh and even unpleasant woman, but perhaps her private sorrows had had a great deal to do with the kind of person she was.

Things had not gone well for Julia, either. In a candid moment about a year into her marriage, she confided to Violet that her husband had been cruel to her and seemed not to love their daughter, Brenda. To Violet, who still believed in fairy-tale marriages, that, too, had been a shock. She was relieved when Julia and Perry divorced soon after. A few years passed. Julia married a man who loved her, though not in the way she would have liked. It seemed to Violet that in some way a curse hung over Julia's family, one that had begun long before Ned Barker's murder.

Ironically, the one person who seemed to benefit from the murder was Celeste Holmes. Not long after the inquest, she married a wealthy man from nearby Burlington who clearly believed in his wife's innocence. By all accounts, he was devoted to her. She had prospered and raised a family, spending years as part of a notable social circle in the Hamilton-Wentworth area. Violet couldn't imagine the awkward Celeste holding court over a group of wealthy socialites, but then stranger things had happened. In later years, following the death of her husband, she opened a hotel, successfully running it till her own death in the early 1990s. Life wasn't fair, decided Violet, who had remained convinced of her guilt. So there had been no justice served after all.

Violet's father had died, too, of cancer in the mid-1950s, while still a relatively young man, leaving behind a bedridden wife with only her daughters to look after her. Then, one day, Violet McPherson married and became Violet McAdams. Eventually, after many long years, Maggie succumbed to multiple sclerosis. By then, Violet and her husband had moved from Nanaimo to Victoria. Following Edgar's death, after nearly fifty happy years of marriage, Violet found herself well looked after. She was comfortable, if not wealthy. Although she and Edgar had no children, Violet's sister and her husband produced five of their own, giving Violet a lively brood of nieces and nephews to keep her occupied. As for happiness, after retiring from teaching she found it in doing community work and, eventually, with her Silver Swans.

Violet still heard from Julia as the years passed, though the cards and letters grew fewer in number. She knew, for instance, that Brenda had given Julia a grandson named Bryson. In each letter, Julia praised Bryson to the heavens and called him her greatest blessing. She kept promising to send Violet his picture, though it never turned up.

Of Ned, they seldom wrote anymore, though Violet remembers one final detail Julia had relayed when asked what had become of his body. Family had claimed him, a brother and sister who buried him in the Cape Breton Highlands. That was his home, despite his claim to have come from British Columbia and trained at the public gardens in Vancouver. It also explained the knotty vowels Violet heard in his speech.

Somehow, seventy years flew by. Violet, the young daredevil who could barely keep out of trouble, had turned into an arthritic old lady complaining of aches and cramps till she sounded like all the old women she had ever mocked as a child. Just deserts, she told herself. We turn into what we deride. When she looked in the mirror now, it was more often to see if she still recognized the old woman she had become rather than to don a smart hat on social occasions. She seldom went out anymore. What was the use?

Loneliness, she decided, was part and parcel of the human condition. There was no way around it. It came with the territory; you simply did what you could to offer a helping hand or speak a kind word now and then. There was always someone in need. It wasn't that hard, really. Sometimes, if you were lucky, you received thanks in return — that was about all anybody could ask. The best thing you could do was learn to enjoy your own company, she believed, because everybody left eventually. Not because they were deserting you, but simply because they had their own needs and reasons for leaving.

Her friends started to go, one at a time, till there was almost no one left but Julia. And then, to no one's surprise, came the note that Julia had died. Too late for Violet even to think of visiting her childhood friend one last time. She was gone, just as if she had never been. Just as Violet would also soon be gone, with no one to remember the story of Ned Barker and the Sulphur Springs Hotel.

How unfair it seemed that it all should pass by so quickly. Violet would like to have looked back on it all with something like pride and tell herself she had lived a life that made a difference. Somehow, she wasn't sure she could do that. Not yet.

THE RIDE TO town doesn't take long. The red Audi delivers her there in less than twenty minutes. Violet gets out of the car and Claire drives off with a wave and a promise to return when Violet calls for her on her cell phone.

The house is small and stylish, with immaculate gardens. She is pleased to see that someone has kept up Enid Browne's gardening skills and her love for plants. She walks up the front steps and rings the bell. After a brief pause, the door opens. Violet catches her breath on seeing that face again.

"Come in, Violet. My mother's just upstairs. She was very excited knowing you were coming."

"Thank you, Bryson. I'm so glad to be here. And I must say the grounds are looking lovely."

"I do what I can, though I'm not really a gardener."

Before either of them can say more, they turn at the sound of approaching footsteps.

"My goodness," a woman's voice says. "Is it really Violet McAdams, all the way from Victoria?"

Violet looks up to see a gracious-looking woman with hair just beginning to turn grey making her way toward them. They shake hands.

"Do you really remember me?" Violet asks.

Brenda beams. "Of course, I do. You came to visit us many years ago. Oh — so long ago now I barely remember. Mother talked of you often. She said you were her only bridesmaid. She always read your letters aloud to me when they arrived. She was so pleased that you stayed friends for life."

"I can't tell you how much I miss her."

"What a lovely surprise to see you," Brenda says.

"Of course, I had planned on dropping by to say hello, so when I met your son, well, I couldn't resist his invitation." Still lying after all these years. It's too late to worry about that now. "I just hope I'm not intruding."

Brenda brushes aside the protest. "You're not intruding at all. Please come in."

Violet steals another glance at Bryson, who has remained standing in the doorway.

"I'll go make tea," he says.

In the living room, Violet thinks she recognizes a few things that were once in the hotel, if that's possible. In particular, a walnut writing desk with a slanted top catches her eye. On top of it are framed photographs of Julia and one of Brenda and Bryson at a younger age.

"Your home is very beautiful. These furnishings are exquisite."

"Thank you. Much of it belonged to my mother."

"Julia always had good taste." She looks around. "I seem to remember a grandfather clock. I don't suppose …?"

"No." Brenda shakes her head. "It was lost in the fire."

"Of course. Along with so much else."

"Sad to say, yes." Brenda smiles. "It was quite the coincidence you meeting Bryson in the coffee shop."

"Yes, wasn't it? Your son is very handsome."

"Don't say that in front of Bryson, you'll only fire up his ego if he hears it."

"It's funny. Your mother promised me a photograph of him many times, but she never sent one."

"Mother was a bit forgetful, I'm afraid. I'm sure she meant to send it to you and just forgot."

"No doubt."

Talk drifts to the past. Violet's stories of her escapades with Julia are received with amusement and gratitude.

"I wish my mother could be here right now," Brenda says. "She loved talking over old times. Even the difficult ones. No matter how bad things got, she could always find a way to laugh over them."

"Things didn't always go well for her, did they? Especially in marriage," Violet says, with what she hopes is a sympathetic tone.

Brenda shakes her head. "No, they didn't. There were early disappointments. But Mother was strong. She didn't often speak of her regrets."

"We women often don't, do we?"

Brenda gives her a searching look.

"What I mean is, we keep things bottled up inside. Things we never forget. And people."

"It's true." Brenda nods. "There was one man my mother never got over. A lost love. 'The one that got away,' she called him."

"Really? What happened to him?"

"She said her mother came between them. Permanently, that is. My grandmother was a real battleaxe, I gather. Then again, I barely remember her. She died when I was still young."

"She had her trials, too."

"They say she killed herself," comes a voice from behind. Bryson stands in the doorway holding a plate of cookies. He sets it on the table. "Some say she set the fire on purpose."

Brenda shakes her head. "We don't know that."

"No, not in any certain sense."

Bryson leaves again. Brenda gives Violet an apologetic smile.

"He tends to be colourful, I'm afraid. It comes from being a policeman."

"Don't worry, dear. I heard about your grandmother's terrible death. Your mother wrote me when it happened. It was a shock."

Brenda holds up the plate of cookies. "Please — help yourself."

Violet looks down, examining the cookies minutely, as though lost in the choosing. After a moment, she takes a lemon cream shortbread. Quietly, without looking up, she says, "Did your mother ever talk about this lost love?"

"Not really. You know how it is. Private thoughts and all." Brenda sets the plate down. "Though there was one night when she'd had a bit to drink — this was after my step-father died — she spoke about him then, but only briefly."

Violet looks up and catches her eye. "Did she? I wonder what she said."

Brenda laughs. "Well, you know mother. He was a bit wild, she said, but a good man. She said she wished I had met him. I would have liked him. No — that's wrong. What she said is that I would have *loved* him. She was sure about that."

"Interesting." Violet nibbles on the cookie. "Did she ever say who he was?"

"Only that he was a soldier. I assumed he had gone to war and never come back, otherwise why wouldn't she try to resume things once he returned?"

"Yes, why indeed?"

"I never heard his name."

Violet pauses.

"It was Ned, dear. Private Ned Barker."

Brenda looks surprised. "Oh, you knew him?"

"Only briefly, but yes. And he was, well, everything she said." She lets the words float in silence.

"Oh, my gosh! I just recalled something," Brenda says. "I can't believe I forgot. She left you something."

Violet watches as she heads to the writing desk, turns a brass key, and opens it. She reaches for a small drawer and slides it toward her. Inside is an envelope.

"Odd that I'd forgotten it till now, but she said if ever you turned up, I was to give you this."

She hands it over. In a large marker scrawl it reads, *Violet McPherson*. Julia has used her maiden name. Beneath this, in bold letters, are the words *TO BE HAND-DELIVERED ONLY.*

Violet's hands tremble as she accepts the envelope.

"Dear me," she says. "What if I hadn't turned up, I wonder?"

"Mother seemed pretty sure you would. I remember her telling me you always got to the bottom of things, even if it took forever. She seemed sure you would be here one day."

Violet opens the envelope and pulls out a photograph of Bryson at what looks like a graduation ceremony. The resemblance to Ned is all too clear. On the back, in Julia's handwriting, are the words: *I always said you would get to the bottom of it.*

But what, exactly, have I got to the bottom of? Violet wonders.

Brenda claps her hands in glee. "There, you see? She hadn't forgot after all. She did want you to have his picture."

"How very kind of her to remember me," Violet says quietly.

"I'm so glad you finally got it."

"And I am too." Violet smiles and turns to look at Brenda. "It's so wonderful to see you again after all these years."

"Tea is ready," says Bryson, entering with a tray.

23

TIME'S WINGÈD CHARIOT

CLAIRE RETURNS PROMPTLY to pick up her aunt. There is time for a brief introduction to Brenda and Bryson, with an invitation to dinner the next time the two of them are in Dundas. The invitation is extended in kind should Brenda or Bryson ever find themselves in Victoria. The goodbyes are just as quick.

Settling in the car on the way back to the hotel, Claire says, "After all you've been through, I hope you're still glad we made the trip, Aunt Vi."

"I wouldn't have missed it for the world. Just seeing Brenda again and meeting Bryson have made it all worthwhile."

"I just wish we could have solved the mystery after all these years."

"Yes, so do I," Violet says, lapsing into silence.

Claire is not content to let the subject lie.

"I still think it odd that no one came up with any other legitimate suspects. What about that director, Willoughby, for instance? You said he showed up almost immediately after you screamed. He must have been close by. Why did no one suspect him?"

Violet watches the landscape passing by outside the window. The valley's greenness is soothing to the eyes.

"That's a very good question," she says. "I wish I knew the answer. Willoughby definitely had his own agenda. I know he tried to frame Ned by hiding the stolen money in his room. It was clear to him that Ned was a professional flirt. Despite her tough exterior, Enid Browne fell for him. Otherwise, I doubt she would have put up with him even if he was good for business. I believe Willoughby thought Ned was horning in on his territory and wanted him gone."

That, she remembers, is exactly what the Silver Swans had said: men kill when they feel possessive.

"Willoughby would not have taken lightly to that, especially if he hoped one day to marry Enid and inherit the hotel."

"Ooh! That's telling," Claire says, clearly enjoying the possibility.

Violet casts her thoughts elsewhere. She is still struggling with the truth, still fighting for clarity after all these years. Why can't she just let it go? That's easy, she thinks. Because she cannot believe that Julia Browne killed the man she loved. In some distant corner of her mind, she would still like to believe that it was Celeste or Willoughby or even a vagrant, as the police claimed.

"It sounds like a soap opera," Claire says. "Do you really think that was his plan?"

"I don't know. You have to remember the police had made up their minds: it was a tramp. They had closed the file on it. And that, as they say, is all she wrote."

IT'S THEIR FINAL morning at the Sherston Arms. Violet gets out of bed and heads downstairs for breakfast. For the first time since leaving the hospital it dawns on her that she's moving far more quickly and easily than she has in years. Somehow, her joints are free from pain and there is a spring in her step.

Claire gapes in awe when Violet mentions it. "Aunt Violet — it's the sulphur springs cure!"

Violet is about to pooh-pooh this, then stops to thinks about it.

"You know, you might be right. I must have lain in that water a good long time till those men were able to get the van and fish me out. Even then, I would have been wearing those damp clothes soaked in the water while they drove me all the way to the hospital. I must have got a healthy dose of it."

She feels gratified knowing the sulphur springs cure was not a bogus claim after all.

Clarice Palmerston emerges from the kitchen wearing an emerald-green outfit with matching earrings. Green for growth. Green for renewal. And true to form, her cleavage is fully visible. Green for optimism.

The guests eat while conversing volubly. The captain is staying on another week. Lucy and Bart are leaving tomorrow. It's Violet and Claire's last day, so they make their goodbyes to everyone. Claire goes upstairs to pack while Violet remains seated till she is the last one there.

"I want to apologize, Mrs. Palmerston," Violet says, when their host comes in to offer her more coffee.

"Whatever for?"

"For any disturbances my stay has caused you. I'm sure you weren't expecting all this rigmarole with hospitals and conservation authorities calling in the middle of the night."

"I have to say, I was on my guard when you showed up wearing that red hat."

They both laugh.

"Don't worry, we'll be off your hands this afternoon. Our plane leaves at four." Violet pauses. "I think you said it was your mother who told you about the Sulphur Springs murder?"

Clarice draws a breath, then says, "Yes, it was. I suspect you've already guessed who my mother was."

238 / JEFFREY ROUND

"I'm pretty sure I have. Your mother was Celeste Holmes, wasn't she?"

"Yes, you're right. She worked as a maid at the spa. She was wrongly accused of the murder at the time, but she was quickly cleared when it came to light that she had left the spa before the killing occurred."

Violet takes this in. "I met your mother, my dear," she says at last.

She nods at Clarice's surprised expression.

"She was a very plucky young woman. You see, I stayed at the Sulphur Springs Hotel once, just before the war. I was there when the murder took place. I'm glad to know she prospered after everything that happened to her."

"Thank you. Mother would be glad to hear that and to know that you remembered her."

"I could never forget her."

UPSTAIRS, VIOLET KNOCKS on Claire's door. She glances at the car keys hanging on the hook inside the entryway.

"Would you mind if I took those?"

Claire gives her a look of concern.

"I'm not going to run away this time, my dear. I just want to pick up something for us to eat on the plane while you pack." Still lying. What's bred in the bone. "That is, if you can spare me."

Claire looks doubtful for a moment, then brightens.

"As long as you promise not to fall in any creeks."

"I promise."

Without really thinking about what she is doing, or why, Violet drives back to the spa one last time. It's not to see it again or even to say goodbye, but rather to convince herself that it had ever been anything but the ruins it is today. But no. That's not quite it. The reason eludes her. Still, she knows there is surely a reason, even if she can't quite articulate it. It's just a feeling she needs to follow.

The grounds are misty. It's fine fall weather. As she walks, her shoes glisten with dew. Somewhere far off, a bell chimes. The sound rings out high and clear. She thinks of the day the storms broke out and extinguished the forest fires all those years ago. The following morning there had seemed to be a promise in the air, if only briefly, of better things to come. Just as there is now. It seeps out of the verdure beneath her feet, fresh and cool. It emanates from the trees and leaves a tang in the air that she can smell. She can't say what it is exactly, but she feels it moving along with her. It's like a fresh start.

As she wanders, an archway appears in the mist ahead of her. A gossamer doorway shot through with rays of sunlight. None of it is real, of course. It's just an optical illusion. A pleasant reminder of all that once was. More of life's mysteries, of which there are so many. Who could say, for instance, which were the true gods and which the false, what in life was truly good and what evil, who a friend and who an enemy? These are unanswerable questions, yet it seems to her that she sees these things clearly at last. It's as if she is looking over mountain peaks into the distance, the vastness ahead of her not as great as it once seemed, yet with still more peaks farther off. And because of this, perhaps, individual peaks seem diminished in importance overall. It all fits into an unending pattern, one vastness offsetting another.

Her life has been a long and, some would say, useful one by any reckoning. In the intervening years, she had married and been loved by the best man she ever knew and had loved him in return. There is nothing to regret, yet somehow it feels as though there's still something missing. What, after all, has been her due? She thinks of all the women she has known, her Silver Swans and others like them, who were left or abandoned, who felt cheated and deceived, whose lives ended unhappy and alone. What of the ones who fell in love with men like Ned and got left behind? Were they to blame for their mistakes? And why does she still remember him so clearly, so vividly? Ned Barker had simply been a man who contributed in some small way to her sexual awakening, and that so long ago. In fact, she had known him for less than a month when he died. In her nearly fifty years with Edgar, she had never felt alone, never been left wanting like so many others.

Julia Browne's life, on the other hand, was in many ways the opposite of what she, Violet, had had. The same might be said of Julia's mother, Enid. And what of Willoughby, so obviously in love with her — she sees it now — and having to watch with frustration as a reckless young man charmed and deceived her? It must have made his blood boil. No wonder he had tried to frame Ned. And then there was the maid, Celeste, who had had no power whatsoever, even to the point of being banished from Sulphur Springs by Enid. Violet recalls the day she found her crying in the library, a simple serving girl, with little education and few prospects. Her world must have seemed impossibly bleak and unfair at that moment.

Violet senses her own anger. It lies deep down, though at what or whom she can't be entirely sure. It's just my nature, she thinks. More of my characteristic petulance. Still, in its way it is reassuring to know it's still there after all this time. She also senses that in some way this is how it should be. I haven't failed, she thinks. I have grown. So, was it an accident then? Did he try to rape her? Was she just defending herself or was it outright murder? *Did you ever figure out who killed you-know-who?* Julia had written in her final letter, still taunting her after all these years. You never thought it was me, did you? she seemed to be saying. You're right, Violet thinks. I didn't. And I refuse to believe it was you,

Julia. Even accidentally. I can't see you killing anyone. Nor does she think Ned was capable of rape, when all was said and done. Somehow, it just doesn't add up. Though in a way she knows it does, if she counts the months from the night of Ned's death to Brenda's birth, from the end of August through to May. Nine months exactly. Any way you look at it, Brenda is Ned's child as surely as Bryson is his grandson.

Then what of Perry, Julia's first husband? They had married suddenly, at the end of October, right before he went off to war. Julia must have known she was pregnant by then. Is that why she married him? Had there been a payment to sweeten the deal? In those days, men were desperate for sweethearts to wait for them while they were gone, just to have someone to dream of returning to, even a girl who was pregnant by someone else. Was that it? Or had she completely deceived him? What must Julia have told him when he returned from war to find himself a father so unexpectedly and unaccountably? It would explain his refusal to accept his newfound station in life, both as a husband and father, though not a true one in either sense. Like the swans that mated for life, perhaps he, too, was unable to accept a substitute for the real thing.

Enid would have to have been in on it at some point, Violet realizes. She doubts that Julia could have kept it from her right up till the end. If anyone paid Perry off, it would have to have been her. Most mysteries, Violet thinks, require silence on someone's part. There are things that may not be spoken of, sometimes forever.

She scuffs the dirt at her feet and is surprised to see a marble tile glinting up, still here after all these years. Perhaps they're all still here, buried under the dirt. That beautiful dance floor, buried under the dirt of the ages. Figures whirl past in her memory. It's a wonder that no one has hauled them off for sale, seeing how they survived the fire. Wally missed a score there, Violet notes. She smiles and thinks of Enid's love for sad songs and her passion for waltzes. The floor would have been quite an extravagance, not just then but even today. There was no doubt that Enid had had a romantic streak under her dour exterior. Enid, whose loneliness had been so apparent to everyone that it must have haunted her to the end of her days and ... and ... suddenly she knows. She sees it as clearly as if it were happening right in front of her eyes. It had been staring her in the face for seventy years. And clever Violet McPherson hadn't seen it. Not then and not till now.

If anyone could figure it out, it would be you, Julia had rightly claimed all those years ago. Of course! She sees Enid blundering into the baths that night and finding the two of them together. Expecting the banished Celeste, perhaps, but finding her daughter, Julia, instead. *He was a monster,* she'd told the police. Picking up a brick, anything at hand, she had struck him on the head, killing him outright. The poor man probably wouldn't even have thought of defending himself from her. But was it done in a rage borne out of a protective urge for her daughter or was it something more? Something darker. Women kill out of jealousy, Sydney had told the Silver Swans that day in the bar. And Violet agreed. *My mother took away my one true love,* Julia told Brenda. *Permanently.* Saying it without actually coming out and saying it. Even Bryson had known somehow: *They say she killed herself.* And she had done that too, burning the spa down around her, taking with her a life she'd despised and felt trapped by. Had it been out of anger, remorse, grief, or all three? What could it even matter now? Violet wonders, though she knows it still does. And of course Willoughby would have known, arriving on the scene, torn between protecting Enid and making sure no blame was laid on Celeste Holmes.

The mist swirls around her. Time is passing by. There's a breathlessness to it, a sense of wonder, as she thinks of all the ages gathered here — ancient rivers and glaciers, Indigenous peoples, the early settlers — each in turn passing on to other ages. Yet they are somehow all still here. She hears the bell calling them all to supper, sees the guests with their withered limbs, sees her mother's fragile hands, her father's concern. She smells the roast beef and Yorkshire pudding, the reek of sulphur and a distant fire as the shadows of birds wing overhead, blotting out the sun. She hears Ned laugh and turns to see him coming toward her through the trees, dressed in his soldier's uniform. She looks into his startling blue eyes, those eyes he has passed on to his grandson. The parade is passing by now. She watches them turn and go on their way, all of them leaving her at last, their voices fading as they go, and she hopes they are going to their rest. Maybe she has done that for them, at least, though probably it has nothing to do with her at all. All she knows is she feels an overwhelming sense of relief.

And then they are gone.

It's not quite over for her, though. There are still things to be done. She must return to the hotel so they can catch their plane on time. When they get back to Victoria, she will get Claire to phone the solicitor and tell them she has changed her mind. "Tell them Violet McAdams has changed her mind," she can hear herself say. "She's not ready for the retirement home." Let them think that she's a dotty, feeble-minded old woman who can't decide what she wants to do. It's not for them to judge. And perhaps she can convince Claire to come and live with her for the near future. They make a pretty good team, after all.

She turns her back on it all: the spa, the springs, the whole colourful past that has survived in her alone all these years up till now. It's time to let them go. She knows she won't be back here again, just as surely as she knows that one day soon, she won't even be at all. She has proved nothing; she has changed nothing. Death has not conceded one inch. Edgar gave her everything and then he left. There was no one to blame for that. Julia had loved Ned and lost him. Enid Browne had done whatever it was she did. That was all. You can't sweep away the past by trying to alter the present. The past is something you have to accept if you can, forgive if you will, or forget if you cannot. The choice, she thinks, is ours alone. That's the way it would always be. If she knows anything, she knows this.

ACKNOWLEDGEMENTS

I'M TOLD THAT messy thank-yous are out of fashion, but I was taught to show my gratitude when and where it was due. Having said that, I offer my heartfelt thanks to Marc Côté for seeing this book for what it was intended to be and placing it on the right path, Sarah Jensen for her astute editorial suggestions, copyeditor Gillian Rodgerson for making me look smarter than I really am, Marijke Friesen for the terrific cover art, Sarah Cooper, Sheetal Nanda, and Dawn Rae Downton for their enthusiasm, Sharon McKenzie for her comments on an early draft, Ed Piotrowski for hosting me in Puerto Vallarta where I first saw aqua-fitness in action, my cousin Gail Price for her insights into family matters, and to Shane McConnell for suggesting a day trip to the Sulphur Springs all those years ago. (You see? I didn't forget.) I also want to thank all the booksellers and marketers for doing a job that often goes unrecognized. I am fortunate to work with three of the best: Basil Sylvester, Diyasha Sen, and Luckshika Rajaratnam. And thanks to you, Dear Reader — *sine qua non*. I hope I've kept you entertained. Mom, I know you wanted a book with polite sex scenes. I hope I succeeded. Hi, Dad. You're in here too.

We acknowledge the sacred land on which Cormorant Books operates. It has been a site of human activity for 15,000 years. This land is the territory of the Huron-Wendat and Petun First Nations, the Seneca, and most recently, the Mississaugas of the Credit River. The territory was the subject of the Dish With One Spoon Wampum Belt Covenant, an agreement between the Iroquois Confederacy and Confederacy of the Ojibway and allied nations to peaceably share and steward the resources around the Great Lakes. Today, the meeting place of Toronto is still home to many Indigenous people from across Turtle Island. We are grateful to have the opportunity to work in the community, on this territory.

We are also mindful of broken covenants and the need to strive to make right with all our relations.